# Three Hundred Years in the Life of a Family

From Michael Kasper of Baden, Germany
to Holly Casper of Minnesota

## James Thomas Casper

Farhaven Press

PEQUOT LAKES, MINNESOTA

James Casper/Farhaven Press
3912 West Lake Street
Pequot Lakes, MN/56472
www.farhavenpress.com

Kate Casper, Copyeditor and Proofreader
Book Layout and Cover ©2020 Kate Casper


Three Hundred Years in the Life of a Family/ James Casper
ISBN 978-0-9994715-2-4

# Contents

*For Karen Hilgers, CSJ*

*an adopted cousin and lifelong friend*
*whose happy heart continues to illuminate these years*

*Get your facts first, then you can distort them as you please.*


—MARK TWAIN

# Foreword

This story has its beginning in 1967 with a visit to the home of my aunt Ivalue Casper Hilgers. When I happened to ask her what she knew about her grandfather Wendelin Kasper, she told me two things, *that he was French and that he had been a judge in the "Old Country."* Though both pieces of information turned out to be mistaken, they were enough to get me started, proving I suppose that even errors can inspire. I was fascinated with the idea of a German grandfather who was actually French and who must have resigned a judgeship to board a ship of another sort, an immigrant sailing vessel heading for America. I was hooked, and from that point on, determined to find out everything I could about the Kaspers and Wendelin, our first Kasper in America. At the time, I had no idea my research journey would seem in some respects as long as his and even lead me back to his birthplace.

To begin, I didn't even know for sure whether our family name originally had been spelled with a C or a K. No one in the family seemed to know, though the many expressed uncertainties pointed to the possibility we had started out as Kaspers. With ever so many questions and so few answers, I was setting out on a long journey of discovery, but the journey between then and now turned out to be much, much longer than I could ever have imagined. Journeying back into the past is like walking toward the horizon, for no matter how far one goes, the destination is always out there ahead, and every question answered leads to yet another question.

Nobody would have been more interested in what follows than Ivalue herself, who I'm sure would have been happy to learn of her mistaken impressions in exchange for everything we now know. Sadly, she did not live to see the story unfold this far. Equally interested would have been my father Holly Casper. Sadly, a project of 40 years duration is bound to extend beyond the lives of some who might have been its most interested audience.

Speaking of mistakes, I am sure that more than a few are still to be found among what I have included here. Family historians would all agree that there's always an error somewhere slipping through despite their best efforts. Rooting out the errors, pulling them out like weeds growing in the family garden, is one of the tasks that accounts for how long a project like this takes. And like weeds, no matter how carefully you work, there always seem to be a few around somewhere the next time you look. If you waited till you got rid of them all, nobody would ever see the rest of it. So at some point, you simply have to say *good enough* and then let go, which is what I am doing here.

Most readers of this will find more here than they ever needed or wanted to know about our Kasper/Casper family and about Wendelin Kasper and his son Elmer in particular. I know this is the case from the number of times I have seen the subject suddenly changed when I have attempted to talk about all this, from the number of sudden yawns, from the pairs of eyes glazing over. Family historians are all just a little crazy. They collect facts the way collectors collect stamps, coins, butterflies, matchbooks, and thimbles. It's perfectly understandable that others would look at the collection and sometimes wonder why anyone would bother. But family historians also recognize how many facts get lost forever because nobody cared enough at the time to keep them safe, and therefore how many now will never be retrieved, no matter how hard they search for them. So the information they do gather, they want to look after and preserve. Better to be boring than leave something out, that then might be lost forever along with so much else.

The truly persistent reader of all this will also notice occasional repetition of details from one section to another. This results from sections being researched and written at different times and in a different sequence from what appears here. Much repetition has been eliminated, but elsewhere it has been retained to preserve each section as a coherent story in itself. This has the advantage of allowing the reader to approach the family story piecemeal skipping around as time and personal interests permit.

So anyone falling asleep while reading this should do so without guilt. Anyone flipping through it, reading a sentence or two here and there, looking at the pictures only, should be equally comfortable. The important thing is that the story is put together now, for anyone who's interested. It's strange to think that more will be known about Wendelin Kasper than about most of us someday, unless another family member comes along, asks someone a few questions, and then gets interested enough to start digging. Who knows? The next Kasper/Casper story of such length might be about you and written a hundred or so years from now. Just in case, I have a suggestion: make a few notes, and leave some facts behind. It seems that Wendelin was too busy uprooting oak trees on the family farm, surviving Midwestern weather, and raising a family ever to get around to keeping a diary.

All the same, I have gotten wonderfully close to him and to many other family who lived and died before I came on the Casper scene. After all these years, Wendelin feels like an old friend, and I'm not about to say goodbye to him or to others I got to know after a fashion. I once placed a handful of stones from the base of St. Jacobus Church in Grafenhausen on Wendelin's grave in Madison Lake, and I like to think he rests there more comfortably now, with a bit of both his worlds nearby. Sentimental stuff, I know, but as I said, you have to be a little crazy to get anywhere with a project like this.

As for his son Elmer, a sketch and memoir of whom is included later on here, I am happy to say that I was born early enough not to miss out on his presence in our lives. This makes me a few years older than I would like to be but leaves me with a lasting impression that he is always somewhere near at hand.

Completing our story of three centuries is an extended sketch of my father Holly Joseph Casper. Since I was born while he was yet nineteen years old, we more or less grew up together, leaving me with more than enough to make a book of its own. Therefore, this family story begins with one sort of problem for the author and ends with quite another. For much of the way I have had to dig around and scratch together enough details to create at least a simple sketch. Then at the end, with my own father in view and so many facts and memories, I was challenged by what to leave out.

Finally, in the genealogical charts, family pages, and census records attached to all this may be found additional sketches of various Casper family. Much of this has been gleaned from conversations with older family members over the years as well as from my own experiences. In the cases of those I have personally known, I have attempted to capture the personalities of each with both sensitivity and appreciation. The reader should keep in mind that memories are elusive and tinged with the hues of those retaining them. Therefore, all my sketches are incomplete and necessarily subjective. I hope I have not been unfair to anyone.

Family history research has been for me a wonderfully interesting and rewarding hobby. It's taken me to distant lands and to the homes of distant cousins. It's introduced me to dozens of wonderful family members I wouldn't have met otherwise. It's been much more for me than simply an accumulation of facts about our family. It's made the present come alive as well as the past.

Our Baden family had lost touch with its American branches for almost a hundred years until that day a handful of years ago when we found ourselves suddenly all standing together again, out in an old Kasper yard, taking pictures, laughing, trying to catch up on all that had happened.

Gerlinde Kasper, who thought she was the last of her family, discovered that she had busloads of family in America. We ate together and drank wine together. Late one evening around the family table, our conversation turned to the last great war and we shared our family losses—my father wounded in Luxembourg; Vera's father-in-law killed in action; Erhard's father gone to the front and forever missing in action, leaving him as a little boy alone with his mother then. Erhard went to his wine cellar and brought out a special bottle of wine. We all drank a toast, and I could not help thinking that for us the war had finally ended.

*James Casper*
*November 2007 (revised February 2009)*

# 1 Main Lines:

# The Baden, Germany Ancestry of Holly Joseph Casper (1921-1994)

In the years 1720-23, **Michael Kasper**, a young shoemaker, settled in Grafenhausen, a farming village situated between the Black Forest and the Rhine River in the southern German state of Baden. Almost exactly two centuries later, Holly Joseph Casper was born in southern Minnesota. Between these two events is the entire Kasper family history as we know it.

Michael Kasper was not the first of his name to settle in Grafenhausen. Village family records list an Anna Kasper born in about 1663 and living there her entire life of sixty years. An Andreas Kasper, identified as a burger, lived there during approximately the same period, and through his son Johannes (1726-1767) began a line of Kasper descendants continuing into the twentieth century and perhaps continuing in the village to the present day. It is not known whether this Kasper line relates to Michael Kasper, the shoemaker, from a period pre-dating earliest records, but it is certainly possible, and may even explain how he came to establish his trade in Grafenhausen.

Grafenhausen, like other Baden villages of this era, by today's standards would have been amazingly self-sufficient, with adjacent farms providing food and raw materials from which products could be made locally to provide for life's basic necessities. The loss of a baker, a weaver, a tailor, a blacksmith, or a cobbler through death or retirement could become a community crisis threatening this self-sufficiency and requiring a time-consuming and sometimes dangerous journey by foot or horseback to an adjacent village. It could also deplete village resources by forcing a transfer of capital. The arrival of a replacement tradesman seeing opportunity in this loss could become an occasion for celebration. We will never know whether Michael Kasper appeared on the scene as one such or as a young man setting up business beside an old man with more work than he could any longer manage. In any event, he used an opportunity and *possibly* a family connection already living in the village to relocate from Prectal, a nearby town.[1] Grafenhausen must have welcomed his arrival. Villagers would not have to look elsewhere for belts, shoes, and harness repair, among the many goods and services a cobbler provided.

Given the tradition of crafts and trades being passed from father to son, from one generation to the next, our Kaspers may have been shoemakers for many generations. They may even have continued as such even after acquiring farmland—as they did over time in Grafenhausen—since farmers in south German agricultural villages often supplemented their agricultural income by maintaining trades and other small local businesses.

Autumn was scarcely a week old in 1723 when Michael Kasper married **Anna Maria Nopper**, possibly a native village girl. From this marriage, six children were born, five daughters and a son named **Johannes** who learned the shoemaker's trade from his father and carried the family name into another generation. Success and social status seem to have come during these years, for subsequent Kasper generations acquired land and became Grafenhausen village farmers, *Bauers* in the German language. The fact that five daughters and a single son formed the next generation might well have furthered this advancement. With their marriages, daughters could form new village connections and family alliances. More than one son would dilute inheritance through division.

To be a *Bauer* or landowner, as opposed to a tenant who rented land and simply raised crops, or a farm worker paid a meager wage, was an important social distinction in German village life. One could only be considered a Bauer by meeting minimum land and livestock ownership criteria. Bauers and their families were among the most prominent of village folk, sharing status with the village priest and beholden only to a local landlord of the aristocratic class.

The first Kasper Bauer was **Joseph Anton Kasper**, one of Johannes' two sons. Joseph Anton married three times, survived his first two wives, and in what seems to have been a most successful life, rose to the level of village mayor. He may have been the source of later family lore concerning the ancestor who had been an "important mayor and judge with so much money it had to be carried around in wheelbarrows."[2] This was probably an exaggeration, but regardless,

---

[1] All specific factual references on this page are taken from *Ortsippenbuch Grafenhausen* von *Albert Koebele, 1971*, a copy located in the research library of the Immigrant Genealogical Society, Burbank, California. Another copy is in the possession of Gerlinde Kasper Joerger. All subsequent references to Wendelin's Grafenhausen family are derived from this important local history source.

[2] I actually heard this story from two aunts, Ivalue Casper Hilgers as previously mentioned, and Agnes Casper, wife of my uncle Milton. Agnes' account was by far the most dramatic. In my childhood years, when I was

Joseph Anton's true importance for later Kasper generations is that his sons and grandsons were the first of the family to settle in America. He and his wife **Katharina Hoegi** are in a very real sense the parents of all our American family.

There are a great many Kaspers and Caspers living these days in the United States. One hears of them all the time and wonders whether we're related. Going back a great many generations, far beyond where any research can take us, it is possible that at least some are distantly related to Holly Joseph Casper and his descendants, but only the descendants of Joseph Anton and Katharina are *closely* related, and among American Kasper/Casper families, only three family branches can be traced back to them. Once these are traced, all close family kin can be identified.

Two branches extend from Joseph Anton's sons **Gabriel** and **Raphael,** born respectively in 1808 and 1810. Bearing their remarkable archangel names, these Kaspers were the first of our family to leave Grafenhausen and settle in what was then a very young country across the sea. We do not know the exact year of their emigration, but it may have been as early as 1830. The third branch extends from the children of their brother **Johann**, born in 1804, and destined to inherit his father's lands.

A tradition, more pragmatic than prescriptive, favored consolidating inheritance to maintain family independence and social status. Farmlands much-divided could become too small to support even one family, and as social historian Ernest Benz points out, this inevitability was of emerging concern in the Baden of our Kasper family era.[3] Family limitation was one solution, and eventually emigration provided another. Over time, the latter became an ever more important option determining who stayed in the village and who emigrated in an era when abundant land and employment opportunities beckoned from across the sea.

This probably explains the departure of Gabriel and Raphael, among the earliest of Grafenhausen folk to set out for America, true pioneers in every sense. A generation later, their presence as established American residents must have encouraged other Grafenhausen men and women to follow in their footsteps. So many followed that a Rhine River boat landing near Grafenhausen became known as *Little America.*

---

staying at her home in Cleveland, Minnesota she shared this account of Wendelin as if it were the most prized of family secrets. "A great judge," she said to my utter amazement, "with wheelbarrows full of money."

[3] *Fertility, Wealth, and Politics in Southwestern German Villages, 1650-1900,* Studies in Central European History Series, (Boston: Brill, 1999). Benz uses Grafenhausen and its neighboring villages of Kappel and Rust as the basis for his study.

Among the many Baden folk departing from there were the niece and nephew of Gabriel and Raphael: Magdalena and Wendelin Kasper were
both in Minnesota by 1870, the eldest and youngest respectively of Johann's three children. Together these four Kaspers *–**Gabriel, Raphael, Magdalena** and **Wendelin***–are the founders of our American Casper family.

Wendelin had been born 05 July 1845, a dozen years after Magdalena and ten after his brother Johann. He was what we describe these days as *the baby of the family*.[4] Whether he enjoyed the special maternal affection late-born sons sometimes have, from mother and big sister alike, we shall never know. The possibility, however, might explain at least some of what followed.

The name *Magdalena*, typically rendered as *Lena*, requires no derivation beyond mention that devotion to St. Mary Magdalene had at times become something of a cult in France and southern Germany. In the former, there is even to be found a church claiming to be her burial place.

Wendelin was named after an obscure, legendary German saint, an itinerant monk of early Christianity who could miraculously cure farm animals of their various illnesses. *St. Wendelin* thus became a sort of German St. Francis, friend of animals and patron saint of farmers and herdsmen. In the era of our Wendelin's birth, children were typically named after their parents or grandparents, local nobility governing area lands, or saints—especially ones whose lives were most connected with the lore and traditions of their region. Statues, murals, and memorials of various sorts in St. Wendelin's honor can still be found in villages throughout southern Germany. In the adjacent state of Rhineland Pfalz, there is even a town named after him whose church claims to have his remains, and where his feast is celebrated each year on October 22. All the same, it doesn't seem to have been an especially common Baden name, and in America it was one that was sometimes shortened to Wendel or Wendell and often misspelled.[5]

All our male Kasper immigrant ancestors, for reasons of expediency and/or convenience, eventually adopted the *Casper* spelling of our name ensuring that anyone these days bearing the name Kasper is not *closely*
related to us and probably does not have Grafenhausen ancestors in our family line.[6]

---

[4] As we shall see, his grandson Holly Joseph Casper was also the youngest of his family by ten years, with a sister significantly older.

[5] In fact, as we shall see, it is even misspelled on Wendelin's grave memorial.

[6] The two spellings often flip back and forth over the centuries, even in the same family line, having much to do with the perceived need to blend in, depending upon location and the fortunes of war, hence both convenience

Gabriel settled first in New York and then in the Hackensack, New Jersey vicinity where he appears to have spent the rest of his life.[7] He worked first as a tailor and then as a grocer, and raised a family of five, among them three sons. By the time of his death, sometime after 1870, he appears to have had more than twenty grandchildren, among them many grandsons to carry on the family name. From the very earliest Federal Census records forward he seems to have adopted the Casper spelling, so all his descendants are Caspers, and anyone encountering a New Jersey native by that name has at least some basis for thinking here might be a third or fourth cousin. The chances improve considerably if they happen to have roots in Bergen County, New Jersey where many of Gabriel's descendants settled and lived all their lives.

Raphael Kasper settled in Mascoutah, a village in southern Illinois near St. Louis. Here, through a life of seventy some years, he worked as a wood turner and carpenter in what was at the time an industrialized rural community.[8] Along the way he raised three sons, one of whom was a Civil War veteran, and all of whom seem to have been lifelong bachelors. Frederick Casper, the war veteran, dying in an old soldiers' home in Fort Leavenworth Kansas in 1927 brought this family branch to an end.[9]

Wendelin Kasper left Grafenhausen in the summer of 1867, traveling up the Rhine River and from there across the Atlantic to America in the company of Jacob Hofstetter, a Grafenhausen cousin. Passenger records of the ship Hermann sailing from Bremen show them arriving in New York on September 7, 1867. Both identify themselves as *farmers*. It seems likely that they would have sought out Gabriel's home somewhere nearby as a place to gather advice and recover from their journey.

It is tempting to imagine a merry gathering in the household of Gabriel, an uncle who had left Grafenhausen before Wendelin was even born. No one took notes and no one we know of kept a diary, and perhaps they never met at all, but we can imagine an experienced, elderly uncle giving advice to an earnest, intent young man who digested both the advice and his first meals in America while cousins gathered around amazed by the appearance of family from a far-off

---

and expedience. The Grafenhausen Kaspers consistently retained that spelling. However, continental European military action—e.g. the Franco-Prussian War and World War I—could create pressures within multi-ethnic American communities for German families to appear less conspicuously German. The Casper spelling could achieve this, as might have Wendelin's evident cultivation of a French identity and perhaps deliberate efforts to obscure his true origins, leaving grandchildren both confused and mystified.

[7] United States Federal Census records for 1850, 1860, and 1870.

[8] Ibid.

[9] Civil War Veteran Death Records.

land they only knew from their parents' stories. Among the oldest of these cousins was Joseph, born in New York in 1839 and no doubt named for his Grafenhausen grandfather.

Joseph, in fact, was six years older than Wendelin, and already had a wife and three children. Something of a bond may have formed between these two cousins in the early days after Wendelin's arrival, for a few years later both would name children *Clara* and *Louis*. This may have been mere coincidence, but it allows us to speculate that the two families kept in touch long after Wendelin had married and settled in Minnesota.

We will probably never know the precise date of Wendelin's arrival in Minnesota, nor whether there is any truth in family lore that he worked for a while in Indiana before coming there. Federal census records for 1870 show him living in LeRay township on eighty acres subsequent Casper generations will occupy for the next hundred years.

Wendelin seems not to have immediately adopted the Casper spelling of his name, and so in various records the name shifts between Kasper and Casper until the early years of the twentieth century when the latter spelling became a permanent change. His signature on a Blue Earth County marriage record is Kasper with an umlaut over the *a*. There is no precedent for such a spelling.[10] No subsequent family members seem to have used the Kasper spelling, and the umlaut never appears again.

In October 1872 Wendelin married **Wilhelmine "Minnie" Cords** whose background and life story may be found elsewhere here. This marriage produced seven children in all, four of whom survived to adulthood and had children of their own. Among Wendelin's sons was **Elmer**, born in 1883 and the father of **Holly Joseph Casper**. Subsequent generations bearing the family name are all descendants of Wendelin's sons **John** and Elmer, since the other surviving son **Albert** had but one granddaughter among his descendants. Among female lines descending from Wendelin, the names **Cords**, **Vogel**, and **Huntington** are the most prominent.

The remaining Kasper/Casper kin in America descend from Wendelin's sister Magdalena who married **Kasimir Schaub**, also of Grafenhausen, and emigrated in 1868 with her husband and five children. This family also settled in LeRay Township, within a mile of Wendelin.

---

[10] Present day Baden family speculate this may have been used at one time in Grafenhausen to distinguish our Kasper family from another of the same name, unrelated. The circumstances of Wendelin's marriage, described later here, may provide a more plausible explanation.

Among the many Schaub family living in the vicinity today, only those who descend from Magdalena relate to the Grafenhausen Kasper line.

In sum, the American descendants of Michael Kasper and Anna Maria Nopper, descending from their grandson Joseph Anton now number well over a thousand. Life being as it is at the beginning of the twenty-first century, these family are scattered all over the United States, with a great many nevertheless to be found still residing in Minnesota and New Jersey.

Meanwhile in Grafenhausen itself lives **Gerlinde Kasper**, the very last of our family to have been born there with the name. The radical depletion of our family bearing the name Kasper in its ancestral homeland, together with its prolific numbers in America today could itself yield a book-length study in the effects of emigration, war, and social upheaval. on indigenous populations.[11]

An account of Gerlinde and Kasper kin of other names living these days in Grafenhausen and elsewhere in southern Germany is included in a subsequent section of this. Suffice it to say for now that with her passing, the name as it refers to anyone of our known family, will die out in the village almost three centuries after the shoemaker Michael arrived, set up his trade, and married a local girl.

A story ends with another well underway.

---

[11] Gerlinde herself has often been teased in a good-natured way about being what we might describe as *the last of the Mohicans* in her family. She was amazed to discover—and with this discovery came a bit of revenge—that "busloads" of her Kasper/Casper family live across the sea.

# 2 Wendelin Kasper (1845-1922)

## Pioneer Founder of the Casper Family
## of Blue Earth County, LeRay Township, and
## Madison Lake, Minnesota

# The Wendelin Kasper Story

## Departure

As previously noted, in the mid-summer of 1867, probably not long after his twenty-second birthday, Wendelin Kasper left his home in Baden, Germany and began a long journey to America. He probably set out from the east bank of the Rhine just outside the village of Kappel, about six miles from his home, an embarkation point still known locally as *Little America*, from the number of Baden folk who left from there to emigrate to the United States.[12] In his company was Jacob Hofstetter, a distant cousin. They traveled together by ferry north on the Rhine, as so many Germans before and after them did, heading to northern ports where ships would take them across the Atlantic. Wendelin and Jacob sailed from Bremen on the ship Hermann and arrived in New York September 7, 1867. On immigration documents completed upon their arrival, both young men listed their occupations as farmers.[13]

Since nothing survives providing Wendelin's word on the subject, we can only speculate about his reasons for leaving home and establishing a new life in America. The few facts we do have in hand, however, give us the basis for a good explanation:

By far the youngest of the three children of Johann Kasper and Katherina Jaeger, Wendelin's options close to home might have seemed especially limited. Grafenhausen, albeit a relatively

---

[12] Interviews with family living in the Grafenhausen area.

[13] Ancestry.com. *New York Passenger Lists, 1851-1891* [database online]. Provo, Utah: MyFamily.com, Inc., 2003. Original data: New York. *Passenger Lists of Vessels Arriving at New York, New York, 1820-1897*. Micro publication M237. Rolls # 95-580. National Archives, Washington, D.C.

prosperous German village, must have contained no more than two dozen or so small farms, all in hands other than his. His brother, Johann seems to have inherited the family farm when his father died in 1861, with Wendelin at the time not yet sixteen. A little over a year later, his mother re-married.[14] His sister Magdalena, wife of Kasimir Schaub, also of Grafenhausen, may have been planning emigration with her family as well, for she, her husband, and their six children arrived in America only a year after Wendelin. As we have previously noted (p. 7), two of his father's brothers, Raphael and Gabriel Kasper, had settled in America some years before.[15]

Beyond all these matters so close to home, was the looming prospect of war between the French and the Prussians of the north, a war which would eventually unite the German state (1871) and into which young men like Wendelin could easily have been drawn regardless of their sympathies and allegiances. And in Baden at this time there might have been more affinity with the Alsatian French of German background than for the distant Prussian Germans under Bismarck. To some extent, even today, there still is. Meanwhile in America, the Civil War had come to an end, and along with it, a period of uncertainty that had seen a temporary decline in German emigration.[16]

So with his father dead, his mother married into another family, his sister planning to leave, his brother now owner of the family farm,[17] the possibility of military service, and family connections already in America, it might have seemed to young Wendelin that he had little reason to stay and every reason to seek a new life for himself in a land where opportunities beckoned. Add to all this a young man's sense of adventure. That alone could have been sufficient. Certainly, his circumstances were far from unusual. In fact, they would have been typical among the hundreds of thousands of Europeans at this time leaving their homelands for America,

---

[14] I mention in passing: my family history research has yielded time and again suggestions that adult children are sometimes upset by their widowed parent remarrying, especially late in life. Inheritance issues are sometimes in this picture, but equally present are misgivings concerning mental health, transfer of affection, and upset of longstanding *status quo.*

[15] *Orstippenbuch Grafenhausen* von Albert Koebele, 1971. Copy located in the Immigrant Genealogical Society, Burbank, California. Another in the possession of Gerlinde Kasper Joerger. All subsequent references to Wendelin's Grafenhausen family are derived from this important source.

[16] Mack Walker, *Germany and the Emigration 1816-1885*, (Cambridge: Harvard University Press, 1964). Walker suggests that German people were overall sympathetic to the Union cause, but naturally reluctant to emigrate while the war was on and its outcome uncertain.

[17] The Baden Germans seem not to have practiced *primogeniture,* the tradition that family property was always bequeathed to the eldest, usually the eldest son. But as Mack Walker points out in his book *Germany and the Immigration 1816-1885,* the fragmentation of family farms into smaller and smaller parcels was becoming a serious problem, since farms any smaller could not support even a single family. Therefore, other arrangements had to be made where younger children were concerned—an inheritance of money or another family enterprise, for example—rather than land. As previously mention (p. 7) emigration became another option, for young men especially.

many of them young men in search of opportunity, land, adventure, even perhaps a wife, since in many parts of Germany—Baden included—there existed at the time, serious financial and social obstacles to marriage.[18]

All the same, we should not think this an easy decision, either for him or other immigrants. He must have known there was little chance he would ever again see his mother, his home, and the family, friends, and familiar places he left behind. He would be leaving everything he had ever known in the years of his childhood and youth to make his way in a largely unfamiliar world, in what was still a frontier environment, among settlers from many countries. There would have been much more uncertainty than certainty and many more questions than answers. It required courage and confidence to do such a thing. Those of us who have the luxury of looking back on it all can sometimes take this for granted.

*A view from the Rhine River north of Baden as Wendelin would have seen it on his journey north toward Bremen and the ship that would take him to America*[19]

Along the great River Rhine as it moves north from France and Germany into a region west of Frankfurt, these days a country of vineyards known as the Rhinegau, the river takes a sharp bend to the west leaving everything out of sight south of there. One can imagine Wendelin and his companion taking a last look as their boat made that turn, the last they would ever see of their Baden homeland.

A new life might have begun with thoughts of the old.

---

[18] Mack Walker, *Germany and the Emigration 1816-1885* and Ernest Benz, *Fertility, Wealth, and Politics in Southwest German Villages, 1650-1900*, (Boston: Brill, 1999).
[19] Nineteenth Century engraving.

# Looking Back: Wendelin's Old World

As we have seen (pp. 5-10), Wendelin's Kasper family had lived in Grafenhausen for five generations, ever since his great-great-grandfather Michael Kasper settled in the community sometime before 1720.[20]

The Kasper family appears to have been as prolific as any other, but more daughters than sons, a possible source of social and financial advancement in the early going (pp. 5-7), also led to a decline in family bearing the name in subsequent generations. War after war and nineteenth century emigration—in Germany called the *auswanderung*—accelerated this decline, while high infant mortality in the family of Johann's remaining Baden sibling all but cinched the matter:[21] As the twentieth century began, our Kasper family name was dying out in Grafenhausen, if not in Baden generally.

*A recent drawing of St. Jacobus (St. James) Grafenhausen, Baden celebrating its two hundredth anniversary, the street leading to it—as it looks today and may have looked in Wendelin's time. On the far right is an old gasthaus named today Le Boeuf, and on the far left nearest the church is the Rathaus (village hall).[22]*

Like most Baden people, the Kaspers were Catholic, and they would have been christened, married, and buried from the village church of St. Jacobus (St. James). This church looks today much as it would have looked in early times. One can see a baptismal font in front of the church to the right of its main aisle where

---

[20] *Orstippenbuch Grafenhausen.*

[21] Ibid. Johann and Theresia Kurz had twelve children, many of whom died in infancy., among them Joseph, Martin, and August Kasper. Adolph, Otto, a subsequent Joseph, and Albert have not been accounted for, but appear to have either died or left Grafenhausen. As far as we know, remaining Grafenhausen family of the Kasper name are descendant from yet another son Franz Xavier and his lone son Ernst Josef.

[22] St. Jacobus Church booklet. The present church (1789) predates Michael Kasper (Abt. 1695-1761).

generations of Kasper family have been christened. One can walk from there down a main aisle to a door from which they stepped as newlyweds and through which years later they would have been carried to their churchyard graves. Today the graves of more recent Kasper family can be located on memorials, but all older ones are gone, obliterated by time and replaced by those that came after. This is typical of many German cemeteries, where new graves over time replace the old.

Wendelin's great-grandfather Johannes Kasper was also a cobbler, but sometime after that, as we have seen, the Kaspers seem to have become successful Grafenhausen farmers, either purchasing land or possibly acquiring it through marriage. This transition from tradesman to farmer/tradesman or farmer may have taken place in the lifetime of Wendelin's grandfather Joseph Anton Kasper who appears to have been quite prominent in village life and even became its Burgermeister (mayor) in 1836.[23] Wendelin's father Johann, his eldest son, inherited the family farm when Joseph Anton died in 1850. Matthias, a remaining brother after the emigration of Gabriel and Raphael, appears to have remained in the vicinity, but already our Baden Kasper family was being seriously depleted.

*Baptismal font of St. Jacobus, Grafenhausen.*[24]

Typical of old European agricultural communities, the Kasper farm would have been small and diversified, located on the main road through the village with its adjoining land extending back from there including cultivated areas and pasture for grazing livestock. There may have been other detached parcels a short distance away and common grazing lands.

An inspection of what remains of the old Kasper farmstead these days suggests that in former times, the family's original living quarters might have been on one end of a large barn, in a portion closest to the road and partially constructed of stone, while animals were sheltered on the other end in a portion entirely of wood. This arrangement

---

[23] It's an interesting facet of Kasper/Casper and Cords family life that over the generations so many have held such positions. Among more recent Caspers, Wendelin's grandson Milton was mayor of Cleveland, Minnesota, and these days, Vera Joerger Schlenker, a great grandniece, serves on the city council and is assistant burgermeister at Kippenheim, near Grafenhausen.  Also among the family of Minnie Cords, Wendelin's wife, several ancestors served as burgermeisters in Ruest and nearby Mecklenburg villages.

[24] Author's photograph.

made it easier to look after livestock in all manner of weather and conserved heat in the winter months. It was common in colder regions, in the Black Forest for example, but according to a surviving contemporary account, also existed in Grafenhausen as recently as Wendelin's era.[25]

*Farm buildings behind the Kasper house (pictured on page 42), possibly from Wendelin's time and offering the suggestion that family living quarters (right) at one time might have been attached to the barn (left).[26]*

Baden farmers in the flat river-bottom land between the Black Forest and the Rhine would have raised cattle, goats, and pigs for dairy products and meat, small grains, flax, grapes, and orchard fruit. Beginning in the early 1800's, tobacco became an increasingly important crop, especially in Grafenhausen, among villages nearby.[27] There did not exist the clear distinction between town and country that we find today in Midwestern rural America. In German villages like Grafenhausen, the farms were a part of the village, and the village part of the farms. To some extent this remains true. Even today one can awaken in Grafenhausen and nearby Kippenheim to the sounds of roosters crowing. Village streets end in farmers' fields.

A firsthand account from Wendelin's era mentions both tobacco and flax[28] as important crops and provides an authentic view of village and family life:

---

[25] Hoehn Family History papers, courtesy of Joseph Hoehn, Madison Lake, Minnesota grandson of Adolph Hoehn who was born in Grafenhausen.

[26] Author's photograph.

[27] Ernest Benz, *Fertility, Wealth, and Politics in Southwestern German Villages, 1650-1900.*

[28] Flax was another important crop ensuring the self-sufficiency of a southern German village. Since it could be spun into thread for making cloth, skilled weavers, seamstresses, and a village tailor could keep the inhabitants clothed.

*The farmers lived in a village [Grafenhausen] mother called a dorf [German word for a small town] and worked the surrounding land with hand tools, their main crops being flax and tobacco. Our grandfather [Hoehn family] had horses and did draying, so they had a hired man and a maid when mother was a child. The church [St. Jacobus] and the school were in their dorf, so they found it quite a hardship when coming to America and having to go miles for either. Their buildings were brick, and the barn was attached to the house. When the girls were old enough, they spun the flax into thread. It was then taken to a distant mill [probably in Rust] and woven into yarn goods. Some of it was dyed and used for outer clothing. The local tailor would come and sew their clothes by hand, sitting cross-legged on the table. The tobacco also had to be prepared by moistening and later it was stripped. This was their main cash crop. When they worked in the evening, grandfather would read to them. When he was out of books, he would borrow from their priest. They weren't too far from the Rhine. On clear nights they could see the lights of Strasbourg on the other side. Their climate was quite mild. On Sunday afternoons, farmers a short distance from there would bring carts of fruit to sell: pears, grapes, and plums.[29]*

The climate, with a growing season months longer, was mild enough to permit the cultivation of things that could not have survived in Minnesota. Baden winter of any sort lasted two or three months, with occasional snow that melted soon after it fell. Summers were warm but seldom as warm as Minnesota's can be. Young Wendelin and other Baden pioneers would have experienced nothing like Minnesota's weather extremes, winters of protracted sub-zero cold and blizzards followed by the parching summer heat so typical of July and August, and then perhaps a first frost as early September. We can easily imagine the challenges faced by farmers adapting everything they knew about agriculture to the reality of a harsh climate in a new world. Much would have to be learned the "hard way."[30]

Only a few miles west of Grafenhausen is the Rhine River and on its other bank the French region of Alsace-Lorraine. To the east, equally close, is the beautiful, rugged Black Forest, probably less forested than today since much of the land in Wendelin's time would have been cleared for grazing livestock. Travel south from Grafenhausen a few miles, and you will come to the

---

[29]Hoehn Family History papers, courtesy of Joseph Hoehn.  Branches of the Hoehn and Schaub families also originated in Grafenhausen and emigrated to the LeRay Township, Madison Lake, Minnesota area. The names of both families can be found on local cemetery memorials, and there is today a Schaub Bakery on the Haupstrasse (main street) through Grafenhausen.
[30] See further pp.22-23.

university city of Freiberg. Yet a little further south is Basel, Switzerland and the Alpine foot-hills. North a few more miles are other great university cities at Heidelberg, Stuttgart, and Tubingen. Closest of all is the beautiful Alsatian French Strasbourg.

It is likely that Wendelin knew of and had possibly been to all these places. Assuming he wasn't a chronic liar, there are too many stories supporting this to be accounted for as mere tale telling. As family lore would have it, he might have been a student at one of the Baden universities. We can speculate, for example, that perhaps he was sent away to university after the death of his father with the hope that he might be trained in a profession, the family farm as a livelihood having gone to his older brother. Some training in law, for example, might have given rise to the rumor that Wendelin had been a judge, while at the same time being of little use to him in America. Nearby Freiburg University offered training in law, and among the children of a Baden cousin Karl Kasper, we find Josef, an attorney at Loerrach.[31] Who knows? Josef may not have been the first.

None of this points more than vaguely Wendelin's way, but he would have been far from alone among German emigrants in setting aside professional prospects—especially with civil unrest nearly chronic in Baden and war always looming—to establish a new life in America. Nothing was simpler and perhaps more expedient, I'm sure, than to identify oneself as a farmer for im-migration purposes, whatever else one might have been or meant to be back home. Tell authorities you're a farmer, and you're unlikely to get a follow-up question. Everyone knew there was farmland available in America, and that's why people came.

Follow-up questions could have been abundant, especially back home where war, revolution, political turmoil, and religious conflict were an almost constant presence in nineteenth-century Baden. Looking back on it now, it's hard to imagine anyone wanting to do more than either keep his head down or run away to a world of more sanguine prospects across the sea in a century beginning with Napoleon and ending with Otto Von Bismarck. Obscurity and distance offered safety. For the more daring and politically savvy, opportunities would have been abun-dant, as would have been risks. Baden was truly a land of the "quick and the dead."

Whatever else he might have brought to America, Wendelin must have come with a head full of ancestral tales and remarkable personal experiences of events viewed both from afar and close up. He and European immigrants would have devoured any news from home helping them put together the rest of a story they had left behind. Even small village newspapers of the era

---

[31] *Ortsippenbuch Grafenhausen*

regularly carried news and features concerning events across the sea. The question must have been asked over and over: where would I be now if I hadn't left?

One can imagine him clustered with other Baden immigrants in a corner of pioneer Madison Lake, all of them speculating, trying to imagine, exchanging news recently arrived from over the horizon, in letters from what some still called home while others called it the *Old Country*. Nearby clusters of recent Irish immigrants would be recounting old tales of the Potato Famine, who among them got out in time and who never made it.

Further accounts from Wendelin's Madison Lake years tell of his ability to speak several foreign languages. This is not surprising, because the world he came from was a neighborhood of several countries joined together by the Rhine, making it an ancient European crossroads. He certainly would have had contacts with people speaking several European languages and many dialects.

In Wendelin's day, as today, Baden was a land of great natural beauty, rural charm, and diverse people, rich in cultural traditions and history. In his youth he would have encountered all this, and in the *New World* so remote from everything he left behind, such experience in itself would have passed for a remarkable education. Ironically, he probably was more cosmopolitan in certain ways and had a greater knowledge of the world in all its diversity than any of his children and many of his grandchildren who grew up more isolated in pioneer-era rural Minnesota.

Beyond all this remains the possibility that he actually did have significant education, perhaps as high as the University level. This would have been a rare thing among Grafenhausen families of the era, but it can't be rejected out of hand, especially given the evident prominence of his grandfather Josef Anton.

This may help explain the stories previously mentioned that circulated in the family among his grandchildren long after his time, perhaps even the story that he had attended university at Stuttgart.[32] He knew about worlds none of his descendants had ever seen. He could describe distant lands, speak foreign languages, and seem familiar with foreign customs. All these things considered, no wonder he seems to have been held in a kind of awe, but for certain this young man of twenty-two when he came to America had never been a judge, though he might have dreamt of being one, and he seems to have lived all his life in his native Grafenhausen, unless perhaps he was away for a time as a university student.

---

[32] This from my father Holly Casper, which up to now I have been unable to confirm.

This is not to accuse Wendelin of embellishing his past, though it would be forgivable if he created a few tall tales for wide-eyed and astounded grandchildren. Even tall tales, though, can have a basis of some sort, and perhaps if anyone embellished Wendelin's past it was his children and even more wide-eyed grandchildren hearing of places they were never likely to see, sometimes spoken of in languages they seldom heard, all from the same man. We're not likely to know more.[33]

More to the point, I think, is the explanation that stories of his wealth and status before coming to America result from generational confusion most family historians encounter at one time or another, in which someone refers to *grandfather*, for example, Wendelin's grandfather, and those hearing it take it as referring to *their* grandfather, in this case Wendelin himself. This particular confusion, once cleared up, would point the story to Joseph Anton Kasper (p. 9), but as will be discussed later, an even more distant Kasper/Casper may be the source.

Our Wendelin himself never claimed to be from Germany on early official records I have seen, because Baden was his homeland, an independent state when he lived there, and not itself an official part of Germany until a few years after his departure, when the modern German nation was first united under the leader Bismarck. People of Wendelin's day might have thought of themselves as German in a general sort of way, but they most often indicated their home German state on immigration and census forms. Thus, on the official records, Wendelin identifies his origins as *Baden*. Grafenhausen, specifically, is not mentioned in anything I have seen relating to him. The only reference to it anywhere is in the Mankato Free Press obituary of his sister Magdalena who died in October 1906 where Wendelin, is mentioned as surviving her.[34]

So small a village is only identified on the most detailed of German maps, and it is in fact one of two Baden villages by that name, the other being further south near the Swiss border in the Black Forest, and not in any way that I know of connected with our Kasper family, even though people of that name have lived there.

---

[33] A future family historian might uncover something of interest in the archives of Baden universities –if any exists from this time—a project beyond my resources.
[34] Located in the Blue Earth County, Minnesota Historical Society.

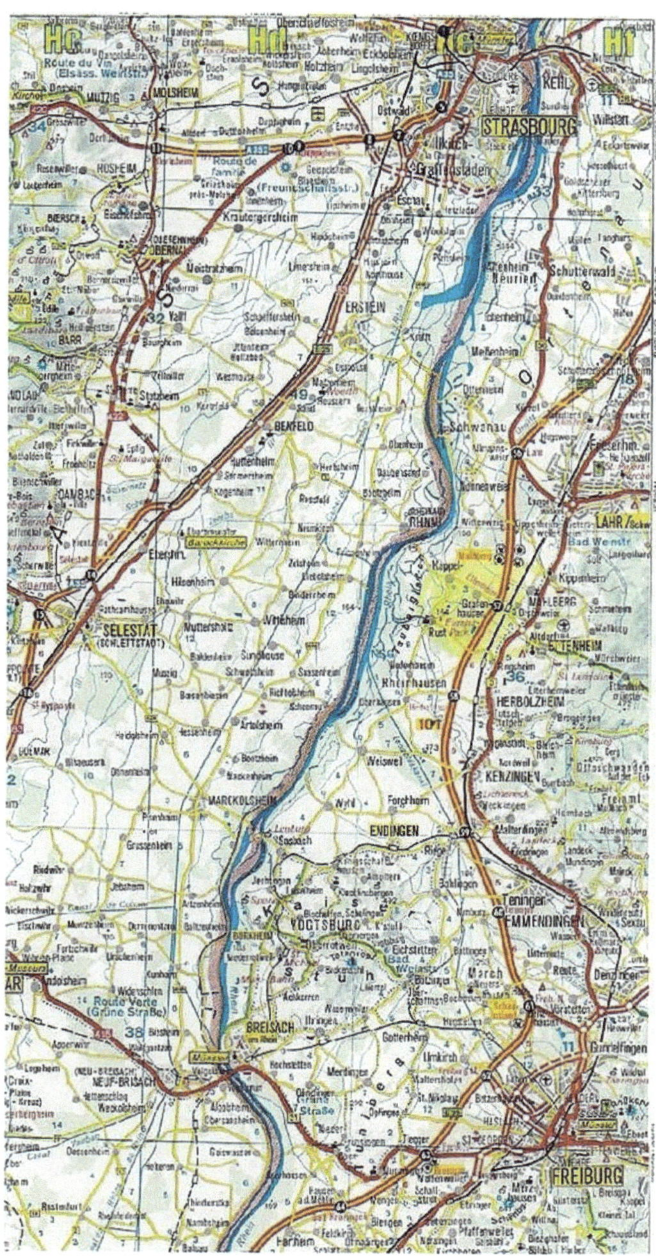

*Wendelin's homeland, the Rhine River (center) and the neighboring lands of French Alsace and Baden. Grafenhausen is in the golden circle center right. To the far right begins the Black Forest. Just south of Freiburg are Basel and the Swiss border.*

Our Grafenhausen itself, as previously noted, is the origin of branches of at least two other Madison Lake families, the Schaubs and the Hoehns. In the greater vicinity, including the nearby cities of Lahr and Offenburg, others—including the Muellerleiles—appear to have their German roots. So traveling in this area today, a Madison Lake native can feel surprisingly at home, with long-familiar names popping up everywhere, in local newspapers and telephone directories, on shop windows, on the sides of trucks, on posters, on war memorials, and on grave markers in churchyards. In Madison Lake itself during the pioneer era this shared past must have led to many moments of reminiscence among the Baden immigrants. But for the presence of so many Irish immigrants as well, Madison Lake might have taken on a good deal more German character than it had in its early days.

*Grafenhausen war memorial on which are displayed many familiar Madison Lake names, victims of the world wars and many of them cousins of Madison Lake settlers.*[35]

---

*Grafenhausen World War II memorial bearing the familiar Madison Lake names Schaub and Moser, among others[36]*

Wendelin's mother died in the spring of 1870, not much more than a year after he settled on 80 acres in LeRay Township of Blue Earth County, Minnesota. At the time of her death, she was married to Jakob Sutter, apparently of the nearby village Kappel. Previous to her marriage with Johann Kasper, she had been the widow of Xaver Kern, by whom she had two sons and a daughter, half-siblings of Wendelin. Thus, in all, she was the mother of six children, only four of whom survived her, Wendelin's half-bothers having died as small children.

Since Wendelin and Magdalena were now in America with their families, what remained of our immediate Kasper family in Grafenhausen were the children and grandchildren of their brother Johann who lived there until his death in 1912. He and his wife Theresia Kurz had twelve children in all, several of whom died in infancy. Nevertheless, throughout Wendelin's lifetime, he would have had many family members in Grafenhausen and the vicinity, most of them nieces and nephews. Contacts between the families seem to have continued at least until the early 1900's. After that, with the deaths of the older generations and the disruption of two World Wars, the Kasper family branches lost contact with each other until the early twenty-first century.

# Looking Ahead: Wendelin's New World

Wendelin's obituary says that he first settled in Indiana.[37] Obituaries are sometimes mistaken, but the report does agree with bits of family lore, including the completely mistaken story that he was married in Indianapolis. It is also possible that the writer of the obituary was confusing Indiana with neighboring Illinois, in the southern part of which lived Wendelin's uncle Raphael Kasper. Raphael (Raph) and his wife Mary appear in the 1870 federal census, and it seems from this record that they were fairly well off by standards of the day, declaring to have real estate valued at $9,000, a considerable sum at a time when an entire farm might have been purchased

---

[36] Author's photograph.
[37] *Madison Lake Times, December 1922.*

in Minnesota for a tenth of that. They may have been in a position to assist their nephew, or at the very least, to offer him a place to live while he made further arrangements.

Immigrants moved and made their way by networking with friends, family, and others from their homelands. It is still this way today, so it is easy to imagine Wendelin staying with one or other of his uncles awhile, either with Gabriel in New Jersey or Raphael in Illinois, perhaps as long as a year or so, perhaps working and saving some money before traveling to Minnesota in 1868-69 when his sister Magdalena arrived there with her family. We're unlikely to ever have any hard facts to fill the gap between his arrival in America and his appearance in Minnesota.

Magdalena and her husband Kasimir Schaub settled on what in later years was the Clare Frederick farm, in LeRay Township about two miles from the Madison Lake village, on a ridge bordering a lowland between the lake itself and nearby Mud Lake. Less than a mile away, by the time of the 1870 Federal census, Wendelin had purchased 80 acres and was living alone on what would be the Kasper family farm for three generations.[38] He was not the first to have owned this land. His is not the first name to appear on its abstract, but he was almost for certain the first to have settled there.[39]

It was a rectangle bordered by roads on its south and east sides. The east road went northeast to the village of Madison Lake, the south road went west to Eagle Lake. Each village was about two miles away. A few miles from Eagle Lake was the already thriving market community of Mankato. A railroad line connecting Mankato with cities to the east as far as Chicago ran past Wendelin's land about a half mile to the south. He could stand looking out from the front door of his cabin and hear the train going by, perhaps even see smoke from its steam engine in a long trail over its cars. Considering all this, Wendelin would have had good reason to think this a good location for his farm, with ready access to a major transportation link taking the place of the Rhine River he knew, and nearby communities where farm produce could be sold and supplies purchased.

By the account of his son Elmer, Wendelin's land was heavily wooded when he began his life there. Building a log cabin and clearing it of trees were his first labors. In the middle of the land was a small woodland pond.[40] The Kasper log cabin was located on the Eagle Lake road. Felling

---

[38] Plat map of LeRay Township lands in the collection of the Blue Earth County Historical Society.

[39] Copy of land abstract, courtesy of Sam Casper, Wendelin's great grandson. Land companies and individual land speculators, often based in the eastern United States, would purchase parcels—often sight unseen—hold them for a time, and then sell them at a profit to emigrants searching for farmland.

[40] Interview with Elmer Casper about 1950.

trees and cutting logs with axe and handsaw, pulling out the stumps without the aid of machinery, would have been hard labor requiring the use of heavy draft animals, horses and oxen. Presumably neighbors helped neighbors and shared their limited resources. With wildlife around in abundance, hunting, trapping, and fishing and would have helped supplement the food supply. Supplement would certainly have been needed, since the growing season was short, as previously noted, and winters long and harsh.[41]

This must have come as a grim surprise to many of these rural settlers, especially those coming from climates as mild as the one Wendelin knew from his life along the southern Rhine. It would not have been possible, for example, to grow grapes for wine, a staple of south German life. Instead, wine would have to be made from chokecherries, wild plums, and rosehips, as it was in the higher elevations of the Black Forest. Small animals without shelter would not survive the winter. Large animals might be kept inside near the living quarters to help provide heat. Roads would be blocked with snow and remain impassable for weeks at a time Medical care was often beyond reach. Women would die in child labor. Outbreaks of diphtheria, smallpox, and scarlet fever would take an especially heavy toll among the children. School and church might be miles away, instead of just a short walk through the Baden farm village.[42] Those early years must have been brutally difficult. Eighty acres was probably more land than many Grafenhausen families had ever owned. By that standard, Wendelin might have felt well off, but by every other standard, his life must have been harder than anything he had known at home. It must have been a life in which achieving even the barest necessities of food, shelter, and warmth was a full-time labor, and good health a matter of luck.

Presumably, not long after coming to Minnesota, Wendelin met his future wife Wilhelmine Sophia Cords, herself only recently arrived in the United States.[43] She had come from the small farming village of Ruest, Mecklenburg, northeastern Germany, bringing with her an infant daughter Anna born in Germany in October 1868.[44] The circumstances surrounding Wilhelmine's emigration from Germany with her daughter will be described elsewhere in this

---

[41] Minnesota State Climatology Department reports for 07 January 1873: *Great Blizzard. Three-day blizzard caused extreme hardship for pioneers from out east who were not used to the cold and snow. Visibility was down to three feet. Cows suffocated in the deep drifts and trains were stuck for days. More than 70 people died, some bodies were not found until spring. Weather conditions before the storm were mild, just like the Armistice Day storm.*

[42] See previous account from the Hoehn Family papers. In my youth, during the 1940's and 1950's, there was an abandoned rural schoolhouse along the Eagle Lake road, less than a mile from the Kasper home.

[43] Precise circumstances of Wilhelmine's (Minnie's) emigration are sketchy and uncertain at this point. We know the date she and her daughter Anna arrived in America (See p. 52), and presume she first found a home with her uncle Frederick Cords' family in southern Minnesota.

[44] Details about Anna's birth courtesy of Betty Lou Cords from her *History of the Cords Family*.

family history. They were married before a judge in Mankato October 15, 1872.[45] Wilhelmine's name on the marriage documents was given as *Mena Kurtz*. This may have been a recording error, but the error seems strange in view of the fact that Wendelin's name, so often entered incorrectly, is here recorded exactly as it should be, and one would think the young couple would have taken pains to have their names correctly written on a marriage certificate especially.[46] In any event, among the Kasper/Casper family, Wilhelmine would be known the rest of her life simply as Minnie

---

[45] Blue Earth County, Minnesota Court House records.
[46] Whether by coincidence or intentionally as part of a broader deception, Kurz is also the family name of Wendelin's sister-in-law Theresia, wife of his brother Johann, still living in Grafenhausen.

**WEST**

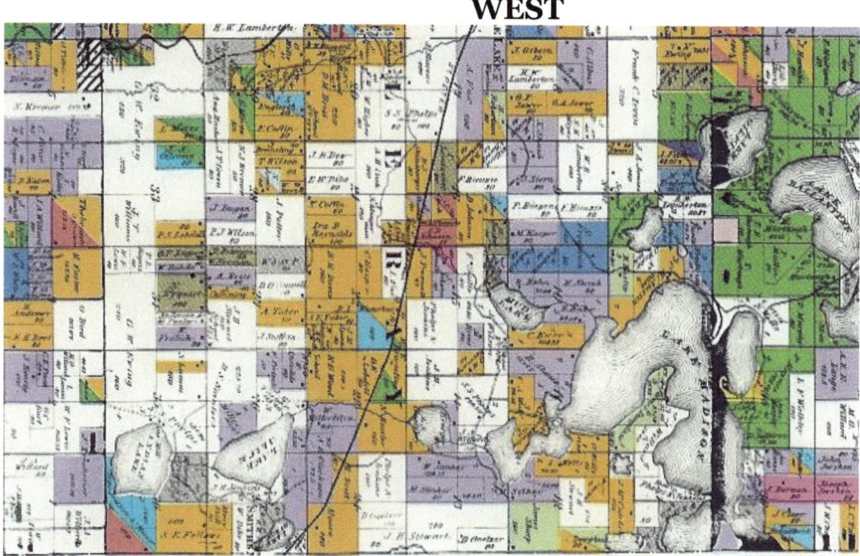

**EAST**

*Map showing LeRay Township lands in 1880. The Kasper and Kasper/Schaub parcels are right of center (violet shaded) southwest of Lake Madison. The location of Wendelin's log cabin is indicated. The railroad line curves through the center.[47]*

In addition to Minnie's daughter Anna who lived with them until at least 1880,[48] Wendelin and Minnie had seven children of their own, born between 1872 and 1885, four of whom survived as adults. The eldest, John and Clara, were baptized in a Mankato Lutheran church. Minnie's brother Charles Cords was a sponsor for John, and Wendelin's sister Magdalena (Kasper) Schaub for Clara.[49] Their youngest children Elmer and Albert were baptized Catholic. In between were Minnie and Lewis (Louis)[50], both of whom died in their youth, and an earlier Albert who died as a baby. These three were buried in a family plot at the Eagle Lake cemetery, and from this we may assume that they were also baptized Lutheran, since Catholics of that era would have been buried in the Catholic cemetery at Madison Lake. So the Kasper family appears to have started out Lutheran, the religion of Minnie's family, and ended Catholic, the religion of Wendelin's.

---

[47] Blue Earth County Historical Society.

[48] 1880 Federal Census for Blue Earth County, LeRay Township, Minnesota.

[49] This information, generously provided by Betty Lou Cords in the course of her Cords family research, was the key detail leading to the discovery of our Kasper family origins in Grafenhausen.

[50] The name of this Kasper son appears in official records with both spellings. On his original grave memorial, however, it is given as Louis. I used the name Lewis in a restoration project, allowing for both possibilities, but perhaps sowing further confusion.

This transition led to the existence of two separate family gravesites, in Eagle Lake and Madison Lake respectively. The Eagle Lake site is the older and more interesting in the respect that it displays the family name spelled as *Kasper* rather than the more recent *Casper* spelling. This is the only family memorial that I know of outside of Baden to have the old German spelling of our name, and its existence certainly establishes that Wendelin did not immediately change the spelling when he settled in America.

*The Kasper/Casper family gravesite at the Eagle Lake, Minnesota cemetery, after restoration by author in 2001*[51]

*Memorial added by author in 2001 restoration. The name Lewis in other family records is also spelled Louis*[52]

---

[51] Author's photograph.
[52] Author's photograph.

*Minnie Kasper memorial preserved during restoration work at Eagle Lake.[53]*

Three times during the early married life of Wendelin and Minnie there would have been a sad little funeral procession down the road from their log cabin to the Eagle Lake cemetery about a mile away. It speaks volumes about the harsh pioneer life of those days to think of children dying this way, of grieving families burying their loved ones and moving on.

In the federal census of 1880, among the children we still find Anna listed as "Annie," age eleven. This is the last official reference to her. She is not mentioned in subsequent censuses, and I have been able to locate no record of her death. Elmer Casper, who was born in 1883, once mentioned in a conversation with his daughter-in-law Marian Casper that a sister of his had "disappeared and was never heard from again."[54] There is every reason to think he referred to Anna, since his other sisters can be accounted for. He may never have known that she was his half-sister only.

And we may never know what happened to Anna, daughter of Minnie Cords and Karl Moller,[55] farmhand of a hamlet near Ruest in Mecklenburg, Germany.[56] It is possible that she was

---

[53] Author's photograph.

[54] Interview with Marion Casper, wife of Elmer's son Holly.

[55] Dieter Garling describes Karl Moller as Minnie's "husband." However, this doesn't mean necessarily that they were actually married. For one thing, both of them were young teenagers at the time of Anna's birth, and for another there were so many regulatory obstacles to marriage in Mecklenburg at this time that many couples had no alternative to simply living together outside of formal marriage.

[56] Details courtesy of Betty Lou Cords family research, further confirmed by Mecklenburg Ruest family historian Dieter Garling.

abducted, but any reference to such a crime has yet to be located in local newspapers of the time. She may have run away from home sometime before the 1885 census where she is *not* listed. She would have been nearly seventeen by then, old enough to make this seem a possibility. She may have been sent away to live with other nearby members of the Cords family. It is also possible that she went to live with her natural father who perhaps still lived in Germany.[57] Each of these explanations seems plausible enough, but given how completely she disappeared from further records, in either the Kasper or Cords families, the last of these scenarios strikes me as the most likely, wherever Karl Moller may have been living. A child who had been abducted, had run away, or had been sent to live elsewhere in the family would have been mentioned from time to time by her mother as the years went by. Even Margaret Casper, a granddaughter who was raised by Minnie, could not recall mention of her. Anna not only vanished without a trace but was seldom spoken of again. It was almost as if she never existed. All of this suggests a secret well kept rather than an unexplained disappearance. We may never know for certain.

The abstract of Wendelin's eighty acres provides an official record of the economic hardships faced by this family throughout the more than thirty years they lived there. A string of mortgage loans involving banks, insurance companies, and brother-in-law Charles Cords tells the story of a farm family struggling to get ahead and never quite succeeding. Each debt paid in full leads to another debt assumed. This is not surprising and certainly no reflection on the efforts of Wendelin who must have worked hard his entire life. Rather it is an indication of the sheer difficulties faced by farming families of this era in which few became rich and most remained poor despite their labors. Success enough was simply raising one's children and leaving them somewhat better off than you had been to begin with. This, unquestionably, Wendelin and Minnie achieved while enduring hardships and overcoming obstacles that we of subsequent generations can hardly imagine.

Also in the property abstract is a record of Wendelin attempting to clear up confusion about his name arising from its being spelled in different ways. Inconsistencies involving both his first and last names abound in all official records. His first name is given about every imaginable spelling while his last begins sometimes with a K and sometimes with a C and sometimes as *Kaspar* instead of Kasper. This has made tracing him through indexed records especially challenging because if he is missing somewhere, one is never sure that he isn't somewhere else with

---

[57] The village cemetery at Ruest, Mecklenburg has a memorial identifying the grave of a Karl Moller whose dates make it possible that this is Anna's father. The name is very common, however, and so this is far from conclusive. Equally possible is that Karl Moller, father of Anna, himself emigrated to America. We don't, at this point, know what became of him.

a different spelling. For certain his name was Wendelin Kasper, and over time in his lifetime and in the family afterwards, the last name came to be spelled *Casper*. Changes of this sort were common in immigrant families as they sometimes opted for less ethnic spellings of their names, identifying themselves more and more with America and less with countries of their origin. World War I, in particular, encouraged this process among German Americans.

Wendelin probably would have been comfortable spelling his name as *Casper*, a version that not only exists in his native Germany, but is more common when the name appears among the nearby French. In some *Kasper/Casper* families living in France-Germany border regions, the spelling of the name flips back and forth over the generations as the family chose to emphasize in turn either its French or its German origins, depending on which served their best interests in that age. When Napoleon was in charge, their name might have been Casper, when Bismarck, it quickly became Kasper. In a region where frequent wars led to leadership and even citizenship changes, it was wise to be flexible. Wendelin must have learned that lesson well.
He applied for, and was officially granted, United States citizenship in 1897, some thirty years after he arrived in America.[58] There is nothing unusual about him waiting so long to do this. Many nineteenth century immigrants never formally sought citizenship. Others waited for years, till perhaps there appeared some formal necessity for doing so.

In his later years Wendelin developed arthritis, a chronic ailment with a long history in the family, and eventually the crippling effects of this forced him to retire from his farm, this taking place in 1906 according to his obituary. From that point, until his death, sixteen years, later he and Minnie lived in the Madison Lake village. They appear in the Madison Lake village census of 1920, residing near their son Bert, his wife Laura Knapp, and infant daughter Margaret, the last living family member to have memories of him when this research was conducted. According to Margaret, their home was located on the southeast outskirts of the village, on a street connecting Highway 60 with another leading to Point Pleasant, not far from where Wendelin's son Elmer lived his last years.

---

[58] Copies of formal citizenship petition are located in the archives of the Minnesota Historical Society, St. Paul, Minnesota.

*The only known photograph of Wendelin seated beside his wife Minnie in a car driven by their son Bert., from probably about 1915.*[59]

Other than that, he was in constant pain and gradually became incapacitated, we know little about how Wendelin spent his final years. His son Elmer ran several businesses of a public entertainment sort during this period, a movie theater and a boxing ring, a pool hall, a nightclub afloat on Madison Lake. Wendelin's older grandchildren recall him sitting around Elmer's pool hall visiting with old friends, telling stories of the old times, speaking with some in the languages he knew from his homeland. He even acquired or cultivated the nickname "The Frenchman," I suppose from speaking Alsatian French.

Among the stories he might have shared was possibly one concerning a certain Monsignor Casper, a man of great prominence in an earlier age in the French village of Obernai, not far across the Rhine from Wendelin's home. Here a main street was named after him, and a prominent memorial erected in his honor. Perhaps Wendelin knew of this famous Casper and had speculated that somehow, he must have been related. This happens all the time, as people imagine themselves somehow related to the rich and famous. Baseless, wistful speculations over time evolve into family lore and are passed from one generation to another, sometimes as tales told to wide-eyed, curious grandchildren. Here we may have the best explanation yet for the report that Wendelin was a wealthy judge in the "old country."

---

[59] Photograph courtesy of Margaret Casper, located with the help of Ivalue Casper.

So telling stories, passing the time among old friends, speaking foreign languages he knew from his youth, repeating legends and himself becoming a legend, Wendelin spent his last years, his beard white enough and grown long enough that he might have been Santa Claus.

Margaret Casper remembered sitting on his lap and playing with that beard until he gently took her hand in his and told her she would tangle it. Gradually his health declined, till at last a stroke left him partially paralyzed, confined to his bed, and sometimes incoherent. The children, among them Margaret, were cautioned not to go into his room, but she ventured there from time to time anyway, and remembers him throwing a lamp at her. Fortunately, the lamp missed her, but the memory remains, of a man suffering in his old age, irritable and perhaps sometimes delirious, ending his life with much less happiness than he deserved. His obituary speaks of his death as a release from pain and suffering, which it no doubt was, of his many friends and his hard work of a lifetime, and the grieving family he left behind.[60]

Wendelin was buried in the Catholic cemetery of All Saints Church, Madison Lake, Minnesota. A large, grey granite memorial marks the place near the southwest corner of the cemetery. Eighteen years later in 1940, his wife Minnie joined him there. Alongside is his son Bert, and nearby his son Elmer. The granite memorial has his name spelled as *Casper*, and as previously mentioned, his given name Wendelin is misspelled on a small flat memorial nearby. His obituary also misspells his name. It seems as if that difficulty, so often encountered in his affairs, stayed with him to the last.

---

[60] Microfilm copies of the *Madison Lake Times*, including Wendelin's obituary, are to be found in the Minnesota Historical Society, St. Paul. Hardbound copies were available for a time in Madison Lake, but I am not sure that these have survived.

# 3 Family Portraits

# Grafenhausen and the German Kaspers
of Today

While the village of Grafenhausen is much changed from Wendelin's day, he probably would still recognize it. He would be surprised to discover a busy German Autobahn (freeway) skirting the eastern edge of his peaceful little place of old. A *Burger King* Restaurant on its outskirts would baffle him, as would traffic on the Hauptstrasse (main street), especially summers when tourists exiting the Autobahn pass through on their way to a nearby amusement park. He would be surprised to hear that for certain administrative purposes his village has been combined with nearby Kappel, and so in some quarters is called Kappel-Grafenhausen. In fields on nearby hillsides, vineyards have been established where cows and sheep once grazed. He might wander about the vicinity for days on end without finding a field where tobacco is grown.

But some things would not have changed so much. A few of the old houses and public buildings of his time remain, albeit painted and remodeled. He would recognize the village church and probably the Rathaus. Perhaps he would point to the old gasthaus *Le Boeuf* and tell us a tale or two about some adventures he had there as a young man. Not far away along the main street stands an old brick dovecote that certainly he would recall. He would recognize names on some of the local businesses, the remnants of village families from his day. As much as anything he would find familiar the flat expanse of farmland all around, rising in the distant east toward the Black Forest, flattening out westward toward the Rhine, the sunrises and sunsets.

*The author standing at the east end of the Hauptstrasse through Grafenhausen. On the welcome*
*sign are displayed The Boeuf (left) and St. Jacobus Church.*
*Above them are official village insignia.*[61]

Most of the old farms are gone, having fallen victim to the same economic forces that threaten family farming in America. This process had begun even before Wendelin's emigration. Already by the mid-nineteenth century, the cottage industries of the old German farm villages were being replaced by more distant factories. Because of the fragmentation of farms resulting from inheritance, many farmers were more than ever dependent upon other livelihoods to sustain themselves and their families. There are, at present, just three working farms in the village where not long ago there were seventeen.[62] One of these is run by the husband of the last remaining member of our Kasper family. The production of pinot blanc and burgundy grapes for Baden wine has replaced much of the old diversified agriculture, though along the main street mornings one can still hear roosters crow. The cultivation of grapes has helped save what is left of family farming, for even small parcels of land turned into vineyards can produce significant cash income.

At least two Kasper houses remain, both extensively remodeled and changed, both on the village Hauptstrasse. One of these, on the western end toward Kappel, was the home of Wendelin and his parents. Over its front door are painted the identifying initials *JK & KJ* (Johann Kasper and Katherina Jaeger). This house has been out of the Kasper family now for several generations. It has been extensively remodeled from the single story it might have been in Wendelin's

---

<sup>61</sup> Author's photograph by Katherine Pomeroy Casper.
<sup>62</sup> According to Erhard Joerger and Gerlinde Kasper Joerger.

time.[63] Presumably at least part of the original Kasper farm adjoined it. An old farm building remains on the property, what appears to be a large barn or shed situated immediately behind the house. Parts of this may be old enough to belong to Wendelin's era.

The other house, to the west, was apparently the home of Franz Kasper, son of the younger Johann. This too has been extensively remodeled but is still in the Kasper family, belonging to Gerlinde Kasper and her husband Erhard Joerger, and housing businesses run by them and their son Dietrich. The key to the family's survival there has been the ability to adapt to changing economic circumstances by developing vineyards and small business enterprises to supplement farm income. This Kasper house now is the location of a farm produce market called *Joerger's Bauernladen* offering locally-grown fruit and vegetables, breads and cheeses, and wine and schnapps produced from the family vineyards.

*View down the Haupstrasse toward the old Wendelin (Johann and Katherina) Kasper home on the far left along the street and much remodeled.*

*In Wendelin's time is was probably a single-story house. Later it would have resembled the first house in the row here[64]*

---

[63]Cousin Vera Schlenker suggests that the original house was single story.
[64] Author's photograph.

*The Johann Kasper /Katherina Jaeger house as it appears to-day at 57 Hauptstrasse, Graf-enhausen, much remodeled and rebuilt but with the initials JK and KJ still above its entrance. Standing in front are the author with his sons Cass (left) and Stephen (right).*[65]

Recently Dietrich Joerger has remodeled the rest of the house into holiday vacation apartments for summer tourists. On the ground floor is an large dining area for group events. Old beams have been exposed, an enclosed spiral staircase added to the exterior, while all around are furnishings and artifacts reminiscent of Baden's rural past. Old wine barrels serve as displays for the family's offerings of wine, schnapps, and specialty Baden liqueurs. Everywhere is a sense of an industrious, hardworking family determined to succeed.

---

[65] Author's photograph by Katherine Pomeroy Casper.

*The Franz Kasper house, from perhaps shortly after World War II, as it looked before extensive remodeling.[66]*

Indeed a dedication to hard work seems to be a Kasper family tradition here, summarized on an inscribed plaque which was long displayed on the house front greeting passersby along the Hauptstrasse.

As we have noted, Gerlinde Kasper Joerger is the last remaining Kasper family in Grafenhausen to have been born with the Kasper name. She is as far as I know the last remaining Kasper descendant of Johann Kasper in all of Germany. She is the great granddaughter of Wendelin's brother Johann and thus a third cousin to Kasper descendants presently living in the United States. The only child of Ernst Josef Kasper and Elise Junele, she has spent her entire life of 77 years in Grafenhausen. Both she and her husband Erhard Joerger are highly respected members of the village community. They have three children and eight grandchildren. Their son Dietrich, as previously mentioned, has joined them in the family farming and business enterprises. Another son Volker has his PhD in viniculture and holds a prominent position in a Freiberg wine institute. A daughter Vera lives with her family in Kippenheim, a nearby village, where she holds a position on the city council and teaches computer science in an area school. The overall family picture is one of dedication to hard work, education, and achievement.

---

[66] Photograph courtesy Vera Schlenker, daughter of Gerlinde Kasper Joeger.

*Plaque formerly displayed on the front of the old Franz Kasper house, now removed I suppose as out of keeping with the holiday apartment rental spirit. A rough would be: "Working and striving is God's commandment. Labor is life and sitting around doing nothing is death."[67]*

Gerlinde is known throughout the area for her culinary skills. You know she is a Kasper straight off because of the value she attaches to potatoes! I hadn't met Gerlinde more than an hour before I came upon her cooking potatoes in her kitchen of the old Franz Kasper house.[68] Among Gerlinde's many specialties are potato (Kartoffel) salad, potato soup, and sauerbraten made according to an old family recipe. She also bakes a variety of traditional German cakes. Curious and appreciative family members have attempted to imitate her successes, but all agree that hers are unequaled. My good fortune has been to sample large portions at her table, followed by the cakes baked from recipe (no box mixes allowed!), all washed down with generous quantities of white wine from the family vineyards. Family history research does have its rewards!

---

[67] Author's photograph.

[68] I have a memory of joining my grandfather Elmer Casper planting potatoes along a strip of high ground bordering a marsh on his Marysburg farm and instructing me with the utmost seriousness that getting one's potato crop established was one of life's more critical chores.  If you had potatoes, you would always eat, he insisted, and for sure we Kaspers have eaten carloads of potatoes over the years.

*Gerlinde Kasper with her characteristic smile and two pans of potatoes cooking.* [69]

Gerlinde and her husband continue to be most active in their community and carry on the family tradition of hard work, even at an age when others might have retired years ago. At work in his vineyards, pruning vines, supervising the harvest and the making of schnapps, Erhard is most often met on his way to work or just coming from it. Each year for many years for the Grafenhausen "Fastnacht" carnival, a weeklong pre-Lenten event, Gerlinde's constructs a life-sized *Hexe* (witch) doll which is burnt in the village square as the culmination of the last night's events.

One other family member of Gerlinde's generation lives in the area, Herbert Schwartz of Freiberg. He is the grandson of Karolina Kasper, daughter of Wendelin's brother Johann. Herbert lived in California for many years where his mother worked as a private nurse, so he is a wonderfully fluent speaker of English. You would hardly guess that he is over eighty years old. He is a most cordial, gentlemanly man, deeply imbued with the history and culture of his native city.

It is possible, given that twelve children were born to Johann Kasper and Theresia Kurz, that other Kasper family still reside in Germany and have in the course of time simply slipped from view of those I met, not surprising given the upheaval and disruption caused by two wars and the subsequent division of Germany into East and West. As previously mentioned, several of these Kasper offspring died in infancy and youth. Others who survived to adulthood appear to have had no children. Among descendants were an attorney at Lorrach named Josef Kasper

---

[69] Author's photograph.

(previously mentioned) who never married—according to Gerlinde—and a Catholic priest Franz Josef Kasper.

*Kasper third cousins (left to right) Herbert Schwartz, the author, and Gerlinde Kasper Joerger seated at a table in the Joerger home.[70]*

The name itself occurs frequently in Germany today, as well as in neighboring countries. As I attempted to make clear at the beginning of this, it would be mistaken to assume that all Kaspers are somehow, even distantly related, and it appears to be, in so far as our family is concerned, a name that lives on in Germany only as long as Gerlinde's lifetime. She is, it must be said, a most worthy last representative of our family name there.

---

[70] Photograph by Katherine Pomeroy-Casper.

*Grafenhausen and St. Jacobus Church today viewed from the south*[71]

---

[71] Author's photograph.

# 4 Family Portraits

# Wilhelmine "Minnie" Cords (1850-1940)

Minnie (Wilhelmine Sophia Friedericke Caroline) Cords was born in Ruest, Mecklenburg 8 August 1850 and christened later that year in her village's tiny Lutheran church. She was the sixth of the seven children born to Johann Joachim Cords and Hannah Catharina Sternberg, a prominent Ruest farming family with a history of several generations there and in nearby villages.

Not long after her eighteenth birthday, the birth of her daughter Anna was entered into village church records. Anna's father was listed as Karl Moller, a farmhand from the nearby village of Dinnies, who appears to have been no more than sixteen. [72]

A village map from 1850 reveals that Minnie's Cords' extended family owned two farms in Ruest village during the period she lived there. Another farm was owned by a Hahn family member, a name prominent in Minnie's ancestral line. The village churchyard (beyond map's right border) whose old cemetery has been preserved in a state of more or less benign neglect gives us a picture of Cords family presence dating as far back as the late 1700's. Among the older Cords gravesites are some that suggest prominence and even wealth with the remains of wrought iron fence work surrounding them and large stone memorials whose dates are badly worn and hard to read. It appears that among the Cords family were men of considerable local, if not regional importance.

---

[72] Dieter Garling, a present-day historian of Mecklenburg families, reports that Carl Moller was the husband of Wilhelmine Cords. I am further indebted to Betty Lou Cords for identifying Ruest as the place of Minnie Cords' origin.

*Painting of an old Ruest farm as it may have looked in Minnie's time*[73]

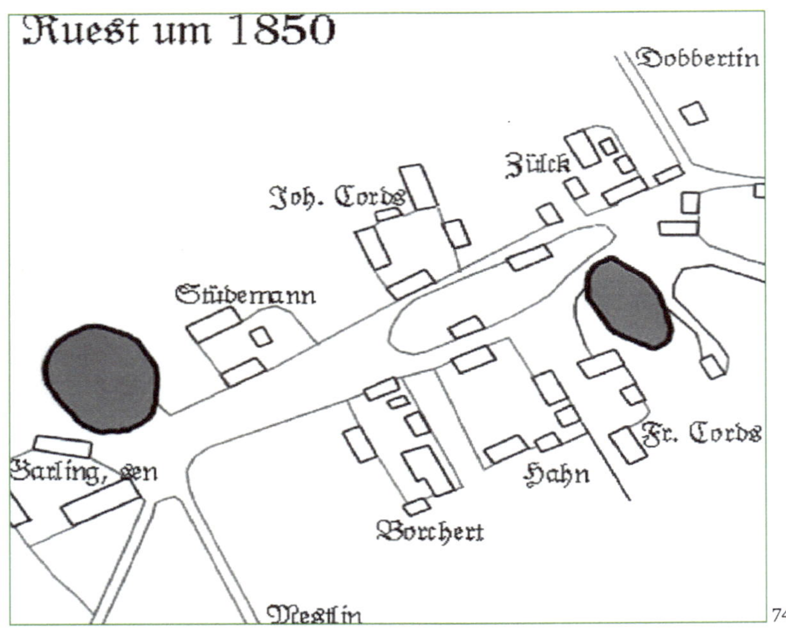


---

[73] Reproduction downloaded from www.emecklenburg.de/Ruest/, a website maintained by Dieter Garling, *et al.*
[74] Downloaded from internet website produced and maintained by Dieter Garling, *et al.*

*Cobblestone road leading to Ruest as it looks in the present day.[75]*

Given the ravages of World War II, especially its horrible aftermath of Russian occupation, collective farming, relocation of entire populations from the countryside into the cities, etc. it's hard to extrapolate from Ruest as it appears today back to what it might have been in Minnie's time. It seems likely to have been quite small and perhaps never large enough to support local merchants and tradesmen. At the same time, its church and its several large brick homes suggest a history of success and even affluence.

*Ruest's Lutheran village church much as it would have appeared in Minnie's time.*

*Both Minnie and her daughter Anna would have been christened here.[76]*

It is possible that Minnie's family was quite well off by standards of the day, a possibility highlighted by the fact that relatively few in this large family chose to emigrate to the United States.

An early family immigrant was Frederick "Fritz" Cords, Minnie's uncle. As often happens, the presence of one family member, settled and established in the "New World," led to others following after, in this case Minnie and her brother Charles.

---

<sup>75</sup> Ibid.
<sup>76</sup> Author's photograph from Ruest, Mecklenburg visit in 1999.

We know little for certain about circumstances surrounding Minnie Cords' departure from her Mecklenburg, Germany homeland except that she must have left in the late summer or early autumn of 1870. She traveled aboard the ship Silesia with her infant daughter Anna, and arrived in New York 18 October 1870, the day after her daughter's second birthday.

*The passenger ship Silesia aboard which Minnie and her daughter Anna journeyed to America in 1870, a year after this ship's maiden voyage.*[77]

Ship's passenger records suggest that she and Anna traveled alone.[78] We are unlikely to ever know her reasons for leaving her homeland. However we can say that while men, especially young men, by the hundreds of thousands emigrated during this period and while entire families emigrating included more hundreds of thousands, a young woman making the Atlantic crossing alone—if that was the case with Minnie—was relatively uncommon, the more so with an infant in her care. In undertaking such a journey, Minnie was already demonstrating the courage and tenacity that seems to have characterized her entire life of ninety years.

By the time of Minnie's arrival. her uncle Frederick, his wife Sophia, and their young family had relocated from a farm in Wisconsin to another McPherson Township of Blue Earth County,

---

[77] Photograph courtesy of Ancestry.com.

[78] *New York Passenger Lists, 1820-1957*, published by Ancesrty.com.  The actual passenger list with the names "Wilhe" and Anna Cords appearing near the bottom is attached in the Charts and Records section following.  The names are difficult to read but unmistakably those of Minnie (Wilhelmine) and her daughter.  This passenger page and those immediately preceding and following list no know Cords family members.

Minnesota.[79] It seems likely this fact determined where Minnie herself would first settle. With a very small infant in her care, the assistance of family would seem especially necessary. The Cords' farm location, near the village of St. Clair, would have placed her within about ten miles south of her future husband Wendelin Kasper who had only recently settled in LeRay Township. They would have met the following year, with their first child John being born in August 1872.

Minnie's brother Cords seems to have emigrated not long after, for he is listed in a Mankato Lutheran Church record as the baptismal sponsor for Wendelin and Minnie's firstborn.[80]

What happened to Karl Moller, Anna's father—whether he died before she left Mecklenburg, or died accompanying her on the voyage to America, or simply stayed or was left behind—seems destined to remain a source of speculation. There lingers in this story, in subsequent events, and in Minnie's occasional references to it late in her life, elements of inconsistency and secrecy and a sense of unsolved mystery. We cannot be sure whether Minnie was running away from events at home or embracing opportunities in a new world. As was so often the case with emigrants, perhaps it was a combination of both. Such journeys as hers could only be undertaken for good reasons. With an infant to look after, she would have needed especially compelling reasons. It must have been reassuring for her to discover in the countryside of Blue Earth County with its gently rolling fields, woodlands, and lakes a setting much like the one she left behind in Mecklenburg.

An account of Minnie's marriage to Wendelin Kasper and their life together will be found elsewhere here (see pp. 25-29 and pp. 93-96). Working in domestic obscurity fulfilling the prescribed duties of wife and mother, most women of Minnie's time left little behind in the way of public records. Every family historian struggles with the fact that much more can be known about family men, concerning whom whole chapters might be written, while so little remains of the life of female family that a few paragraphs will suffice, much of that conjecture. So it is with Minnie.

Minnie and Wendelin left their farming life and retired to Madison Lake in 1905. For the next seventeen years, until Wendelin's death in late December of 1922, they appear to have rented a home in a residential neighborhood near Point Pleasant. The 1910 Federal Census lists their

---

[79] This Cords family is listed in the 1870 Federal Census for Blue Earth County.
[80] Information generously provided by Cords family historian Betty Lou Cords.

son Albert, age 25, living with them. By the time of the 1920 Census, Albert, now married to the former Laura Knapp, is living next door with a daughter Margaret.

Two family deaths brought major changes to Minnie's life in the next decade, first Wendelin's and then that of her daughter-in-law who died of appendicitis late in pregnancy while giving birth to a fourth child in 1924. This left four grandchildren, including a newborn, next door without a mother. Minnie, now in her early seventies, stepped in to fill the void and by all accounts raised a second family. By the time of Minnie's death in 1940, the youngest of these, a granddaughter Violet, was sixteen.

We have but four accounts of Minnie from her last sixteen years. The first from her granddaughter Margaret Casper who recalled with deep admiration how Minnie, at about the age of eighty, confronted a neighbor woman who was beating her daughter by bolting down into her basement and pulling her out into her yard for a tongue lashing. For Margaret this memory captured both Minnie's courage and her sense of duty toward the innocent and helpless. In a second memory from Margaret, we hear Minnie cautioning her in her adolescence. "Don't do as I did," she said referring to what she regarded as mistakes from a time in her life back in Germany when she was about Margaret's age. "God punished me," she said.

Next, we see her very late in life, now possibly suffering from dementia, at the old Madison Lake school interrupting routine of the school day to ask if Violet can come out. And finally, we have a memory of yet another granddaughter brought to visit her, "a little old lady, dressed in black, sitting by herself in a darkened room."

In her last years, it appears Minnie lived with her son John in a little house near the Madison Lake fire department and water tower. Family lore reports that upon her death, her daughter-in-law Rosetta, burnt her personal effects. If so, we have another instance of how conflagrations erase the record and leave family historians with so many missing puzzle pieces that what might have been a portrait becomes a mere sketch. Fortunately, a short time before this alleged fire, Margaret Casper secretly removed the picture of Wendelin and Minnie included here on page 34.

*Probably Minnie's 80th birthday[81]*

Minnie, who lived to her ninetieth year, is buried alongside her husband Wendelin in the All Saints Church cemetery at Madison Lake.

---

[81] Casper family photograph.

# 5 Family Portraits

## Elmer Francis "Cass" Casper (1883-1953)

### A Biographical Sketch and Memoir of Wendelin's Son

It's hard to know where to begin with our story of Elmer Francis Casper, except to say that among the many recollections of him, I have yet to find one that does not recall him with warmth, affection, and a hint of respectful amusement.

He was born December 27, 1883 in his parents' log cabin on the Kasper homestead in LeRay Township between Madison Lake and Eagle Lake, the second youngest of the children of Wendelin and Minnie Kasper. At the time of his birth, he had two brothers, John and Louis, and two sisters, Clara and Minnie. Also possibly still part of his family was Anna, a half-sister born in Germany. Two years later, with the birth of Albert, another brother, his family would be complete. Sometime between the censuses of 1880 and 1885, Anna would disappear, and before Elmer himself was twelve years old, both Louis and Minnie would die, she in 1887 and he in 1894.

These must have been very hard times. A land abstract of the family property lists a string of mortgages, one after another and year after year, debts paid off and new debts made. To Wendelin and Minnie, children were born and children died. Hardship, hard work, outbreaks of diseases like diphtheria and smallpox, loss, heartbreak, the economic depression of the 1890's --all these things had to be part of Elmer's upbringing, and yet for all that, and from beginning to end, he seems to have been an optimistic, lighthearted man.

I cannot say for sure where Elmer attended school. His parents eventually became members of All Saints Catholic parish in Madison Lake, but I don't, at the time of this writing, know when the Catholic school there first began operation, and it's hard for me to imagine him being sent that distance (three miles), especially winters in these days before automobiles. I'm quite sure that there was a "one room" schoolhouse much closer at that time, just down the road from his family's log cabin, and perhaps whatever he had for formal education was provided there. The abandoned building, on the old Eagle Lake Road, was still there in my youth, but has long since disappeared.

Elmer once shared with me his own version of his education: "I walked in the front door of the school, spit tobacco on the floor, and then walked out the back door." He chuckled when he said this, and then his tone grew serious. "Education," he said, "is the one thing they can't take away from you." It might have been something his father said to him, for certainly his father coming from Baden, Germany had brought an education with him to the "new world," and certainly in the course of time this young immigrant family had discovered how much else could be given and how much taken away.

One summer when he was about sixteen, Elmer worked with a local threshing crew, by all accounts intense, unrelenting, backbreaking work. He said that he began that summer as a boy, and ended the summer a man. Working on a threshing crew for a young man in those days could be a "rite of passage," and it seems to have been just that for him.

*An early photograph thought to be of Elmer*

As a young man, he was not only athletic, but had a strong interest in athletics. He played baseball for a Madison Lake team which seems to have achieved prominence in the area, and later on, he managed both the Madison Lake baseball and basketball teams. And pretty good teams they were. He was also interested in boxing and may have been an accomplished boxer himself. He seems to have taught my father (Holly Casper) how to use his fists, and the latter had memories of accompanying his dad to St. Paul in the late 1920's where Elmer—well into his 40's now—would work out as a sparring partner for some of the prominent boxers based there. In this era, St. Paul was a major center for boxing promotions.

*Young Elmer in his baseball uniform (photo courtesy of Faye Casper Michaletz).*

In mid-November 1904, a few weeks before his twenty-first birthday, Elmer married Estella Knapp, daughter of prominent Madison Lake resident James K. Knapp, drugstore proprietor, local school board member, and justice of the peace. One would have to surmise that for Elmer and the Kasper family, his marriage was a significant step up the local social ladder.

*Wedding photo of Elmer Casper and Estella Knapp.*

I haven't discovered where the young couple lived immediately after their marriage, but soon afterwards, if not beforehand, Elmer was at work building a home. I don't know that he ever considered himself a builder, but he certainly went on from there to build things aplenty. In Elmer's day, of course, people often had no alternative to doing for themselves tasks which in the present time other people are hired to do. A man needing a home for his young family wouldn't necessarily hire a mason to lay its foundation and a carpenter to put up its walls and roof. More than likely, he would get advice and help from family, friends, and neighbors, and do it himself, learning the skills he needed as he went along. So it may have been with Elmer.

The little bungalow he built for his young wife was located on the south end of the Wendelin Kasper homestead, across the old Eagle Lake road from the site of the log cabin where Elmer himself was born. In fact, Elmer's bungalow displays features possibly reminiscent of south German domestic architecture, especially in its main gable facing the road, with its unusual slightly curved lower lateral surface. This tempts one to think that Wendelin provided some design pointers from memories of his homeland. And why not? He probably was still living just across the road while his son was at work. Many a time he must have walked over to give advice and lend a hand.

An unusual feature, not revealed in the accompanying photograph, is a ground floor window built diagonally across the corner of the house in such a way that the corner itself is replaced by the window's lateral surface. I know of but one other example of a house with a window placed this way, in an old Madison Lake home in a neighborhood where Wendelin seems to have lived his last years. Perhaps this is yet another structure that Elmer and his father had a hand in building, and for all I know at this time, it may in fact be where Wendelin himself lived in his retirement.

The room on the far left in this picture, an entryway, appears to be a later addition from long after the time Elmer's family resided there. Other additions are also evident, suggesting that the original structure may have been simply the part formed by the main gable. In any event, it appears that Elmer and Estella's first three children —Milton, Ivalue, and Dayton—were all born here, making it possible to place the dates of the family's occupancy from 1905 until sometime after 1911.

*According to several family sources,
this house,
these days in the Buskey family,
was built by Elmer Casper and was the
home where he and his wife lived when
their oldest children were born.*

Another of Elmer's building projects may have been the store on Front Street in Madison Lake that housed for a time the pharmacy of his father-in-law James K. Knapp, and in later years was known as the Dick Brinser store. A third, built about 1920, was the home on the northeast corner of the Kasper homestead where my father grew up, and where subsequently our family lived till about 1967. He also may have built, or had a hand in constructing, the building on the north end of Front Street in Madison Lake, once the Herman Muellerleile Hardware, and later the Red Barn, a furniture store. His last building project was the white stucco "Spanish" style house with a tile roof on a hillside at the edge of Madison Lake where he himself lived, though he left it unfinished from the time his wife died in 1946.

All his homes had interesting features and could fairly be described as distinctive for the periods in which they were built. The "Spanish" style house, as it came to be called in both community and the Casper family, would have been more accurately described as *art deco*, something far more unusual in a small Midwestern farming community. In fact it might have been the most interesting piece of domestic architecture ever built in the Madison Lake village. It has long since been demolished but in the twenty or so years of its existence, it became a village landmark.

*The front entrance of Elmer's "Spanish" house, clearly instead an art deco design. Note its black trim and decorations, the circular roof over its front entrance, the black metal lattice work.*

Only the first of Elmer's homes, the bungalow, still survives, and when I was in it this past year, I noticed that the unusual corner windows give its living room a subtle hexagonal feeling. This is the house that Margaret Casper says contains within it remnants of the old Kasper log cabin, a claim I wasn't able to confirm, and which I now doubt.

*The Elmer Casper home on the northeast corner of the original Kasper family farm, shortly after its construction in about 1920. These must be among the first of Elmer's turkeys raised there.*

Speaking of the 1920 home where I grew up on the other end of the old Kasper farm, Elmer always assured my mother that it was built well and would never blow down in a storm. And though it was a drafty, poorly insulated place for the bitterly cold winters we endured there, it was charming enough to look at in its prime. Many a terrific summer storm did have a go at it, but it took a bulldozer in the late 1960's to do what the gusting winds failed to accomplish.

From at least the time of his marriage in 1904, Elmer became deeply involved in the life of Madison Lake. Perhaps in order to be closer to his many enterprises he moved his family into the village sometime after 1911, settling in a home on Lake Street where Louis and Holly, the last of his five children, were born. While raising his family—Louis dying of scarlet fever in infancy—Elmer started and ran various recreation and entertainment businesses, and also for a time may have been involved in an automobile dealership and a short-lived taxicab operation with his older brother John.

A June 1914 *Mankato Free Press* article mentions that he is the Madison Lake proprietor of the Rex Billiard Hall, and then announces that he has recently purchased in St. Paul the necessary projection equipment to bring Madison Lake its first regular "movies," every summer night in a 40 by 65-foot tent he has also purchased, and will set up along the right-of-way of the Great Western Railway. Clearly Elmer was making his presence felt as an entertainment entrepreneur, not only in Madison Lake but throughout the area.

Elmer's movie pavilion project may have been temporarily "derailed" when the Great Western Railway folks read of his plans to locate it along their right-of-way. If so, he wasn't about to be stopped, and soon found another place to pitch his tent, in a vacant lot behind the Madison Lake municipal tavern. Nor would he restrict his offerings to moving pictures, for he also featured boxing matches and the sort of vaudeville-style, live road shows that were common in that day. It was Madison Lake's first and only entertainment venue. Elmer himself might have participated in some of the boxing matches, and perhaps he was able to book well-known fighters from St. Paul, using his connections there.

Given the well-documented involvement of gangsters in the boxing world, it is fair to assume that Elmer was familiar with some notorious St. Paul underworld figures of the Prohibition Era. This possibility is supported by an anecdote preserved in the Dayton Casper family. It seems that at some point during Dayton's ownership of a local landmark called the *Nine Mile Corner*, a filling station and tavern located at the junctions of Highways 14 and 60, he may have been threatened by gangsters selling "protection." The nature of this kind of racket was *either you pay us, or something bad happens to you and your business*. Apparently, Dayton informed his dad, and when these thugs returned at their appointed time to either collect payment or do their worst, Elmer himself confronted them. That was all it took to end the threat, once and for all. Perhaps they didn't like the thought of tangling with Elmer, the boxer, a raw-boned, imposing man, with hands the size that used to be described as "meat hooks," but I think it also possible that Elmer had connections with people these crooks were even more wary of upsetting, and so they turned tail and were never seen again at the *Nine Mile Corner*.

Other Elmer enterprises also involved tented structures, most remarkable and memorable of all, his legendary *Noah's Ark*, a huge, tent-covered platform built upon barrels to float as a dancehall on the lake itself. *Noah's Ark* is said to have been the most famous enterprise ever to appear in Madison Lake. People came from miles around just to gawk at the prodigious, canvas-covered barge whose dance bands included that of the legendary Lawrence Welk. With a strong wind blowing and a lively crowd aboard dancing, it would sometimes break loose from its moorings and float out across the bay till it was grounded on the opposite shore. One can only imagine the delighted couples splashing ashore at night's end, knowing already that they had a good story to tell years later when their grandchildren came along.

Even taken off the lake, Noah's Ark lived on as a dance hall and a roller rink re-constructed near the *Nine Mile Corner*, and many years after it was torn down and carted away, it still lived on in local legend. Mention to anyone that you were one of Elmer's grandchildren, and you were almost certain to hear another tale about *Noah's Arc*. In fact, if Elmer had done nothing else in his remarkable life, his floating dance hall alone would have secured his place in local legends. But in fact he did many things, and along the way became the subject of many local legends.

Elmer Casper's "Noah's Ark"--the floating dance pavilion on Madison Lake, 1925. It was located by the present North Shore Park. This was the canvas roof stage. The lake was down then. Note long plank walks over the water pools.
Photos by Dayton "Mike" Casper

Madison Lake in these days was a rough-and-tumble German/Irish community, and businesses of the sort Elmer ran would be bound to attract unruly types. It's pretty safe to conclude that his management duties included acting as a bouncer, and from everything I know about him—his large hands, his rawboned physique, his athletic prowess—I would think it very seldom that anyone seriously challenged him.

At the same time, he was a 'gentle giant," full of good humor and a sense of right. A well-documented local story describes a rally of rural Nonpartisans in the streets of Madison Lake, in the course of which tempers flared between the demonstrators, who included women and children, and their opponents who opened up the village fire hydrants and turned hoses on them. It is said that Elmer waded through the riot and turned the water off and almost single-handedly protected the women and children from the mob. No one there would have challenged him -- that was the sort of man he was, combining *strength, courage, a keen sense of justice, and compassion.*

There was no end of need for such virtues in these days called the "Roaring Twenties," followed by "Prohibition," the "Great Depression," union turmoil, racketeering, local women's temperance committees, the morally outrageous, and the morally outraged. Elmer's businesses would have been right in the middle of this turbulent mix, attracting the thugs and the disorderly and attracting the attention of local do-gooders and law enforcement. There must have been more than one unscheduled fight at his pavilion, and there certainly were a few out on Madison Lake where Noah's Ark floated less peacefully than its biblical namesake. After two successful years, the county sheriff shut it down, or at least ordered it off the lake, so the story goes, in the "interest of public safety."

Elmer must have always loved shows and entertainment, though in his later years—and perhaps never—he wasn't the sort to make a show of himself. Still, I think he had an exuberant side which even in old age would sometimes surface. I remember him in our yard bursting out with a line or two of a song called "Wait till the Sun Shines, Nellie," while telling me about a film he had seen or was about to see. And he once told me about having seen "Buffalo Bill's Wild West Show," including the famous female sharpshooter Annie Oakley. He had brought the silent films of early Hollywood to his village pavilion, and later when his son Dayton offered free outdoor movies behind the *Nine Mile Corner*, Elmer would often be there among the Friday night crowd watching the likes of Tom Mix and Gene Autry. He lived long enough for television to become a fact of life even in our home, and so I once saw him watching *Roller Derby* in our living room with rapt attention, no doubt thinking the old roller rink he owned in bygone days.

We sometimes shake our heads in amazement and believe that the latest gadgets of our age would have positively flummoxed our grandparents, had they lived to see them. Not so with Elmer, I think; he might have had his doubts about the wisdom of computers and mobile phones, and people sipping martinis on passenger jets, but there was nothing he couldn't have taken in his long stride.

Somewhere in the course of his middle years, perhaps for peace and peace of mind, Elmer turned more and more to farming. His father Wendelin died shortly after Christmas in 1922, and the north 40 acres of his land passed into Elmer's hands, while the south 40 went to Elmer's younger brother Bert. With his house completed there, Elmer began to raise turkeys on his portion.

In the dry summers of the 1930's, he would put his turkeys out "on range" along the shore of Madison Lake just south of Point Pleasant. Among the local lads he hired to tend them there were my father and Ted Roemer, one-day postmaster of Madison Lake. Ted Roemer himself wrote and published in the *Madison Lake Times* an appreciative memoir of Elmer from which are taken some of these details.

*The Casper turkey farm on the north end of the original Kasper homestead, sometime during the 1930's. I remember the little barn being there till the late 1940's, but not after that.*

During this time also, Elmer joined other enterprising locals in harvesting seed from reed canary (phalaris) grass which grew in the many sloughs and lowlands scattered throughout the area. This could be done either by hand, or by mechanical means using a custom made "binder" that could be drawn out into the sloughs in early summer and used to cut the seed-laden heads from this tall grass. At times, the prices paid by local seed dealers were high enough to make even hand harvesting pay off, as much as a dollar or more per pound, which was truly a lot of money in those days.

My first—but by far not my last—memory of phalaris grass, is of Elmer gathering up a bundle of seed heads in one of his large hands and holding them near my face. He told me that the seed was worth money, and if I could gather enough of it, I would have a pocket full of silver dollars. Then he made a gesture toward the plants still standing nearby, a sweep of his hand, as if holding an imaginary scythe, to show me how it could be done even by hand.

Elmer's wife Estella Knapp inherited from her family another parcel of 80 acres northwest of Marysburg, about 5 miles from Madison Lake. He also farmed this land for many years, one of its perennial crops being the seed from a phalaris grass marsh that made up about 30 of its acres.

*Elmer, his son Holly, and wife Estella,*
*out among their turkeys sometime in the 1930's Depression era.*

So what with one enterprise and another, Elmer made his way through the first half of the twentieth century, raising his three sons and a daughter to a adulthood and finally losing his wife to cancer as World War II was coming to an end and his youngest son Holly was recovering from his wounds near the battlefront in France. He had always taken an active role in the affairs of his family, including helping in various ways to raise the children of his brother Bert whose wife had died in 1923 leaving four little ones—including a newborn baby—in the care of Elmer's mother. By these, he was remembered affectionately as "Uncle Elmer," who once caught his niece Margaret in a local Protestant church and pulled her out by the ear. Others, in his family and around Madison Lake, called him warmly by his nickname "Cass."

During his last years, living alone in his unfinished "Spanish" house in Madison Lake, he mourned his wife deeply. The house, as I recall it, had but four rooms, and Elmer confined himself to what would have been the kitchen. Beside the kitchen, a pair of lovely French doors led into a living room sparsely furnished with whatever was left from the life he and his wife had shared for 42 years. I remember a little writing desk, a chair or two perhaps, a little table, odds and ends, but mostly a sense of emptiness. Down the hall from the kitchen—where I never dared wander the few times I was there with my father—there must have been a couple of bedrooms. There was no plumbing, no phone. Elmer got water from a red iron hand pump out in the yard where along the road a cherry tree grew. An oil burner in the kitchen served to keep him warm enough, but left a faint kerosene smell in the air, and in his clothing. He slept on a cot nearby beneath a jumble of old blankets.

He helped his son Holly settle with his family on the old homestead and farm the Marysburg land. In the course of these endeavors, I often spent time with him. We saw a lot of him in those days working out in our farmyard which he had left to us such a short time before that he must have had much that still concerned him there. One of his favorite expressions, when picking up a piece of angle iron or an old tool and hanging it on a hook nearby, was "this will come in handy some day." He had learned not to throw such things away.

If my mother was frying donuts, he would sit in our kitchen, place several of them like large rings on his finger, and one by one dunk them in his coffee, which otherwise he would cool by pouring it into a saucer. He chain-smoked, often lighting one cigarette with another, but we didn't mind. His warm, mellow presence overwhelmed all other impressions, even the bizarre way he would eat dinner at our table, by first dishing everything up, and then mixing it all together with the side of his fork so that it became an indescribable slurry mounded on his plate. At other times he would accept invitations for Sunday dinner at the nearby homes of his other children.

Most summer evenings with the sun going down you would find him out on Front Street of Madison Lake, sitting on a bench, visiting with his friends, in front of Herman Muellerliele's

Hardware or Pearl's Restaurant, a little red brick building he may have built. If we happened to be in town that evening, he would find in the deep pockets of his very baggy pants, enough change for us to have an ice cream cone at Gifford's Drug Store. Generosity was an instinct -- he didn't have to think about it.

*Elmer relaxing outside the home of his daughter Ivalue Casper Hilgers,*
*rural Eagle Lake, early 1950's.*

There seemed to be about him in those days a warm glow that persists now even in distant memory, his stoicism, his kindness, the smells of his tobacco smoke and old wool, something like saintliness.

There can be no doubt that he cared deeply for others and neglected himself. He would never see a doctor. He let his hair grow long, till with his wire-rimmed glasses, and his tattered clothing, he resembled the "hippies" of an era that was twenty years in the future. He drove old cars whose lights seldom worked all at once, cars that would backfire if they started at all, and then lurch forward with the engine racing as he let the clutch out, cars that sometimes just blew up, and wound up with weeds growing around them in our yard or his.

A large tree, long dead in our yard, once crashed to earth where he had been sitting not five minutes before. He believed enough in Providence that he could survey the scene coolly afterwards, smoking a cigarette, and say that it mustn't have been his time. Another day a crippled old turkey came chasing after me, unwisely it turned out, for once Elmer heard of it, the *turkey's time had come*. He was quick to defend those he loved, yet not reluctant to criticize them when it came to that. When his son Holly came home with a sporty new Buick convertible in 1949, Elmer was dismayed. He pointed to his old Model A Ford out in our driveway, and said that such a car was good enough, cost hardly anything, and would last for years. What business did his son have throwing his money away on flashy cars? Not long after, he drove his old jalopy out behind our house, where the engine promptly blew up. Such was life for Elmer, but nothing dismayed him for long.

Elmer loved growing things. There still thrives in what used to be our yard along Highway 60 a spruce tree he brought there from his own yard in Madison Lake. Standing by that morning, watching him unload it from his old truck and ease it into the black soil, I asked him how old it was. "As old as you," he said, which I took to mean it was ten. I was taller than the tree at the time, but not for more than a year or two. Behind our house for many years was a little orchard of plum and apple trees which he also would have planted; and also the cherry tree along the road by his Spanish house; and, for all I know, even the spruce and lilacs which are still in the yard of the first house he built. Every spring, till the year he died, he had his potato patch. His sweet corn, vegetables, and muskmelons (which he called "mushmellons") would appear on the doorstep of the Catholic school nuns' convent in Madison Lake. His wife's grave at All Saints Cemetery, from the time of her death in 1945 to the day of his own, was ever so carefully tended, with flowers every spring and summer, and *arbor vitae* flanking her memorial.

What Elmer lacked in formal education he more than made up for in personality, common sense, imagination, generosity, and plain hard work. He seemed always ready to give new things a try, whether it was baseball and boxing, or phalaris grass and turkeys on a lakeshore. He began his life in a rough log shanty and ended it in an art deco house of his own construction, which even if simply built, was easily the most interesting dwelling design in Madison Lake. In between, he had a movie theater, a floating nightclub, and a roller rink. He raised potatoes and melons. He raised hell with crooks and bullies. He was always quick to lend a hand, and slow to ask for help himself. He appreciated simple things —a good cup of coffee, a good cigarette, a doughnut fresh from the cooker, a day ending in a chat with friends. He planted trees and memories, many of which live on to this day. He created legends.

The morning he died, in May 1953, he was supposed to come from Madison Lake to join my father and me for a trip to the Marysburg farm to get started with the spring planting. When he didn't show up at the appointed time, my dad drove in to see what the matter was. Returning soon, he came with the news of his death. I can still hear his voice in our kitchen saying, "Pa is gone! Pa is dead!" --words like that resound across the days and years ever afterwards. I can still hear them. When you are very young, things like this stick with you because you are still unacquainted with how suddenly everything can change forever. With Elmer gone, the world changed forever. A lot of people felt that way, I think. The book of those who attended his funeral visitation contains dozens upon dozens of names. And everyone who signed it could have told you dozens of stories about him, some of them amusing, some heroic, all of them heartfelt.

*Elmer in his last years.*

Later on, some neighbors told us that they had seen his old truck pass by coming out from Madison Lake that morning, and then return right after. It may be that he didn't feel good, and simply didn't want to bother us with how he felt --a Casper trait for sure-- or perhaps he knew he was dying, and just wanted to have a last look at where it all began --looking back over your shoulder, another trait I share with him, for how else could this all be written? Out in the yard behind our house I cried from grief for the first time.

One evening when I was a little boy, he shared an account of what life on our farm was like back in his early days. Probably some of what he told me were stories he had heard from his own father who had settled on this land thirteen years before he was born. One would have to think by the time Elmer was old enough to remember, much of the land had been cleared of its many large trees, and that the rattlesnakes he mentioned to amaze me had long been overwhelmed by the bull snakes he said were brought in for that purpose. Though most likely the little pond he told me about, once located right in the middle of our 80 acres, was still there when he was a little boy, shimmering in three seasons and frozen solid in the fourth. For all I know, he might have skated on it. He certainly would have been the sort to put on a pair of skates and go flying out across it.

The Kasper pond has long since been drained by a system of tiles, and apart from springtime periods of heavy rain, is seldom again seen, much less skated upon by any of my generation and younger. It only shows up in the wettest of springs, glimmering there over an acre or two for a week or so before the tiles beneath thaw sufficiently to carry it all way again.

I like to think the pond was there that early spring morning when he had his last look and said his last goodbye, and that in his mind he could see himself gliding out across it again, and behind him the little log cabin where it all began, with a trail of smoke flowing skyward from its hearth.

*Last photograph of Elmer Casper, in his old Mackinaw coat and hat with earflaps, as most of us recall him, from the early spring of 1953. Picture taken by the author.*

Some people who are part of your life, however briefly, seem to stay there forever, even long after they're gone. What they leave behind seems to be more than mere memories, but rather a part of themselves, who they were, and the way they saw the world, which because they shared it, becomes in turn part of who you are and the way you see the world. For those of us fortunate enough to have lives that Elmer's overlapped, that's the way it is. You simply can't forget him. He always seems to be nearby.

# 6 Family Portraits

# The other Wendelin and Minnie Kasper Children

## An Album

*John Casper (1872-1940) as a young man* [82]

As was most common with men of his generation in rural village America, **John Charles Casper** dabbled in a variety of ventures. He seems briefly to have held an automobile dealership in Madison Lake, also briefly ran a taxi service there possibly in partnership with his brother Elmer, once ran against a cousin (Frank Cords) for the office of county sheriff, and may have been a farmer at other times. He seems to have had a litigious side, frequently engaging in lawsuits making their way into local newspapers and apparently going nowhere.

His nephew Holly Casper recalled him owning a team of white horses.

---

[82] Photo courtesy of Judy Bushlack, great granddaughter of John Casper

*Clara Leona Casper Cords (1873-1963)*

The only daughter of Wendelin and Minnie Casper to survive to adult-hood. **Clara Leona Casper Cords** lived most of her adult life in St. Clair, Minnesota, among Cords family of her husband Johann Heinrich (Carl John) Cords. She is reported to have suffered from severe rheumatoid arthritis, a condition probably inherited from her father, and for which she was at time confined to hospital. She was survived by only one of her five children.

*Albert "Bert" Casper (1885-1963) with a local threshing crew (third from left).[83]*

---

[83] *Photo courtesy of his daughters Margaret and Violet.*

The family life of **Albert "Bert" Casper** took a tragic turn when his wife Laura Knapp died of appendicitis late in her pregnancy with their last child Violet who survived. This left Bert with four small children, the oldest not yet six years old. These children, as was common practice in those days, were raised by their grandmother Minnie Casper, then in her seventies. For much of his life, Bert lived around Madison Lake. I used to see him from time to time around, wearing in those days a western-style hat. I have no notion of how he made his living, but the picture above suggests that at least part of the time he worked as a farmhand. Late in life, he lived with his daughter Margaret in New Ulm, and died as a result of an automobile accident between there and Mankato.

*John Casper in later years with his mother Minnie*

# 7 The Next Generation

# Holland "Holly" Joseph Casper (1921-1995)

America has been called the *Great Melting Pot*, for reasons easily illustrated in our Kasper/Casper family story. Even the transition in the spelling of that surname represents a stage in the process of assimilation and loss of ethnic identity. The name Casper exists in various versions in a multitude of ethnicities, whereas the Kasper spelling is distinctly, if not exclusively, German. Wendelin himself showed every sign of a desire to blend in. If we can trust family lore, he portrayed himself as having a French background, and for good measure may have further obscured his native origin by ambiguous references passed on to his children and grandchildren, so much so that at the beginning of this, I thought he might have come from Alsace-Lorraine, Luxemburg, Belgium, as well as the Saar Valley, none of which turned out to be true, and most of which would have left him looking less German than he actually was.

As has been narrated elsewhere here, little more than thirty years after Wendelin arrived in America, his son Elmer was playing the great American sport of baseball for a Madison Lake team. Elmer was the last of our direct Casper ancestors to be entirely German, and with his marriage to Estella Knapp in 1904, our branch of the family now calling itself *Casper* loses its exclusively German character.

The surname Knapp is of Germanic (Anglo-Saxon) origin, and while to this day there are many of that name in Germany, the name is also common throughout Europe and in the United Kingdom. Estella's Knapp family had distinctly British roots and had been in America from almost the time of the Mayflower pilgrims. On her mother's side, the names Murphy and O'Connell are almost iconically Irish. Including Estella's grandparents and great grandparents, later family generations become a distinctly American mixture of German, English, Scottish, and Irish. All this was passed on to their children, three sons and a daughter, Holly Joseph Casper being the youngest of them. We now turn to his life story.

All his life he went by the name Holly, yet a family record—most probably written by his mother--indisputably lists his name as *Holland Joseph Casper*. Even she, it seems, always called him *Holly*.

Everyone called him Holly. His first name was one of the more immediately memorable things about him. It's a wonderfully happy-sounding name with its suggestions of Christmas merriment and eternal life, but you don't often meet a man named Holly. Much of his life, I suspect, he had to tolerate the inconveniences of such a name. He must have been teased as a boy at school, and perhaps from that his feisty side developed, and I'm sure he never quit encountering confusion in people who assumed from looking at his name before they actually met him that they were dealing with a woman. Yet I think he was fond of being Holly, for it appealed to his flamboyant, carefree side --the part of him that showed in the red shirts he would wear at Christmas in his later years.

He never said how he happened to have this name. I think he probably didn't know and was curious. Late in life he discovered the existence of a John Holly Knapp house in western Wisconsin, named after a nineteenth century lumber baron who had built it. We both speculated about whether his mother had heard of this Knapp, a distant cousin perhaps, and had named her son after him. He would have liked the thought of being named after someone so rich and famous. Clearly he didn't know for sure.

He might have been named Holly simply because he was born on November 29 at the beginning of the Christmas season. His mother had recently lost a young child Louis, had mourned him deeply --we've been told-- and may have really wanted to celebrate an end to this sadness with the birth of her new son. My mother quotes her as once saying, "I had my Holly for Christmas." This may be part of the story, but perhaps it has an earlier chapter.

*Earliest known picture of Holly, probably on the front walk of his grandparents' home on Lake Street in Madison Lake at about the age of 1.*

The surname Holly exists in early Knapp family records from Connecticut and New York where a Samuel Holly Knapp was born in 1800 to a Richard Knapp and a Mary Holly, daughter of Joseph Holly. None of these are more than most distantly related to our Knapp family branch, but memories we know nothing about may have come west with Knapp ancestors and been passed down to Holly's mother in stories she heard as a young girl.

Given the strong inclinations of people in those days to carry forward old family names in naming their newborn, this is at least a possibility. Nevertheless, naming a son Holland despite the inevitable nickname Holly was a pretty extraordinary thing to do, even if its symbolic side was endorsed by now forgotten family tradition.

Of further interest is a small Alsatian village named Holland not far from Wendelin Kasper's origins on the opposite side of the Rhine River. This French village may somehow have figured in Wendelin's history—in ways we may never know-- and been sufficiently memorable that it entered another generation as my father's name.

Estella Casper had previously reached far afield in naming her children, coming up with the names of *Dayton* and *Ivalue* for two of Holly's siblings. You won't often run into those two either. Names this unusual encourage speculation.[84]

Holly's middle name Joseph has a prominent place in Casper/Kasper family history, for Joseph Anton Kasper, a great great grandfather, was a prominent ancestor, perhaps the legendary mayor or judge who had so much money that he would have needed a wheelbarrow to cart it around—family lore. More than likely, though, Joseph was intended to give Holly a saint's name, there being no St. Holly to satisfy Catholic Church baptismal naming requirements.

One of the first things I recall about my father was his often-repeated rhyme: "Never worry, never fear, when Holly J. is the engineer." He would say this in the midst of some difficulty, when the car wouldn't start or had a flat tire, or when a pipe in our house was frozen --as happened equally often in those days. "Don't get excited," he would say, and then as often as not he would get more excited and worry more than just about anyone.

About the earliest recollection of him from any source comes from one of his few remaining first cousins who remembers him when he was about ten years old on an occasion when her family from California visited his. "He was such a kind and courteous little boy," she said. "He took me and my sister fishing." These two recollections say much about him, for he was a kind

---

[84] I recently asked Dayton's son Sam if he had ever asked his father how he came to be named Dayton, a name less used than his nickname "Mike," and Sam answered that he thought Grandma Casper had come upon it somewhere in a novel she'd been reading.

and gentle-hearted man, courteous and personable, always something of a charmer, with strong feelings on many subjects, a sense of humor and a sense of irony, and more than a tendency to get excited. He could in fact explode.

*Holly on the shore of Madison Lake*

As the youngest in his family, he would have been heavily relied upon by his parents to help out with chores no longer performed by brothers and a sister who had left home and already married before he was ten years old.

One of the pictures in this scrapbook, the only of him with both his parents, shows him on the turkey farm at about the age of 16. Some of these Depression era summers were hot and dry, and during those periods the turkeys were moved to the south shore of Madison Lake where water was always at hand. Ted Roemer, retired Madison Lake postmaster among other "old-timers" recalls being hired as a sort of turkey shepherd to watch over the turkeys there. I think Dad's job even involved staying there over night with them.

*With his parents out among turkeys, shown being raised "on range," in open fields with moveable shelters. Here for the first time we see his characteristic*
*"hands-on-hips" pose.*

He dropped out of school (All Saints of Madison Lake) after the eighth grade, about 1936, a common enough thing in those days, especially for rural boys. All Saints at that time had a high school, in fact, but the only one of his family to graduate was his sister Ivalue. This seems strange today, but young women of this era frequently remained in school longer than their brothers who were expected to help on the farm or begin earning a wage, while the women were destined to become homemakers, something their parents were often more interested in postponing.

Since financial opportunities were few in those days, many stories of his youth, mirror those of others who lived through the Depression, having to do with ways of earning money --raising turkeys, cutting reed canary grass for its seed, trapping turtles, muskrats, and skunks. He had stories about all such things. By the time he and his future wife met, when she was sixteen and living with her family that summer in the Lysdale place on Duck Lake, he had saved enough from trapping and odd jobs to buy a Ford Model A.

If you mention this to Mom to this day, you will almost certainly hear the tale of going on a date with him and discovering several dead skunks in the trunk. After that he became a more conscientious suitor, disposing of the skunk carcasses and spraying his Model A with cologne before picking her up! Thus their courtship thrived.

Dad and Mom married young, though not exceptionally so for couple of that time: he was a few months past 18, and she a few days short of 18 on that July 10, 1940 when they eloped to be married at Estherville, Iowa.

It was an extremely warm, muggy day as they drove south from Madison Lake to the Iowa border. With them in the Model A Ford were Drusilla Brouse, Marion's sister, and Richard "Chuck" Morson, Drusilla's boyfriend, later her husband. They would serve as witnesses to the marriage.

Their arrival in Estherville began with a bit of bad luck. Holly made a "U" turn and was stopped by a town cop, who fined him fifteen dollars. The merest reminder of this incident would make him angry the rest of his life. Eventually, even if it continued to anger him, I think he managed to enjoy everything about this incident, including his own towering rage that a small-town cop would defile his wedding day.

In any event, that legendary "U" turn, so very symbolic of much that has happened in this family, begins the story of the Casper-Brouse family, bringing together everything else that is to be found in these pages, for shortly thereafter Holly Casper and Marion Brouse were married. The fifteen-dollar fine nearly might have stopped them though --they were so poor at the time they had barely enough left to pay for a marriage license and ceremony before a justice-of-the-peace

On their way home that day, chugging through the fields of southern Minnesota, they would hardly have been aware that the land they were passing through had been the setting for much of the family history their marriage had joined forever. Marion's great grandparents, the Campbells and the Hicks had settled in southern Minnesota near the Iowa border the century before, and a bit farther north about the same time the Murphys, Cords, and Knapps from Holly's side had moved in to homestead and set up their front street businesses in villages that were just then forming and had now become small towns of twentieth century Midwestern America.

But the thoughts of Holly and Marion could hardly have been on family history this day—of all days—as they drove home. They must have been wondering how they would tell their parents, none of whom knew. Their thoughts must have been on the sort of life that would await them in the years ahead. And of course, there would have been just the sheer excitement of it all. On the way home they stopped at a rural nightclub and danced till early in the morning. Then they went first to Marion's home on Duck Lake, near Madison Lake where her mother Jessie Lozira awaited them, fretting with a headache so bad they found her lying on her living room floor having little luck getting over it as long as she didn't know where her daughter Marion was. We don't know if the news they brought helped the headache or made it worse!

Late the next morning they drove to Holly's home to break the news. They decided to tell his mother Stella first, feeling a bit more comfortable about her reaction. They didn't have to tell Elmer. She accomplished that by shouting to him—let's assume he was outside somewhere working in the yard, and that she shouted from the back door, "Cass, do you know what these kids have done? –They went and got married!"

*Holly and Marion at the beginning of their more than half century together. Far right is the Model A. Always a flashy dresser, Holly is wearing a double-breasted pinstripe suit, a lapel handkerchief, a hat at a sporty angle, and a broad smile. Marion, demure in jumper and coat, with schoolgirl "bobby socks."*

After their marriage, they lived briefly with Holly's parents on the farm southwest of Madison Lake, in a house which at the time had no indoor plumbing or electricity. This period is the source of many of the stories that come down to us about Estella who would die but a few years later from breast cancer. She and Marion spent a lot of time around the house together, cooking and engaged with other household chores. Estella must have been impressed with her new daughter-in-law.

Nonetheless the young couple moved out on their own soon enough and lived in a succession of cabins and cottages around Madison Lake. To one of these I was brought home from my birth at St. Joseph's Hospital in Mankato. Later the three of us lived in a small one-room cottage with a gabled roof built with the help of my grandfather Al Brouse. This too had no plumbing, and I'm not sure it even had electricity. When last I caught sight of it years later it was sitting with weeds growing around it in the abandoned Roscoe Davis Stockyards on the Duck Lake side of Madison Lake.[85]

By the time of my birth the Depression was all but over, World War II had begun, and within a few weeks Japan would attack Pearl Harbor. Dad and Mom kept moving around and lived for a time with my aunt Ivalue and her husband Ed on their turkey farm near the village of Eagle Lake where they all went through the legendary "Armistice Day blizzard" in which Uncle Ed lost about 500 turkeys.

With a young family to look after (My sister Anne was born in November of 1942), Dad wasn't going to sign up for military duty. Instead he traveled out to San Francisco, looking for

---

[85] I took a slide picture of it in a wasteland of weeds which one day I hope to include here.

employment in the shipyards there, and staying with his Knapp cousins. When that didn't work out for him, he returned to Madison Lake where he was finally drafted in the spring of 1944. It was just like him to stay out of the military as long as he could, and then when he finally got in, to be a top-notch soldier. He returned home with two "purple hearts," a bronze star and "oak leaf cluster" for bravery in combat, and an array of other medals.

After the war, while his family grew to six children, he tried his hand at various ventures—feed salesman, farmer, cattle-man, janitor for the J. C. Penney store in Mankato, intermittent worker on his brother-in-law's turkey farm, and finally running a consignment and sales business from his front yard in Pillager, Minnesota, chiefly selling lawn mowers he bought and re-conditioned. Through all this he was troubled by side effects of his war injuries growing progressively worse.

He was never one to lie in bed or take what is called a "busman's" holiday. Despite severe arthritis in his later years, he kept phenomenally busy. After living near Madison Lake for his first fifty years, he moved nearly a dozen times in the next twenty, living in intervals at Pillager, Brainerd, Montrose, and St. Cloud, Minnesota, sometimes two or three times in some places. When he wasn't tinkering around his house and workshop, he would be shopping, roaming especially the food aisles of nearby supermarkets. He kept an eye on prices and current events and held many strong opinions on the dismal state of national affairs.

He disliked black cats and commotion of any kind. He traveled from time to time, but seldom far from home. When he got to wherever he was going, he could hardly wait to head back. He and Mom once drove from central Minnesota to Hot Springs, Arkansas, where—by her account—he parked his car, went into a Woolworth store, purchased a transistor radio, and then headed home as if this had been all along the point of it. On a hot summer day in his last years Mom spied him leaving a jar lid of water for a toad he found marooned on the windowsill of his garage.

True to his name throughout, his showy side never left him. He purchased large automobiles—Lincoln Town Cars, Cadillacs, and the like—put tiny American flags on their bumpers, and might have been mistaken for a Government ambassador in a parade, except for the outrageous appearance of a set of Texas longhorns fastened to the front end. Once he actually found himself in an Independence Day parade quite by accident when he pulled from his parking place at the Brainerd Post Office directly into a line of floats. The big car, the flags, even the long horns, left no doubt in anyone's mind that he belonged there. In no time at all they were waving from sidewalks and he was waving back. He never tired of telling that story. Nor about the time he was on his way home after a few drinks in a local bar, and a highway patrolman collided with *him*, leaving the patrolman apologizing and Holly still in the driver's seat beyond the arm of the law.

His life was like that: spells of bad luck and moments of amazing good luck. When he was wounded in Luxemburg as General Patton's Third Army raced to the Battle of the Bulge, he was the last soldier in a line of a dozen or so. Every man in front of him was killed by machine gun fire. Had the gunner kept his finger on the trigger an instant longer, this would also have been his fate. Another time, he was posted as a guard at a doorway or gate. Less than a minute after he moved to another position, an artillery shell completely destroyed the place he'd been standing. He was involved in more than one automobile accident that might have left him crippled for life or even killed when instead he walked away relatively unscathed. On the other side of life's ledger, so much he attempted, especially as a farmer, failed as a result of bad weather, pestilence, and plain rotten luck.[86]

He died of a stroke at a St. Cloud hospital, and now rests in the Catholic cemetery at Madison Lake. At his grave side I couldn't have been the only one thinking he'd already become a legend. The local parish priest who'd never met him even had a piece of it to share, recently picked up from one of his parishioners. Years ago, he said, Holly wanted to cash a check at a local bar. it was an age when every business owner kept a pack of generic checks for customers to access their bank accounts by filling in all the blanks. "Which bank?" asked the bartender. "Doesn't matter," said Holly, "They all have money." We all stood there chuckling just before his grandson Stephen played *Taps*. This was Dad, always larger than life, and Holly in every sense of the word.

---

[86] A more complete account of all this can be found in my personal memoir *Through the War and out the Other Side*.

*A photograph published in the Brainerd Dispatch during his last years,*
*showing him as he always was, busy to the end.*

# 8 Further Ancestral Notes and Records

## Holland Joseph Casper (1921-1995)

There is in what follows here much repetition resulting from the way I have preserved a digital record of my research notes as a basis for the preceding narratives. Any discrepancies between these notes and the narratives should be resolved in favor of the narratives which represent my most up-to-date findings and conclusions.

I considered omitting biographical notes for Wendelin Kasper, Minnie Cords Kasper, Elmer Casper, and Holly Joseph Casper since most of what is to be found there simply repeats what is included in their respective narratives. Eventually I decided against this because sometimes the notes demonstrate the evolution of the narrative, showing the various zigs and zags I have encountered along my way to getting at the truth and creating the most complete picture I can assemble. This will hardly interest anyone, but still in its own way, this is *the story of the story*, and it seems mistaken to leave it out.

Much from this point on will not interest any but the most avid family historian, except in the case of biographical notes concerning family members not otherwise dealt with in longer narratives. I have included a few photographs from a much more extensive collection to be found in my family history albums and in the "scrapbook" sections of my digital family files using the program Family Tree Maker.

*Generation No. 1*

**1. Holly Joseph Casper,** born 29 Nov 1921 in Mankato, Minnesota; died 21 Sep 1995 in St. Cloud, Minnesota. He was the son of **2. Elmer Francis Casper** and **3. Estella Mary Knapp**. He married **(1) Marion Valerie Brouse** 10 Jul 1940 in Estherville, Iowa. She was born 13 Jul 1922 in Duluth, Minnesota. She was the daughter of Allan George Brouse and Jessie Lozira Boutin.

*Generation No. 2*

**2. Elmer Francis Casper,** born 27 Dec 1883 in LeRay Township, Blue Earth County, Minnesota; died 14 May 1953 in Madison Lake, Minnesota. He was the son of **4. Wendelin Kasper** and **5. Wilhelmine Sophia Friedericke Caroline Cords**. He married **3. Estella Mary Knapp** 15 Nov 1904 in Madison Lake, Minnesota.

**3. Estella Mary Knapp,** born 20 Nov 1884 in Rochester, Minnesota; died 23 Jul 1945 in Madison Lake, Minnesota. She was the daughter of **6. James K. Knapp** and **7. Margaret J. Murphy**.

Further on **Elmer Francis Casper**:

One summer when he was about sixteen Elmer worked with a local threshing crew, by all accounts intense, unrelenting, backbreaking work. He said that he began that summer as a boy, and ended the summer a man. Working on a threshing crew for a young man in those days could be a "rite of passage," and it seems to have been just that for him.

As a young man, he was not only athletic, but had a strong interest in athletics. He played baseball for a Madison Lake team which seems to have achieved some prominence in the area, and I think later on he managed the Madison Lake baseball team. He was also interested in boxing, and may have been a pretty accomplished boxer himself. I think he taught my father (Holly Casper) how to box, and the latter had memories of accompanying his dad to St. Paul in the late 1920's where Elmer—well into his 40's now—would work out as a sparing partner for some of the prominent boxers based there at that time. St. Paul in this era was a major center for boxing promotions.

From at least the time of his marriage to Estella Knapp in 1904, Elmer became deeply involved in the life of Madison Lake. I don't know that he ever considered himself a builder, but he certainly built things. Among the first of these may have been a little bungalow for his young wife and family on the south end of the old Wendelin Kasper homestead, on the very site of the log cabin where he had been born. Another may have been the building on Front Street in Madison Lake that housed for a time the drug store of his father-in-law James K. Knapp. A third, built about 1920, was the home on the northeast corner of the Kasper homestead where my father grew up and where subsequently our family lived till about 1967. A fourth was the white stucco art deco style house on a hillside at the edge of Madison Lake which he himself lived though he left it unfinished from the time his wife died in 1946. All his homes had interesting features and could fairly be described as distinctive for the periods in which they were built. Only the first of these, the bungalow, still survives, and when I was in it this past year, I noticed that it has windows unusually built into the corners of its living room, giving the room a subtle hexagonal feeling. This is the house that Margaret Casper says contains within it remnants of the old Kasper log cabin, a claim I wasn't able to confirm. Of the 1920 home where I grew up on the other end of the old Kasper farm, he always assured my mother that it was built well and would never blow down in a storm. And though it was a drafty, poorly insulated place for the bitterly cold winters we had there, it was charming enough to look at in its prime, and it took a bulldozer in the late 1960's to do what no summer storm could ever accomplish.

While raising his family of five children—including one named Louis who died of scarlet fever in his infancy—Elmer started and ran various recreation and entertainment businesses, and also for a time may have been involved in an automobile business and taxicab operation with his older brother John. Among the enterprises for which Elmer was most remembered would be a kind of pavilion he constructed behind the Madison Lake municipal tavern and "Noah's Ark," a floating dance hall. The pavilion offered boxing matches and films, and perhaps was Madison Lake's first and only movie theater. I would think that Elmer himself might have participated in some of the matches, and perhaps he was able to book well-known boxers from St. Paul given his connections there.

Madison Lake in these days was a rough-and- tumble German/Irish community, and businesses of the sort Elmer ran would be bound to attract unruly types. It's pretty safe to conclude that his management duties included acting as a bouncer, and from everything I know about him—his large hands, his rawboned physique, his athletic prowess—I would think it very seldom that anyone seriously challenged him. At the same time, he was a 'gentle giant," full of good humor and a sense of right. A well-documented local story describes a rally rural socialists in the streets of Madison Lake in the course of which tempers flared between the demonstrators, who included women and children, and their opponents who opened up the village fire hydrants and turned hoses on them. It is said that Elmer waded through the riot and turned the water off and almost single-handed protected the women and children from the mob. No one there would have challenged him—that was the sort of man he was, combining strength, courage, a keen sense of justice, and compassion.

There was no end of need for such virtues in these days called the *roaring twenties* followed by *Prohibition*, the *Great Depression*, union turmoil, times of gangster activity, local women's temperance committees, the morally outrageous, and the morally outraged. Elmer's businesses would have been right in the middle of this turbulent mix, attracting the thugs and the disorderly and attracting the attention of local do-gooders and law enforcement. There must have been more than one unscheduled fight at his pavilion, and there certainly were a few out on Madison Lake where Noah's Ark floated less peacefully than its biblical namesake. After a time, the county sheriff shut it down, the story goes.

He must have always loved shows and entertainment, though in his later years—and perhaps never—he wasn't the sort to make a show of himself. Still I think he had an exuberant side which even in old age would sometimes surface. I remember him in our yard bursting out with a line or two of a song called "Wait till the Sun Shines, Nellie," while telling me about a film he had seen or was about to see. And he once told me about having seen "Buffalo Bill's Wild West Show," including the famous female sharpshooter Annie Oakley. He had brought the silent films of early Hollywood to his pavilion, and later when his son Dayton offered free outdoor movies behind his tavern called the *Nine Mile Corner* Elmer would often be there among the Friday night crowd watching the likes of Tom Mix and Gene Autry. He lived long enough for television to become a fact of life even in our home, and so I once saw him watching *Roller Derby* in our living room with rapt attention.

Somewhere in the course of his middle years, perhaps for peace and peace of mind, Elmer turned more and more to farming. His father Wendelin died shortly after Christmas in 1922, and the north 40 acres of his land passed into Elmer's hands, while the south 40 went to Elmer's younger brother Bert. With his house completed there, Elmer began to raise turkeys on his portion. When the drought of the 1930's struck, he put his turkeys out on range along the shore of Madison Lake just south of Point Pleasant. Among the local lads he hired to tend them there were my father and Ted Roemer, later postmaster of Madison Lake and local historian.

During this time also, Elmer joined other enterprising locals in harvesting seed from reed canary (phalaris) grass which grew in the many sloughs and lowlands that were scattered throughout the area. This could be done either by hand or by mechanical means using a custom made "binder" that could be drawn out into the sloughs in early summer and used to cut the seed-laden heads from this tall grass. At times the prices paid by local seed dealers were high enough to make even hand harvesting pay off, as much as a dollar or more per pound, which was truly a lot of money in those days.

Elmer's wife Estella Knapp inherited from her family another parcel of 80 acres northwest of Marysburg, about 5 miles from Madison Lake. He also farmed this land for many years, one of its perennial crops being the seed from a phalaris grass marsh that made up about 30 of the acres.

So what with one enterprise and another, Elmer made his way through the first half of the twentieth century, raising his three sons and a daughter to a adulthood and finally losing his wife to cancer as World War II was coming to an end and his youngest son Holly was recovering from his wounds near the battlefront in France. He had always taken an active role in the affairs of his family, including helping in various ways to raise the children of his brother Bert whose wife had died in 1923 leaving four little ones, including a new born baby, in the care of Elmer's mother. By these he is remembered affectionately as "Uncle Elmer," who once caught his niece Margaret in a local Protestant church and pulled her out by the ear. Others, in his family and around Madison Lake, called him warmly by his nickname Cass.

During his last years, living alone in his unfinished art deco house in Madison Lake, he mourned his wife deeply. The house, as I recall it, had but four rooms, and Elmer confined himself to what would have been the kitchen. Beside the kitchen a pair of lovely French doors led into a living room sparsely furnished with whatever was left from the life he and his wife had shared for 42 years. I remember a little writing desk, a chair or two perhaps, a little table, odds and ends, but mostly a sense of emptiness. Down the hall from the kitchen—where I never dared wander the few times I was there with my father—there must have been a couple of bedrooms. There was no plumbing, no phone. Elmer got water from a pump out in the yard where along the road a cherry tree grew, heat from an oil burner in the kitchen, sleep on a cot nearby beneath a jumble of old blankets.

He tended his wife's grave, planting flowers there each spring and some arbor vitae which grew quite large and long after he himself lay there was taken down. Out on his farm at Marysburg, he would plant potatoes and vegetables, bringing a portion of his harvest each summer and fall to the nuns in the convent of All Saints parish. He helped his son Holly settle with his family on the old homestead and farm as well the Marysburg land. In the course of these endeavors I often spent time with him. We saw a lot of him in those days working out in our farmyard which he had left to us such a short time before that he must have had much that still concerned him there. One of his favorite expressions, when picking up a piece of angle iron or an old tool and hanging it on a hook nearby, was "this will come in handy some day." He had learned not to throw such things away.

If my mother was frying donuts, he would sit in our kitchen, place several of them like large rings on his finger, and one by one dunk them in his coffee, which otherwise he would cool by pouring it into a saucer. He chain-smoked, often lighting one cigarette with another, but we didn't mind. His warm, mellow presence overwhelmed all other impressions, even the bizarre way he would eat dinner at our table, by first dishing everything up, and then mixing it all together with the side of his fork so that it became an indescribable slurry mounded on his plate. At other times he would accept invitations for Sunday dinner at the nearby homes of his other children. Most summer evenings with the sun going down you would find him out on Front Street of Madison Lake, sitting on a bench, visiting with his friends, in front of Herman Mueller-liele's Hardware or Pearl's Restaurant, a little red brick building he may have built. If we happened to be in town that evening, he would find in the deep pockets of his very baggy pants, enough change for us to have an ice cream cone. Generosity was an instinct—he didn't have to think about it.

There seemed to be about him in those days a warm glow that persists now even in distant memory, his stoicism, his kindness, the smells of his tobacco smoke and old wool, something like saintliness. There can be no doubt that he cared deeply for others and neglected himself. He would never see a doctor. He let his hair grow long, till with his wire-rimmed glasses, and his tattered clothing, he resembled the "hippies" of an era that was twenty years in the future. He drove old cars whose lights seldom worked all at once, cars that would backfire if they started at all and then lurch forward with the engine racing as he let the clutch out, cars that sometimes just blew up, and wound up with weeds growing around them in our yard or his.

A large tree long dead in our yard, once crashed to earth where he had been sitting not five minutes before. He believed enough in Providence that he could survey the scene and say that his time wasn't ready. He loved planting things. There is still growing in what used to be our yard a spruce tree he brought there from his yard in Madison Lake. Standing by, watching him unload it from his old truck and ease it into the black soil, I asked him how old it was. "As old as you," he said, which I took to mean it was ten. I was taller than the tree at the time, but not for more than a year or two. Behind our house for many years was a little orchard of plum and apple trees which he had also would have planted; and also the cherry tree along the road by his art deco house; and --for all I know-- even the spruce which is still in the yard of the first house he built.

The morning he died in May 1953, he was supposed to come from Madison Lake to join my father and me for a trip to the Marysburg farm to get started with the spring planting. When he didn't show up at the appointed time, my dad drove in to see what the matter was. Returning soon, he came with the news of his death. I can still hear his voice in our kitchen saying, "Pa is gone, Pa is dead"—words like than resounding across the days and years afterwards. When you are very young, things like this stick with you because you are still not acquainted with how suddenly everything can change forever. Later on, some neighbors told us that they had seen his old truck pass by coming out from Madison Lake, and then return right after. It may be that he didn't feel good, and simply didn't want to bother us with how he felt—a Casper trait for sure—, or perhaps he knew he was dying, and just wanted to have a last look at where it all began—looking back over your shoulder, another trait. Out in the yard behind our house I remember crying from grief for the first time.

When I was a little boy, he shared with me one evening an account of what life on our farm was like back in those days. Probably some of what he told me was a story that he had heard from his father who had settled on this land thirteen years before he was born, for one would have to think by the time he was old enough to remember, much of the land had been cleared of its many large trees, and the rattlesnakes he mentioned to amaze me that evening had been overwhelmed by the bull snakes brought in for that purpose. Though most likely the little pond that lay right in the middle of our 80 acres was still there when he was a little boy, shimmering in three seasons and frozen solid in the fourth. For all I know he might have skated on it. He certainly must have been the sort to put on a pair of skates and go flying out across it.    The Kasper pond had long since been drained by a system of tiles, and apart from springtime periods of heavy rain was never again seen, much less skated up by any of my generation. It only showed up in the wettest of springs, glimmering there over an acre or two for a week or so before the tiles beneath thawed sufficiently to carry it all way.

I like to think it was there that early morning when he had his last look, and that in his mind he could see himself flying out across it and behind him the little log cabin where it all began with a trail of smoke flowing skyward from its hearth.

Notes for **Estella Mary Knapp**:
Biographical Sketch:

As the daughter of James K. Knapp and Margaret Murphy, she would have shared in their lives prior to her marriage to Elmer Casper in 1904.

Four or so years after her birth in Rochester, Minnesota in 1884, the youngest of four children, her Knapp family settled in Madison Lake, about eighty miles northwest. She probably had few if any memories of life in Rochester.

We know nothing of J. K. Knapp's decision to re-locate, but his wife's sister Ellen lived there from 1888, having married Patrick Murphy (no known relation) of rural Madison Lake that year. J. K.'s widowed father and at least one brother were living in nearby Mankato.

One can imagine, J. K. attending this wedding, liking the place, seeing business opportunities there, and taking up residence not long after this wedding. Equally probable is that he was familiar with the town from his previous residence in Mankato.

Madison Lake in the latter part of the 19th century would have been an attractive resort community on the shores of a lake bearing the same name, rough-and-tumble to be sure, and yet promising from both the standpoints of business prospects and as a place to raise a family.

Estella would have begun school there, and we know she continued in school until at least 1900 when age 16 she is identified as a student in the Federal Census for Anacortes, Washington. It's worth noting that the same census also lists her older sister Genevieve as a student, suggesting that their parents placed great importance on the education of their daughters in an era when many children left school after the eighth grade.

(I am not alone among family historians in regarding with frustration laws keeping school records private even regarding family members long deceased. School newspapers and yearbooks are an exception, but small town and rural schools seldom published the like. On a visit to

Anacortes, Washington I did come across a class picture with possibly Estella's sister Genevieve in it, but no sign whatsoever of Estella herself.)

If we can trust family lore, the various seashells and rock specimens lying around on tabletops, in curio cabinets, and even sometimes in children's toy boxes in our family when I was growing up were the remains of Estella's collection gathered during her few years in the Pacific Northwest. Many of these items—large seashells, abalone shells, pieces of quartz—wound up in the possession of her daughter Ivalue who had a way of "confiscating" anything appearing in our midst somehow connected to the family. Ironically, most of these things as far as I know have now been lost.

One item, a piece of petrified wood, once bearing a handwritten label, may still reside somewhere in my brother Grant's family. Another—perhaps the most striking item in her collection—I somehow managed to keep, a geometrically cut piece of black rock, which my father thought was a "polished meteorite," but which seems to be obsidian as far as I can tell. At least as far as I have determined, it has none of the characteristics of a meteorite.

Thus we know our Estella Casper had a rock and stone collection, or we can assume so if we're not once again dealing with confusion over the word Grandma, making the whole thing her mother's collection instead of hers, a possibility not to be dismissed. Otherwise I have a photograph of her standing in the yard of her recently-built home in rural Madison Lake, the very one I grew up in, with a walkway of sorts appearing to be outlined by rows of abalone shells each placed about three feet apart. This photograph unfortunately is not among those included in the scrapbook here, so I cannot have a look to confirm my description. I do recall, though, a great many abalone shells, no longer in our yard, but scattered among our household stuff before my aunt, ever alert, carted them away to their present oblivion. We managed to keep one, I think, sometimes pressed into service as an ashtray when company appeared.

I wouldn't be at all surprised to learn that Estella's father was not particularly pleased about her marriage to Elmer Casper whose rural Madison Lake farming family must have been a social notch beneath the Knapps. There is no record of this, and it is entirely speculative on my part, but parents who kept their daughters in school as long as Estella and her sister appear to have been, must have been hoping they would "marry up" as the expression puts it. In neither case did this seem to happen. Both married into rural Madison lake farming families, of modest means or less. The Caspers were distinctly poor. Albeit Elmer, from all we know about him—athletic, happy-go-lucky, enterprising, and ambitious—must have caught the eye of more than one young lady in town. From their viewpoint, Elmer must have been a "catch". And who knows, but even J. K. himself might not have been able to resist liking his new son-in-law?

Surviving from that happy day is a spectacular wedding picture (to be found here) as well as a wedding invitation (also pictured here). I can't say whether it was common to omit mention of the groom's parents, but we find no mention of Elmer's in this one, and six years later in the 1910 Federal Census, J. K. himself as local census-taker is at a loss to correctly spell their names. We have instead both of them garbled to a degree suggesting they hardly knew each other.

The marriage of Estella and Elmer produced five children, four of whom survived to adulthood. Anecdotes of Estella from this period suggest a personality somewhere between Annie Oakley and Betty Crocker. On the former side, we hear of her out on the back step of her home, six-shooter in hand, shooting off the head of a snake lurking in her yard some distance away. On the Betty Crocker side are stories from my mother in the early days of her marriage fixing meals alongside Estella in her kitchen when the newlyweds briefly lived there.

My father seems to have been much closer to his mother than to his father, and this suggests to me that she must have been a kind and caring sort who perhaps kept him especially close because he was by far the youngest of her children, only leaving home long after the others had married and moved away.

I have but two memories of her, both of them treasured. Possibly the earliest of the two has me toddling around the yard of her rural Madison Lake home and pulling open the door of an "outhouse" to discover within a startled lady shooing me away we both hands upraised. I promptly closed the door and wandered off, hardly imagining that I carried with me a moment I would never forget. The lady could only have been she. The other memory, the last and only other time I saw her, has her visiting our Glenwood Avenue home in Mankato during the Second World War, standing just inside the door with a bunch of bananas raised high in her right hand, dangling by the stem. Her eyes were bright, her smile animated, and the bananas so intensely yellow I can see them to this very day. Perhaps I owe it to the bananas that I have never forgotten this moment. She must have been very ill with cancer at this time.

She would have died a few months later while my father was away at war. That he never got home to see her before the end was one of his life's great regrets.

Estella like most women of her time left little behind in the way of a public record. Her many cares and accomplishments are lost in time. What I can say is that among the many of our family's next generation whose early lives were lived in her midst, I have never heard anyone speak of her without respect, admiration, and affection.

I have but two memories of her, and consider each of them a treasure. In the first, I must have been toddling around the farmyard of her home, in the course of which meandering a pulled open an "outhouse" door to discover what must have been my grandmother sitting within. She lifted up both hands to shoo me away. I promptly closed the door and toddled away, little realizing I brought with me a lifelong memory.

More About Elmer Casper and Estella Knapp:
Marriage: 15 Nov 1904, Madison Lake, Minnesota

Children of Elmer Casper and Estella Knapp are:
>    i.     Milton Francis Casper, born 24 Nov 1905 in LeRay Township, Blue Earth County, Minnesota; died 25 Jan 1960 in Mankato, Minnesota; married Agnes Boda 10 Jul 1926 in Detroit, Michigan; born 01 Feb 1906; died 09 Jan 1975 in Mankato, Minnesota.

As a young man, Milton settled for a time in Evanston, Illinois where he may have worked in sales. There are pictures of him and his wife and daughter Faye from this period.

He returned to Minnesota at still a young age and made his home in Cleveland, a small town about eight miles across country from Madison Lake. At various times he owned automobile dealerships in Cleveland and nearby LeCenter. He was also mayor of Cleveland and owned a large farm nearby (large for those days) on which he raised registered Hereford cattle and a few show horses. He had a private pilot's license and one or two planes.

Occasionally he would "buzz" our house, and these were certainly some of the most exciting and memorable events of my childhood. Every time we heard the distant drone of a small plane, we would wonder if Uncle Milton weren't about to descend upon us. If the drone grew louder and finally became a window-rattling roar, we knew for sure it was he taking aim straight at our gable. We would run out into the yard and find him swooping in toward us as low as the corn tassels, pulling up at the last minute to clear by a few feet only the large trees in our yard.

The earth seemed to shake, the treetops to bend in fright, the dog would bark and head for a hole under our house, our breaths would stop in our throats, and if he actually landed—as he sometimes did—out in a field nearby, not Charles Lindberg himself could have been regarded by us with more awe.

Milton and his wife Agnes lived in what was easily the largest house in Cleveland, a white Victorian large enough to seem a mansion to us when we visited occasionally. I most remember its porch swing and its piano, both of which seemed novel luxuries to us. Milton was fond of hunting and fishing, and later in life would spend his summers at Walker where he ran a launch service for people wishing to fish on Leech Lake.

When I was growing up, everything about the man seemed to represent adventure and success, illusions that were hard to come by in my family. He had lived in a big city—Chicago; he was a daredevil pilot whose license might be imperiled if not his life; he sold new cars and raised high class cows; he hunted in Wyoming; he fished the big northern lakes; he had been a mayor. All this was such wonderful, impressive stuff—you could have daydreamed about being his friend—and certainly no one in our family could have topped any of it.

"Cass" was his nickname, one shared by his father Elmer. He liked to show off, I'm sure. He night visit us wearing a sport jacket, and once when he did so, he reached absently into his lapel pocket and pulled out a folded check whose presence there seemed to surprise him. It turned out to be a check for a hundred dollars he had absently left there from several months ago. He had forgotten about it. This was as amazing as his nosedives into our yard, the thought that this Cadillac-driving uncle could actually lose track of so much money.

Notes for **Agnes Boda**:

Of Hungarian origins, and like many women of her family background a wonderful cook in an old-fashioned, farmhouse vein. Agnes was always ready with a warm greeting for visiting family. Dessert might be expected to follow. She and her husband always remembered nieces and nephews at Christmas with gifts left under the family tree. She was an intensely fervent Catholic in the tradition of her central European roots.

More About Milton Casper and Agnes Boda:
Marriage: 10 Jul 1926, Detroit, Michigan

ii.  Dayton James Casper, born 23 Nov 1907 in LeRay Township, Blue Earth County, Minnesota; died 12 Apr 1994 in Yuma, Arizona; married Georgia A. Greenig 05 Sep 1931 in St. Peter, Minnesota; born Abt. 1912; died 03 Oct 2004 in Mankato, Blue Earth County, Minnesota.

Notes for **Dayton James Casper**:

Here we have yet another uncommon Casper name. His son, my cousin Sam, thinks Dayton's mother found it somewhere in a novel she was reading. Whatever its origin may be, he usually went by the name of "Mike."

Uncle Mike was a gruff sort, not really unfriendly, but not approachable without the feeling he wished you hadn't, as if you were interrupting him in the middle of changing a tire or in the middle of a thought. This made it hard to come near, except on tiptoe with an apology close at hand.

His most memorable enterprise was the "Nine Mile Corner," an almost legendary tavern, restaurant, dance hall, entertainment center, and filling station at the intersections of Highway 14 and 60 about nine miles east of Mankato. I feel fortunate to have a photograph of it, taken at a later time, when it belonged to Kevin Neary --Mike's second cousin, though Mike himself appears not to have known this and wouldn't have much cared for the idea.

I sense the hand of his father Elmer Casper in both the design and construction of this building and in its business purpose. It wouldn't surprise me in the least to learn it was another of Elmer's projects and entertainment schemes, this one intended to be a livelihood for his son. Like so much belonging to my childhood days, it has been demolished, with even the land upon which it once stood so re-arranged by road construction as to be unrecognizable today.

*"Nine Mile Corner" after Uncle Mike's time, when it had been sold to a second cousin Kevin Neary.*

Years ago, though, in more than one way the Nine Mile Corner held a prominent place in Casper family life. I first became aware of it as location for free movies on weekend nights, these projected on a screen nailed high up on a back wall facing a grassy area with benches and parking places for cars. It was, at least for our locale, the first outdoor movie theater, years ahead of a time when such entertainments were common but for all that years after Elmer himself had shown films in a large tent by the railroad tracks in Madison Lake. Its memory merges with another memory, of Elmer Casper promising to take me there for a "show." He didn't always manage to do this, but it happened often enough that I can still reconstruct the scene with dusk descending over the back lot, country boys in darkened cars with their girlfriends, people on benches and on blankets spread out over what remained of grass after so much driving and trampling, a black and white picture flashing and fluttering from the open rear doors of an old panel truck where a projector aimed at the screen. The movie was almost always a "Western" of the sort saving production costs and wear and tear on actors by having most of the action scenes occur in the dark with flashes of gunfire, the thud of well-aimed punches, and groans to leave you wondering whether your hero or the villain had come to a dismal end. Between times, frequent intermissions offered moments of relief, lights would illuminate the back lot, young romancers in their cars would scramble for cover, and the rest of us head inside where Uncle Mike would sell refreshments from behind his tavern bar. I cannot imagine a personality less suited for the role of congenial tapster. The effort must have stretched Uncle Mike to some extreme beyond himself from which at night's end he could only retreat grumpy and exhausted.

From all I know of my grandfather Elmer Casper, the enterprise had his notions written all over it. What it must have failed to acknowledge is how unprepared his son would have been to engage in it.

It may well have been this, more than the emergence of authentic outdoor theaters in the Mankato vicinity, that brought an end to Mike's Nine Mile Corner days. The free movies flickered out while I was yet very young, and I recall first a gypsy encampment of small trailer houses briefly parked in Uncle Mike's back lot and then the place resembling a neglected cow pasture with weathering benches lurking among wildflowers and arching grasses. (So much forming a part of Casper family history has gone this way, first a promising idea, and then tall grass overgrowing a dream.) Perhaps the whole inspiration passed away with Elmer in 1953, for it wasn't long after the death of his father that Uncle Mike sold out.

With the old man's disappointment no longer a risk, he attempted to raise turkeys on his half of the old Wendelin Kasper homestead. He hung a large bell to one side of a structure called a poultry confinement and named it the Silver Bell Turkey Ranch. In a year or two the bell tarnished to a frosted white, and then several more years later whole sections of the empty turkey pen collapsed one by one in plain view of the road. It might have been yet another attempt to follow in his father's footsteps before he discovered a path of his own. Having dabbled in these various enterprises, he moved his main business interests to Mankato where at one time or another he owned a Standard Oil gas station and a package liquor store in a shopping mall on the edge of town.

When I was a student at Loyola High School, I sometimes caught without a ride home in the evening, my steps would lead up Madison Avenue to Uncle Mike's gas station where he would be shutting off the lights and locking up at ten o'clock. He never greeted me with more than a nod, but never refused me a ride home in his pickup truck, and at times he may even have taken me the extra half mile between our place and his. But few words ever passed between us as we bumped over the pavement ridges of Highway 14 and then dodged chuckholes in the old Eagle Lake road. Uncle Mike stayed safely out of sight in his thoughts, and I in mine. "Thanks," I would have said at the end of it. And that was truly the end of it.

He lived in Yuma, Arizona in his retirement years, died of geriatric leukemia, and is buried near his daughter Sharon whom he survived.

*Uncle Mike & Aunt Georgia in Arizona*

Notes for **Georgia A. Greenig**:

An amateur painter of rural scenes, most notably perhaps a large canvas of Madison Lake rolled onto a corrugated downspout and used as a curtain for plays All Saint School. I remember her being a little dark-haired woman with lips she could manage to purse into straight lines even while seeming to smile, as if the smile went up into her eyes and left her mouth unaffected. This gave her a matter-of-fact, take life as it came, resigned look.

More About Dayton Casper and Georgia Greenig:
Marriage: 05 Sep 1931, St. Peter, Minnesota

       iii.      Ivalue Margaret Casper, born 27 Jun 1911 in LeRay Township, Blue Earth County, Minnesota; died 01 Feb 1980 in Mesa, Arizona; married Edmund Hilgers 26 Dec 1930 in Madison Lake, Minnesota; born 29 May 1908; died 28 May 1981 in Mankato, Blue Earth County, Minnesota.

Notes for **Ivalue Margaret Casper**:

Her name is yet another of the unusual names Estella Knapp found for her children. In my extensive family history research, where I must have come across ten thousand names, I have never noted another Ivalue., nor have I ever met anyone quite like her. Her middle name was no doubt meant to honor the memory of her grandmother Margaret Murphy Knapp.

The first thing you remember about Ivalue is how excitable she was and how fast she talked. We used to say—out of amazement, I think, rather than cruelty—that her tongue must have been hinged in the middle, so that she could talk from either end. A conversation with her became mostly Ivalue's monologue. If you could get a few words in now and then, you felt pretty good about it.

She worked hard all her life, raising with her husband Ed three adopted children. She had in the family a reputation for keeping a close eye on her money, but you could hardly shed such a habit if you grew up poor as she must have and then lived through the Depression in the first ten years of her married life. If you visited her and Ed, no matter how unannounced, you could be sure of a warm welcome and their interest in how your life was going. She loved gardening—vegetables, berries, and flowers especially. More outgoing and bubbly than most Caspers, she once got herself on the sixties television show "The Price is Right" by standing on her chair in the audience far in the back of an auditorium and waving and shouting so vigorously that she was selected to participate. Naturally, she came closest to guessing the price of whatever could be won for the guessing.

She deserves a special place in this family history because of her own interest in it, especially the Knapp, Murphy, and O'Connell branches. She preserved the Knapp family bible by wrapping it in cellophane and keeping it in her freezer—I'm not sure if that really helped, but it was a remarkable thing to see her reach down into her freezer and pull it out for my inspection. Elsewhere here you will find reproduced the family record pages from that bible and the Richard Moxley letter to his daughter Jane which was also kept by her. She was most fond of the thought that we were all directly descended from Daniel O'Connell, the "Irish Liberator," something that as far as I now know turns out not to be true—though we are related to him. She died before I knew that, but I wouldn't want to have corrected the impression in any event. She provided me with some of the first family history facts I gathered, and even searched through the family for the only photograph we have of Wendelin Kasper, at that time in the possession of her cousin Margaret.

As my details about the family bible illustrate, she had her eccentric side. You wouldn't dare get sick around her because she kept a medicine cabinet full of left-over medications, every pill, capsule, and cough syrup that she hadn't the heart to throw away. These would all be brought out for your cure—if they didn't kill you first! According to my cousin Sam Casper, she died after returning to Arizona from Las Vegas where she had won a substantial pile of money. His story makes it sound as if the excitement of all this was just too much for her, which well it might have been, but I sense the possibility of exaggeration. This fits a bit too neatly with her reputation for loving money, but I would think more than one family member chuckled over the possibility. Still she always looked younger than her years, and most of us were shocked to hear of her passing before reaching even the age of 70.

For myself, I have often wished she might have lived long enough to know about our family the many things I now know. She would have been most interested. In a strange sort of way you can still hear Ivalue—in the "you-who" spring song of the chickadee. She would shout "you-

who" for one of us to come from wherever we were around the turkey farm, and it sounded just like that. Ever since I have thought of the chickadee as the "Ivalue" bird.

In this last picture of her here in her scrapbook, she begins to resemble her aunts and her grandmother, the Murphy women. She really did look very Irish, much like one of those dark-haired, hook-nosed Irish women one encounters all over Ireland. She would have liked to hear that I'm sure, all but the hook-nosed part that is.

Ivalue had a strong sense of family loyalty. At various times her home became home to extended family in need, to her cousin Margaret, and to her brother Holly in the early years of his married life. She always hoped that what remained of the original Wendelin Kasper homestead would stay in the Casper family. This might have been the case had she not died before her husband who had other plans.

**Notes for Edmund Hilgers:**

"Uncle Ed" had a corner on reliability in our family—in many ways its most responsible citizen. If trouble was brewing anywhere, you would want Ed nearby to figure out what to do next. In many, many ways he helped our family through the troubled times in which we grew up. For this, among many things, he should be remembered fondly.

A practical, no nonsense sort, he nonetheless had a sense of humor, most frequently seen when he detected a bit of nonsense. He wouldn't hesitate to laugh before pointing to a change of direction. For example, he much enjoyed the fact that his daughter Karen and I spent most of the summer day chatting endlessly between cascades of laughter when we were supposed to be working for him. His enjoyment didn't prevent him from assigning us to separate jobs at opposite ends of his turkey farm. In later life, he never failed to laugh about the many coats of paint I applied to his sheep shed while attempting to cover over the gnats and flies finding a permanent home on the wet siding. I must have used ten gallons of paint for every gallon required, and when I finally gave up, there were still flies and gnats visible everywhere. "Never had to paint it again," he would say with his quiet, amused laugh. Nor would he ever again put me to work painting for him. Painting old farm buildings wasn't a job for perfectionists.

He and my aunt Ivalue built a brick home near the highway between Mankato and Eagle Lake in the 1930's and began raising turkeys on their farm of ten or so acres. They also raised three adopted children, and for the next forty years or more made a life of this before retiring to Arizona.

A solid work ethic was the rule of life for them and their family, but not so firm a rule that time was not set aside for ball games in a sheep pasture, vacation trips to fishing cottages, and family gatherings at which Ed, who had a pleasant voice, would sometimes join in group singing. In later years Ed and Ivalue developed an interest in Mexico and traveled extensively there.

Their turkey farm became something of a local institution with customers coming from great distances to buy their freshly-slaughtered birds, especially for Thanksgiving and Christmas. These commanded premium prices, the general opinion being they were well worth both the extra money and the trip. As their business grew, it demanded more hands than the family could provide, and extended family and Eagle Lake "locals" were hired to form a work crew at peak times. This employment, in difficult days, became a good local income source for many people over the years, for housewives whose children were raised or in school, for underemployed men, and not the least for my mom and dad and some of their older children. When they retired and quit their turkey business, they had both employees and steady customers who had been around for more than twenty years. I can well imagine for years after, there would be customers stopping by the Hilgers Turkey farm saddened to discover the signs down, the doors locked, and no more birds to provide a special touch for their holiday tables.

Ed was the kind of practical, conservative, small businessman that helped America prosper in the post-Depression and World War Two years. He saw success as something people earned by their hard work, not something they were either entitled to or denied by birth. When I once described for him some supposed hardship I had endured, he looked me over with an amused glint in his eye as if to say, "Pull your socks up, kid. You ain't seen nothing yet."

He enjoyed amazing health throughout most of his life. I am not sure if the Wheaties he bought by the case and ate for breakfast every morning over decades had anything to do with this. He might have been expected to live to one hundred. Instead he survived his wife by little more than a year, died of cancer at his Eagle Lake home, and is buried by her side in a Mankato cemetery.

*Edmund Hilgers and Iva Casper:*
*Marriage: 26 Dec 1930, Madison Lake,*
*Minnesota*

iv.    Louis George Casper, born 02 Oct 1917 in Blue Earth County, Minnesota; died 09 Feb 1920 in Blue Earth County, Minnesota.

v.     (1) Holly Joseph Casper, born 29 Nov 1921 in Mankato, Minnesota; died 21 Sep 1995 in St. Cloud, Minnesota; married Marion Valerie Brouse 10 Jul 1940 in Estherville, Iowa.


*Generation No. 3*


**4. Wendelin Kasper,** born 05 Jul 1845 in Grafenhausen-Kappel, Baden, Germany[1]; died 26 Dec 1922 in Madison Lake, Minnesota. He was the son of **8. Johann Kasper** and **9. Katharina Jaeger.** He married **5. Wilhelmine Sophia Friedericke Caroline Cords** 15 Oct 1872 in Mankato, Minnesota.

**5. Wilhelmine Sophia Friedericke Caroline Cords,** born 08 Aug 1850 in Ruest, Mecklenburg, Germany; died 18 Feb 1940 in Madison Lake, Minnesota. She was the daughter of **10. Johann Joachim Carl Friedrich Cords** and **11. Hannah Catharina Dorothea Sternberg.**


Family lore concerning **Wendelin**:

Family tradition had it that he emigrated from the Saar Valley region of Germany, or possibly Alsace Lorraine. Another family tradition, which appears to confuse him with perhaps a parent or a grandparent, is that he was an important judge or a mayor—possibly in Belgium or Luxembourg—and, as my aunt Agnes Casper told me years ago, had enough money to fill a wheelbarrow. All of these stories have turned out to be mistaken, though it is interesting to consider their origins and whether they represent confused references to other family members.

Certainly the reports that Wendelin was a famous mayor or judge could not possibly be true. He was only 23 years old when he arrived in America, hardly old enough to have achieved such status. He seems to have been relatively poor all his life. Perhaps as an old man he loved to delight his grandchildren with tall tales about himself. Or perhaps these stories apply to an earlier generation, or came from Minnie and concerned someone in her family.

Nevertheless, all such stories wherever they occur in family history merit further research since they may possibly point to an earlier generation's or another family branch. It is true that Wendelin's grandfather Joseph Anton Kasper was a sort of mayor in the village of Grafenhausen, but the village would have been so small that this could hardly have made him more than a local figure. Nevertheless, not far away across the Rhine in France, in the town of Obernai, there once lived a wealthy, influential Casper who even succeeded in having a street named after him. Monseigneur Casper he was called, something of a local nobleman, I would think, with an impressive local cemetery memorial. Perhaps the Grafenhausen Kaspers had visited Obernai and fancied they had a connection with him. Perhaps there really was a connection, now lost to us, but in either case the story passed from generation to generation, growing more and more confused, till at last Wendelin himself became the distinguished ancestor.

Memories of **Wendelin**:

My aunt Ivalue Casper once told me that around Madison Lake Wendelin was known as "The Frenchman" because he was fluent in the French language.

My father Holly Casper said that he was, in fact, fluent in five different languages. And it was also from my father in one of my last conversations with him that I learned that Wendelin had attended the University of Stuttgart.

My father claimed to remember Wendelin and to once have seen him in the pool hall at Madison Lake speaking several different languages to another man in town who was also fluent in these languages. Clearly what my father recalled here was not something that he actually experienced, but rather a memory of someone else's account of this. When Wendelin died, my father was barely one year old! In any event his fluency in a variety of languages seems to have impressed people in an age when it wouldn't have been unusual for people who were recent immigrants to be fluent in at least one, other than English. And the impression that he knew so many languages may have been created by a bit of fluency in several, which is usually enough to impress those who know nothing about it. Wendelin's Baden homeland had been for centuries a European crossroads, and this fact would have given him ample opportunity for exposure to several languages, for example French, Alsatian German, Belgium French, Italian, and Swiss dialects.

Wendelin's granddaughter Margaret Casper, about the last person left having any memories of him, recalls sitting on his lap when he was quite an old man living with his wife in Madison Lake. She says that at that time he had a long white beard, "like Santa Clause," and that when she would stroke it, he would caution her not to get it all tangled up.

From 1875 through 1900 Wendelin lived on this eighty-acre farm, probably having cleared all of it during the 1870's. Census records show his family growing and shrinking decade by decade as children are born, die, and leave home. The children of Wendelin and Minnie will be found listed on the family page to which these notes are attached. We also know that Wendelin applied for citizenship in 1897, 30 years after his entrance into this country (naturalization records).

More memories and conjectures:

I can't myself recall the origin of another story about Wendelin's strength, strong enough to grasp a large, heavy wooden barrel loaded with who knows what? — feed or buttermilk or turtles trapped and packed for shipment to Chicago restaurants—and hoist it by himself up onto a truck or trailer. Nor can I recall the origin of the story that he was a stocky, barrel-chested man. His sons John, Elmer, and Bert—I remember the latter two—were well-built men.

Wendelin's obituary says that he first settled in Indiana. This agrees with the family tradition, but the obituary says that he married Minnie Cords in Mankato, while my father said that the marriage took place in Indianapolis. There's interesting confusion about this marriage.

According the Margaret Casper, Wendelin and Minnie lived out his last years in a small house in Madison Lake. Heading east into Madison Lake on highway 60, you would find the location by taking the first street right—on the edge of town, roughly across from the site of the Hoehn nursery, then up the hill and down. Wendelin's house would have been on the right as the street heads down toward Madison Lake, across from what is presently a vacant ground where the Earl Zuel mink farm was once located. He and Minnie had moved there, "into town" from the family farm homestead southwest of Madison Lake. This homestead of what was originally 80 acres was located on the west side of Highway 60 about 2 1/2 miles southwest of Madison Lake in what I think is LeRay Township. The northwest corner of the homestead would have been at the intersection of Highway 60 and County Road 13 which goes to Eagle Lake, from that corner a half mile along Highway 60 toward Madison Lake and a quarter mile along Highway 13 toward Eagle Lake.

When Wendelin and Minnie first homesteaded this land in the early 1870's it was heavily wooded and needed to be cleared. This according to my grandfather Elmer Casper who gave me an account of all this when I was a little boy, and he was babysitting while my parents were out for the evening. According to Elmer Casper, there were huge hardwood trees on the property and even a small lake which had been drained by tiling the field. He seemed especially eager to tell me about all the snakes inhabiting the land, rattlesnakes by his account which they eradicated by importing bull snakes that preyed upon them. I head this story from my grandfather in the late 1940's, and I can remember that in rainy seasons in those days and sometimes in spring after the snow melted, you could still see the lake—really a large pond—where it had originally been located, now there only briefly while the winds evaporated it, and the tiles carried the rest away.

My grandfather Elmer Casper was said to have been born in a log cabin on the south end of this homestead along what is presently county road 13. Today on the site is a small home which my father told me was built by Elmer himself and is now the Gib Buskey retirement residence. At any rate, Wendelin, Minnie and their children apparently lived on this homestead for a good many years until 1905, the date given in his obituary for their move to Madison Lake. This was occasioned by his failing health.

Wendelin's last years appear to have been painful ones. He was most likely crippled by arthritis for which in those days there was little pain relief. He was confined to bed for the last two years of this life, may have had a stroke, and according to his death record in the Blue Earth County courthouse also suffered from senility. Putting it all together, it couldn't have been a happy ending to a long life that began across the ocean in Germany.

Margaret Casper remembers the last period of his life when he was confined to a room which she and the other children were not supposed to enter. From time to time she would go in anyway, and she recalled that he would become very upset, and one time threw a lamp at her! I suppose he could be excused for being out of sorts, and who's to say what sort of mental shape he was in after all he'd been through. All in all, I think it's fair to say he was a hardworking and highly respected member of his pioneer community. The thrown lamp, as far as I can tell, missed Margaret, and we leave it lying on a floor somewhere in the bedroom of a house where I have never been.

Wendelin we leave lying in the Catholic cemetery at Madison Lake, his wife Minnie beside him, his son Bert to his right and Bert's wife Laura to Minnie's left. There is a large, impressive grey granite family marker, and foot stones marking each grave. I have but one photograph of Wendelin, its original in the possession of Margaret Casper, and that is located in the scrapbook section of this file.

In later years, the family homestead was divided among descendants, the south forty going to Wendelin's son Bert and the north forty to Elmer. By the time I was old enough to remember anything, the south 40 acres was owned by Elmer Casper's son Dayton who lived and raised his family there in a house which still stands --though in run-down condition, at the intersection of Highway 60 and county 13. The north forty passed to my father Holly and his sister Ivalue upon the death of Elmer. Eventually Ivalue purchased Holly's twenty-acre parcel, except for an acre or two where we all lived. Here was where I grew up --a large spruce tree is about all that's left of the spot. The tree was planted by Elmer Casper when I was 10 years old and standing by watching him. Upon Ivalue's death, the homestead passed completely out of Casper hands after about a century of their stewardship.

## Conclusions:

Here near the end of my research into the background and personal history of Wendelin Kasper, it is possible to solve most of the puzzles that surrounded his life as I pieced together its various elements from family anecdotes and documents mentioned above:

Wendelin himself was never a judge or a mayor: he was beginning to end a farmer. This story may have been an exaggeration concerning his Grandfather Joseph Anton Kasper who appears to have been an important figure in Grafenhausen. Or it may have been mistakenly applied to him by grandchildren who heard it from his wife Minnie who instead was speaking about one of her own Mecklenburg ancestors. Also a possibility is that it was a Kasper family conjecture concerning the important Monseigneur Casper who lived in Obernai, Alsace on the other side of the Rhine. Every family historian knows how much rumors of connection to the rich and famous become the sworn facts of subsequent generations.

Wendelin and his family signed the Kasper name with an umlaut over the "a" probably to distinguish it from other Kaspers living in the village who were not family. This was explained to me one evening in Grafenhausen by Herbert Schwarz, a Kasper cousin.

Wendelin himself, like a great many German people in America when World War I was underway, probably thought it in the best interests of his family to obscure its German origins, so the name began to be spelled Casper while the family's origins were allowed to shift across the Rhine into Alsatian France encouraged by Wendelin's "The Frenchman's" knowledge of French. And so, after a fashion, Wendelin himself became the famous Monseigneur Casper of Obernai.

There is no known connection between our Kasper family and the Kaspers of Albertville/St. Michael.

Notes for **Wilhelmine Sophia Friedericke Caroline Cords**:
Biographical sketch:

Minnie (Wilhelmine Sophia) Cords came from Ruest, a small farming village in the lake country of Mecklenburg, northeastern Germany. She was among the youngest of two large Cords families living there on nearby village farms.

While she was yet seventeen, she gave birth to a daughter named Anna. Anna's father was even younger, a farmhand named Carl (Karl) Moller. We do not know if Minnie and Carl were subsequently married. That would have been the necessary outcome in this strict northern German Lutheran culture, but perhaps his extreme youth or social barriers of the era did not permit it. We do not have a marriage record for them, but Dieter Garling, a local Mecklenburg historian with access to more records than I have seen, refers to Karl Moller as Minnie's husband, and Casper family anecdotes have Minnie referring to herself has having been married when she was 15, hardly accurate in any case, but when she said this anyone who heard would have assumed she spoke of her marriage to Wendelin. She would have left it that way.

She left Ruest and even Karl Moller it seems in 1870 with Anna still an infant in arms and emigrated to America aboard the ship Silesia. Ship's records suggest she and Anna made the voyage alone. It's a matter of conjecture that they at first settled on farm near St. Clair in the care of her uncle Johann Joachim Friedrich Cords recently re-located there from Wisconsin with his family. He had been the first of our Cords family to arrive in America.

Shortly thereafter Minnie somehow met Wendelin Kasper who had settled on 80 acres in LeRay Township about nine miles northeast of Mankato and little farther from St. Clair. They married before a judge in Mankato on 15 October 1872. Minnie's daughter Anna would have been four days from her fourth birthday, and previously in August a son John had been born to them.

Minnie's name in the Blue Earth County marriage record is given as Mena Kurtz. It is easy to see how the German pronunciation of Cords might have been rendered that way, but when one considers how her husband's name, first and last also easily misspelled, is recorded precisely correct, one wonders if Minnie's wasn't deliberately provided that way and left uncorrected. This is but one of several suggestions that Minnie was not at ease with her past. Witnesses to this marriage were Frederick and Helen Heinze of Mankato. Helen Heinze was a Schaub family member with origins in Wendelin's Baden hometown of Grafenhausen.

I think it likely, as Dieter Garling suggests, that Minnie had been married to Karl Moller in Germany, and was genuinely perplexed about how to manage that fact in the first years of her relationship with Wendelin. She came from a strict Lutheran background, Wendelin from what might have been only a slightly more liberal Catholic one. Then she and Wendelin had a child. They resolved their problems by having a civil marriage outside both their faiths and obscuring Minnie's name in the official record. Their attempt to conceal Minnie's past went further with Anna (Annie) listed as a Kasper daughter of Wendelin in both the 1875 Minnesota Territorial Census and the 1880 Federal Census.

One can only feel compassion for them, struggling with this problem by candle and lamplight in their log cabin on the Kasper farm at the outset of their life together. How they must have worried that Minnie's past would return to haunt them one day. Many more problems would follow in a pioneer life that must have been filled with more heartache and pain than most of us could endure. The graves of three of their young children in a family plot in the Eagle Lake cemetery remind us of this.

Sadly, I think it likely that Minnie's past did cause them further pain—in the form of the "disappearance" of her daughter Anna sometimes between the 1880 and 1885 censuses. All my grandfather Elmer Casper (born in 1883) knew of this was that he had had a sister who disappeared without a trace, a fact he once mentioned to my mother. John and Clara, the older surviving siblings, would have remembered Anna and probably knew more. Someone certainly knew she was not to be counted among the offspring of Minnie and Wendelin because in the latter's obituary in the Madison Lake Times mention is made of seven children, four surviving and three deceased. Anna would have been an eighth.

Given all the German folk in the vicinity at the time, many of them with connections back to Minnie's world in Mecklenburg, I think it possible that word of her marriage reached Karl Moller, and a bargain was struck: Anna would be returned to her father in exchange for silence.

Supporting this is a ship's record of one Karl Moller arriving in America "to visit" in 1882, albeit Karl Moller is a common name, and this might have been another. An alternative happier explanation for Anna's disappearance might be that Minnie—in old time Lutheran fashion—began to fret so much about the other children discovering her past, as they grew older that finally Anna at about the age of fourteen was sent to live with another part of the Cords family. Betty Lou Cords, the Cords family historian, thinks this most likely, and even wonders if Anna might not be an Anna Ludtke who has an unexplained presence among her records. We will probably never know for sure, but having looked in vain through local newspapers of this period for report of Anna's disappearance, I think this was simply a story given to the other children in place of something that could not be revealed.

All this helps us to understand why Minnie in later life could seem evasive and full of secrets and innuendo, and why she even had difficulties revealing her correct age. Some of her grandchildren thought she and Wendelin had been married in Indiana. One remembered her describing how she and Wendelin had gone boating on the Rhine River, something that could never have happened. Stories lay upon stories. Inevitably tales became mixed and inconsistencies surfaced. To this day there are people in the family who think she lived to an age older than she was. In later years she would often confront the behavior of her granddaughters Margaret and Violet by veiled references to her own past and the punishment God visited on such behavior.

These matters, interesting as they might be to anyone with a taste for mystery, obscure the broader features of Minnie's life and the remarkable woman she was. To live for America with a small baby in her circumstances required great daring and fortitude. In Minnesota with Wendelin she raised her pioneer family in the midst of continuous hardship, and in later years when her son Bert's wife died, she raised a second family of his four children. Family anecdotes reveal a devoted, determined woman who had no reason to hide anything or apologize to anyone.

Marriage Notes for **Wendelin Kasper** and **Wilhelmine Cords**:

The official record of a civil marriage between Wendelin and Minnie can be found at the Blue Earth County courthouse in Mankato, Minnesota. The date of their marriage, the marriage record itself, and various conflicting reports circulating in family lore all point to the fact that Minnie had been previously married and had given birth to a daughter Anna at a very young age in her native Mecklenburg. Otherwise in this era, it is hard to explain their reluctance to marry before the birth of their first child.

An account of Minnie's circumstances can be found elsewhere here.

Arriving in America in 1870 with her infant daughter, and separated from her first husband who may have stayed behind in Germany, she was probably supported by a Cords uncle (Johann Joachim Friedrich) who had recently settled in southern Minnesota on a farm near St. Clair, not more than a dozen miles from where Wendelin purchased eighty acres in 1869. Somehow the young couple met, perhaps at a village dance or another gathering used by pioneer settlers to provide social opportunities for young people who were otherwise isolated with their rural families.

She and Wendelin must have established a common household sometime between the 1870 Federal Census (where he is listed as living alone) and the birth of their first child John Charles in August 1872. Minnie's daughter Anna is listed with them in both the Minnesota Territorial Census of 1875 and in the 1880 Federal Census. In both instances her name is given as Anna or Annie Kasper.

The official marriage record gives Minnie's name as Mena Kurtz whereas Wendelin's name, often misspelled, is written out exactly as it is supposed to be. Census-takers and others grappling with an array of accents made frequent mistakes, but it's hard to imagine a young couple standing by with witnesses not correcting what seems to be an entirely different name for Minnie. Even though the name Minnie might be pronounced to make is resemble Mena and Cords could be pronounced Kurtz, I think the error is deliberate, and also clever since it can be so readily explained away. All this well ahead of our era of "plausible deniability"!

Witnesses to their marriage were F. and H. (probably Frederick and Helen) Heinze, residents of Mankato. Wendelin's family name is spelled with a K rather than a C, and most interestingly an umlaut (two dots) have been placed over the a in Kasper, rendering it as an *ae* for pronunciation. Family and Grafenhausen are at a loss to explain this, except perhaps as a local custom of this period to distinguish the name from that of other, unrelated Kaspers in the village. An explanation closer to whom may have been a further effort at disguise on the part of the young couple. We're unlikely ever to know.

Helen Heinze, born Helen Schaub (1852), was also a Grafenhausen native, having come to America with her parents Xaver and Helena Schaub. Xaver was the brother-in-law of Wendelin's sister Magdalena, and so a family connection existed to explain their presence as witnesses. Helen Schaub died not long after the marriage of Wendelin and Minnie, and she is buried in the Glenwood Avenue cemetery in Mankato. She and Frederick had an infant daughter at the time of her death. He re-married and went on to become a prominent, successful Mankato community citizen.

More About **Wendelin Kasper** and **Wilhelmine Cords**:
Marriage: 15 Oct 1872, Mankato, Minnesota

Children of Wendelin Kasper and Wilhelmine Cords are:

    i.    John Charles Casper, born 26 Aug 1872 in LeRay Township, Madison Lake, Minnesota; died 22 Jun 1940 in Janesville Township, Waseca County, Minnesota; married Rozetta Florence Compton 10 Jan 1897; born 1878; died 08 Nov 1970 in Minneapolis, Hennepin County, Minnesota.

Notes for **Rosetta Florence Compton**:

Perhaps should be best remembered for burning a great many Casper family photographs left with her from a time when her widowed mother-in-law Minnie lived with her. This allegation comes from her niece Margaret Casper whose pilferage saved from that conflagration our one and only photograph of Wendelin.

I have been unable to determine whether her first name was spelled Rosetta or Rozetta.

More About John Casper and Rozetta Compton:
Marriage: 10 Jan 1897

    ii.    Clara Leona Casper[2], born 26 Sep 1873 in LeRay Township, Blue Earth County, Minnesota; died 02 Dec 1963 in St. Clair, Blue Earth County, Minnesota; married Johann Heinrich Carl "John" Cords 15 Mar 1894; born 1868 in Blue Earth County, Minnesota; died 1939 in St. Clair, Blue Earth County, Minnesota.

Notes for **Clara Leona Casper**:

For much of what precedes and follows here in the Cords line I am indebted to the meticulous research of Betty Lou Cords, work she has most generously shared.

Various family reports suggest Clara suffered from the rheumatoid arthritis inherited in the Casper line. She also seems to have suffered from severe chronic depression.

Notes for **Johann Heinrich Carl "John" Cords**:

For much of what both precedes and follows here in the Cords line I am indebted to the meticulous research of Betty Lou Cords.

Marriage Notes for Clara Casper and Johann Cords:
A marriage of first cousins once removed.

More About Johann Cords and Clara Casper:
Marriage: 15 Mar 1894

> iii.    Minnie Kasper, born 10 Jan 1877 in LeRay Township, Madison Lake, Minnesota; died 21 Jan 1887 in LeRay Township, Madison Lake, Minnesota[3]

Notes for **Minnie Kasper**:

Reported by Margaret Casper to be buried in an unmarked grave on the south side of the Eagle Lake cemetery. This turned out to be only partially correct as her memorial marker was located and included in my restoration of the family grave site (see scrapbook).

Margaret Casper thought she was a drowning victim sometime after running away from home. But thanks to Betty Lou Cords (February 1998) we now have every reason to doubt this, for Minnie was barely 10 years old when she died. So the story that Margaret heard from Minnie's mother was either invented to impress Margaret with its moral, or it was misunderstood, and in fact it concerned a family member of an earlier generation—perhaps a sister or cousin who met such a fate in the Mecklenburg lake country where Minnie Cords was born. Such misunderstandings are common as family lore passes from one generation to the next.

We don't yet know for certain whether Minnie or the older Anna "Annie" was the sister who "disappeared," but Anna is the one who can't be accounted for in any known records. It's still possible that Minnie met with foul play, and the story I heard concerning my Grandpa Casper having a sister who disappeared and was never seen again really was that she disappeared and was never seen *alive* again. The weight of evidence, described elsewhere, however, suggests the story concerned his sister Anna.

It seems likely that Minnie was the victim of one of several childhood diseases afflicting pioneer families: scarlet fever, diphtheria, or smallpox.

| | | |
|---|---|---|
| iv. | | Lewis "Louis" Kasper, born 1879 in LeRay Township, Madison Lake, Minnesota; died 12 Jun 1894 in LeRay Township, Madison Lake, Minnesota. |
| v. | | (2) Elmer Francis Casper*, born 27 Dec 1883 in LeRay Township, Blue Earth County, Minnesota; died 14 May 1953 in Madison Lake, Minnesota; married Estella Mary Knapp 15 Nov 1904 in Madison Lake, Minnesota. |
| vi. | | Albert Casper, born Abt. 1884 in LeRay Township, Blue Earth County; died Abt. 1884 in LeRay Township, Blue Earth County. |
| vii. | | Albert A. "Bert" Casper, born 04 Jul 1885 in LeRay Township, Madison Lake, Minnesota; died 04 Oct 1963 in New Ulm, Minnesota; married Laura J. Knapp; born 22 Feb 1899 in Deerwood, Minnesota; died Abt. 17 Mar 1924 in Madison Lake, Minnesota. |

Notes for **Laura J. Knapp**:

Laura Knapp died from complications of appendicitis during late term pregnancy. Her four children were subsequently raised by their grandmother Minnie Cords Casper.

**6. James K. Knapp,** born 18 Feb 1845 in Madison County, New York[4]; died 11 Mar 1927 in Madison Lake, Minnesota. He was the son of **12. Ambrose Knapp** and **13. Jane Ann Moxley**. He married **7. Margaret J. Murphy** 03 Jul 1868 in Cedarburg, Ozaukee County, Wisconsin.

**7. Margaret J. Murphy,** born 15 Oct 1849 in Milwaukee, Wisconsin[5]; died 05 Oct 1931 in LeRay Township, Blue Earth County. She was the daughter of **14. John Henry Murphy** and **15. Catherine O'Connell**.

Notes for **James K. Knapp**:
Biographical Sketch (revised January 2009)

James K. Knapp, man of many parts, was the sort of townsman a thriving community of the pioneer era required. Public-spirited, entrepreneurial, versatile, indomitable, and energetic, he was a nineteenth century, Midwestern Paul Revere who even made an heroic horseback ride to warn settlers of an impending threat.

At various times in a life of 82 years, spanning the breadth of the continent, he was a Union soldier, a local newspaper publisher, a druggist, a veterinarian, a justice of the peace, village clerk, census-taker, and local school board member. Family lore says he even for a time established a fish canning business during a brief residence in the Pacific Northwest. This list would probably be longer if better records had been left behind, or if we could ask "J. K.", as he was often called, to give us an account of all he did.

He was born in New York in 1845 in an era when the state did not maintain birth records, though sketchy evidence suggests the south-central part of Upstate. His parents were from Connecticut, and appear to have moved from there not long after their marriage, as part of the westward migration of even long-established New England families searching for work and new opportunities as populations grew and resources dwindled in areas where their families had first settled.

His ethnic background was predominately English and Scottish and more distantly northern European.

His Knapp family had already been living in the United States for more than two centuries prior to his birth, and was, by the mid-nineteenth century, widely dispersed throughout New England and the Middle Atlantic States. The first Knapps to settle in colonial America were probably Protestant "dissenters" from eastern England arriving about 1630. The name from there in various spellings can be traced back to Anglo-Saxon times. Ambrose Knapp, James K.'s father, had been baptized a Quaker, but there is no evidence of Quaker practice in subsequent family generations.

His mother Jane Ann Moxley, a first-generation immigrant, bore an Anglo-Irish name, but though her Moxley family has a long history in Ireland extending up to the present day, the name is of English origin, and Jane's parents were both born in England. Her family was Anglican, though she in later years became a Methodist.

His paternal grandmother Eunice Campbell was Scottish, but aside from the existence of a sister Maturah, the deceased first wife of James K.'s grandfather Ebenezer Knapp, we know little about her. In many records, Maturah is erroneously recorded as Ambrose's mother.

James K.'s middle name has yet to be found on any record, but since he was born the year of James Knox Polk's inauguration as President of the United States, we may conjecture that the initial K stood for Knox. In these days naming a son after a prominent public figure was commonplace. He never to my knowledge used his middle name, suggesting that he disliked it.

James K. Knapp's father was a ship's carpenter who perhaps fell victim to the declining shipbuilding industry in coastal New England. This came about in part because of the depletion of forest resources as more and more nearby wooded land was cut over. Like many others of this time, he appears to have moved west where his carpentry skills would be in demand as new villages were being established.

After the birth of two or three children, James K. among them, he settled in Wisconsin where the family appears in an 1850 Federal Census. The family into which James K. was born was in a time of transition, and he himself would have come to Wisconsin as an infant with no recollection whatsoever of life in the eastern United States. We do not know precisely when Ambrose Knapp's family joined him in Wisconsin, but given these dates, it would appear that he was there for a while ahead them. Afterwards the family moved around the state, living at various times in Milwaukee, Osceola, Eureka, and Buena Vista before finally settling on a homestead near Madelia, Minnesota in 1861. Shortly afterwards a Sioux Indian uprising forced the family to move to Mankato for safety.

Young James K. became heroically involved with military operations in the local and regional Indian conflicts of this period. A local history records that on August 18, 1861 he rode to New Ulm (presumably from Mankato) to warn the settlers there of the threat of a massacre, and from there he rode another 30 miles to St. Peter to summon aid from a military outpost. This was brave stuff for a lad of less than eighteen. Afterwards he was involved in various military operations involving the Sioux and Chippewa Indians until he was discharged at Fort Snelling on November 28, 1863. His grave site in the cemetery at Madison Lake identifies him as a Civil War veteran.

After the local Indian uprisings and the Civil War (1865) he farmed 80 acres near Madelia until 1872. In the summer of 1868 he married Margaret Murphy, daughter of John Murphy and

Catherine O'Connell. Not long after the father had died, the Murphy family --Margaret, her brothers, sisters, and mother-- had settled early in the decade within twenty miles of Madelia on a farm near St. Clair. I can only speculate that the couple may have met in Mankato during the Indian uprisings. Even so, my records indicate their marriage took place in Cedarburg, Wisconsin where presumably a great many Murphy family still resided.

After 1872, James K. worked as a veterinarian, first at Mankato (1872-73) and then in Rochester, Minnesota from 1874 to 1887. It should be mentioned that little in the way of formal requirements existed in the world of veterinary medicine at this time. One could become a veterinarian by simply adopting the title. From this circumstance arose the derogatory term "horse doctor" applying to anyone practicing medicine and considered a "quack."

During this period of Rochester residence, three of his four surviving children were born. Moving to Madison Lake in 1887-88, he is said to have continued his veterinary practice. He also ran a pharmacy on Front Street and edited a weekly newspaper called the Madison Lake "Breeze." I have yet to discover a copy of this newspaper. An article in the Mankato Review of April 16, 1889 reports his prosecution for selling liquor without a license in the form of a concoction called the "Wine of Life," apparently some sort of patent medicine consisting mostly of alcohol, which—the article claims—was developed and marketed to circumvent laws governing the sale of alcohol. The article concludes that James K. Knapp was appealing the case to district court. I would think that this misadventure might have placed him somewhat at odds with elements in the Madison Lake community, and possibly contributed to the eventual migration of the family to Washington State. On the other hand, documents bearing his signature indicate that the was serving as Madison Lake village clerk as late as 1892, proving that nobody selling liquor will stay unpopular for long!

An interesting coincidence in all this is that in colonial Massachusetts, some 250 years before, Nicholas Knapp, James K.'s great great . . . grandfather was arrested and fined for selling a patent medicine claiming to be a cure for the scurvy, but found to be "of no value."

I have not yet discovered precise dates for the Knapp family's movement to Washington State, but believe that it may have begun as early as 1892-93 with James K.'s sons James E. and then George W. leading the way. Both appeared to have learned the carpenter's trade, owing perhaps to the influence of their grandfather Ambrose. The 1893 Seattle city directory lists among its residence a carpenter named James Knapp, and about ten years later lists another carpenter George W. Knapp. Between times the latter must have been settled in Anacortes on Puget

Sound north of Seattle, for the family bible lists a daughter Lila Mae born there on August 21, 1900.

The 1890's were a period of recession, depression, and general hardship in many parts of the country, Seattle had experienced a major fire in 1889 which had destroyed much of the city, so there must have been significant opportunities in the building trades in the years following. At the same time Anacortes, some sixty miles to the north, had been founded and almost overnight become a boom town, with literally thousands of new residents moving in to work in the fishing and timber industries or to cater to the needs of this mushrooming population. The Anacortes "boom" soon came to a "bust," and it may have been that the Knapps arrived on the late side, missing the best times and facing the worst.

My theory is that James K.'s sons George W. Knapp for sure, and possibly James E. (if one and the same with the James referenced in the Seattle city directory) headed west from Minnesota in search of work. Having learned the carpenter's trade as a skill passed from generation to generation in the family and having inherited as well the Knapp instinct toward land speculation and entrepreneurship, the brothers were drawn there by news of the many opportunities opening up. They also may have been afforded a foothold by the presence of other Knapps, possibly distant cousins from the East Coast branch of the family who had previously settled there. Seattle city directories list many Knapps in residence there during the 1890's, some of them notably successful, an attorney named Frank H., for example, and others in real estate.

*The Knapp Drug Store building in later years.*

Later on, circa 1897 to 1902, the Knapp brothers were followed there by their parents and sisters. James K.'s biographical sketch (History of Blue Earth County) attributes his move to the burning of his drug store in 1899. This may be so, but on the other hand a story in the Madison Lake Times reports the sale of his house on Lake Street to his sister-in-law Kate Murphy in August 1896. He may have owned more than one house, so this date might not determine when he moved west either. Regardless, it seems safe to say that he, his wife, and two daughters were in Washington State, possibly in Seattle, and certainly in Anacortes as the last century came to an end, and they are in fact listed in the 1900 Federal Census for Skagit County,

Washington. They must have returned to Minnesota circa 1902, in time for his daughter Estella to meet and marry Elmer Casper in 1904.

Both James K.'s biographical sketch and family tradition agree that he and his wife had an "interest" in a clam cannery in Anacortes. Having been to that city and researched its history, I can say with some confidence that this is not to be taken as indicating any particular financial success or affluence. In the 1890's the Anacortes waterfront was teeming with fishing industry businesses of all sorts, including a multitude of fish canneries, large and small, a few of which grew very large and survived well into the next century and many of which went out of business almost as soon as they began. A fish cannery at the time could have been little more than a shanty along the bay with a stove, a large pot, and some canning utensils. Family tradition also says that James K. owned a square block of downtown Seattle, currently the site of either the Seattle Post Office or the King County Courthouse. I haven't been able to verify this, but my hunch is that this tale confuses him with some other Knapp, possibly one of the successful East Coast distant cousins concerning whose presence there I have previously speculated.

Had James K.'s years in Washington State led to any notable success I doubt that he would have returned home so soon, and to judge from further reports in the Madison Lake Times, he returned, resurrected his Knapp Drug Store on Front Street, and escaped the disastrous town fire in the business district shortly before Christmas 1910. He also served for a number of years as village clerk and local justice of the peace, a position which would have seen him carrying out a variety of local judicial activities, including—presumably—performing civil marriages. His biography acknowledges that he was a lifelong Catholic and supporter of All Saints Parish in Madison Lake.

His granddaughter Ivalue (in a conversation with me) once referred to him as being a "healer," I presume in the sense of thinking he had the power to cure people of illnesses. On the other hand, she may have confused this bit of family lore with a detail concerning Wendelin, her other grandfather.

Sometime between 1910 and the end of World War I, James K. retired from business and his assorted other enterprises to live out his remaining years in his house on Lake Street in Madison Lake. At times it would have been a house full of small children, aftermath of the deaths of his daughter Genevieve and his granddaughter Laura Knapp, both in childbirth, as well as continuing financial and personal problems of his son James E. who having returned from the West Coast is residing there with his family in the 1910 Federal census.

What little else we know of his business activities relates to his having a dock of some length extending out in the lake below the bluff in front of his house. He is reported to have rented fishing sites from this, and the story goes that he may even have dumped a dead horse in the water nearby to attract fish for his clientele. Ted Roemer, now in his eighties, recalls as a young boy once fishing from that dock without paying. James K. caught him and delivered a swift kick to his backside, enough to send him flying into the water.

Toward the end, he may have been confined to bed much of the time. A granddaughter Betty Ezelle recalls visiting the house on Lake Street when she was a very small girl and meeting her grandmother Knapp but not her grandfather who was in his room confined to bed. He died in early March of 1927. His burial site alongside his wife Margaret in the Catholic cemetery at Madison Lake acknowledges his service in the Civil War.

If there were two men of his generation in the family whose memory was maintained with a sort of awe, one of the certainly was James K., the other being the legendary Kasper judge who was confused --I'm sure-- with my other great grandfather Wendelin Kasper. Despite his "run-in" with the law over the intoxicating medicine sold in his drug store, I have never heard him spoken of with less than great respect. His heroic Civil War era service, his civic and business interests, all served to secure his reputation among his family and in his community. He was in many respects the quintessential Knapp, displaying most of the characteristics my research attaches to this family: adventurous, independent, strong-willed, adaptable, entrepreneurial, resourceful.

Notes for **Margaret J. Murphy:**
Biographical Sketch (revised January 2009)

My father used to say with conviction that she came from County Cork, Ireland, an error I only uncovered after he was gone. Both he and my aunt Ivalue would have been surprised to learn that she was in fact born near Milwaukee, Wisconsin. This is another one of those confusions arising from ambiguities involved in use of the words *grandmother* and *grandfather*. Probably both my dad and my aunt heard their mother say something like "Grandma was born in County Cork," and though she was talking about her grandmother (Catherine O'Connell), they mistook it for theirs. This sort of thing goes on all the time in family stories about their ancestors. I have had to deal with it several times in these pages.

Margaret "Maggie" Murphy's anecdotal record was all but lost by the time I began this project since so many who might have remembered her had passed away. I think Margaret Murphy would have been described by people close to her as courageous, determined, and deeply religious. I surmise that she had strong family instincts and throughout her life kept in close touch with her brothers and especially her sisters Kate and Nellie. Margaret Casper remembers that she made dandelion wine, which she kept in jugs in a sort of back shed of their house on Lake Street of Madison Lake, and once Margaret as a small girl having sampled the contents of one such jug, passed out in the garden and had to be carried into the house.

Otherwise what we know of Margaret Murphy is that she was known as "Maggie," she accompanied her husband and family to the Pacific Northwest where they settled briefly at the end of the 19th century, possibly in Seattle for a time and also in the village of Anacortes north of there on Puget Sound where she is said to have been involved in seafood canning, a detail I have no reason to doubt but have never been able to confirm.

Ivalue had a story about her death, one of those haunting anecdotes of the immediately before or the immediately after sort, with suggestions of premonition and word from beyond the grave, but I heard this a long time ago, and can no longer remember the details. But I do remember Ivalue declaring, "Grandma always said that when her time came she would turn her face to the wall, and die like a man." And so, by her account, she did.

Recently I heard this story from Margaret Casper about her namesake's death in the very home in rural Madison Lake where I lived as a boy, and probably in the very bedroom where I slept. It seems that much of the family had gathered that evening to await the end. Ed and Ivalue were there, possibly newlywed. Margaret Murphy's daughter Estella and her husband Elmer Casper would have been there for sure, for this was their home, and I presume my father Holly would have been on hand, being a boy of ten years old still living at home. Margaret was at her great grandmother's bedside and had been asked to sing to her "When it's Springtime in the Rockies." This apparently was one of Margaret Murphy's favorite songs, and I like to think that it brought back cherished memories of her own trip across the Rockies when she and her husband James K. Knapp journeyed to the Pacific Northwest. Margaret says that while she was singing, the old woman appeared to fall asleep. She kept on singing, and a little while later she was taken by hand out of the room. Margaret Murphy had died.

The only other thing I know for sure about her at this point is that the year before she died, she traveled by train across the country to Redwood City, California to attend the funeral of her son George who had been killed in an automobile accident. This would have been quite a journey for someone of her years and says something about how determined she was when family mattered. Bob Knapp once told me that he thought his father Frank accompanied her on that trip. At the time, I think her sister Nellie would have been living in nearby Palo Alto with her husband Patrick Murphy. My guess is this would have been the last time these sisters saw each other. Since her sister Catherine ("Aunt Kate" of the Madison Lake dress shop) had died in 1929, these Margaret and Nellie (Ellen) were the last left of the John Henry Murphy / Catherine O'Connell family in that generation.

Women of Maggie's generation if they had daughters and themselves lived to old age often found themselves raising their daughter's children if they passed with a young brood to look after. In those days the widowed husband almost never took over, and the responsibility of childcare was transferred to "Grandma." This seems to have happened to Maggie when her daughter Genevieve died in childbirth, leaving a newborn daughter and three sons, the oldest barely five.

Maggie herself was about sixty-three when these four little Muellerleiles probably arrived on her Lake Street doorstep. The children's paternal grandmother, if still living, would have been yet older. Otherwise the only other family women possibly available to help, would have been Genevieve's sister Estella, herself with three small children, and Maggie's granddaughter Laura Knapp, about age 13, and perhaps living in Madison Lake at the time. There may have been other Muellerleile family in a position to help.

The 1910 Federal Census records Laura, her siblings and parents already living with James K. and Margaret Knapp, six of them at the time. It's not clear where they had gone, or even whether they were gone, at the time of Genevieve's death. It could have been an amazing house full at the Knapp home in Madison Lake in the early summer of 1912! Maggie would have had many mouths to feed and no end of things to think about, assuming of course she had much leisure to think.

Somehow all these children, the little Muellerleiles and the Knapp's grew up, and Maggie, an indomitable spirit for certain, lived on to see all this, have a strong hand in it, and keep going a few years even after her husband died. Before that happened, she may even have helped out rearing the four motherless children of her granddaughter Laura who died in the spring of 1924. How else could Margaret have gotten into that dandelion wine as a young girl?

The public record leaves little trace of the likes of women like Maggie Knapp and her Casper family counterpart Minnie Casper. Yet from the little we know, we cannot help but be awed by their courage, spirit, generous natures, and tenacity.

More About **James Knapp** and **Margaret Murphy**:
Marriage: 03 Jul 1868, Cedarburg, Ozaukee County, Wisconsin

Children of James Knapp and Margaret Murphy are:

  i.  James E. Knapp, born 14 Feb 1872 in Madelia, Minnesota; died 30 Dec 1945 in Redwood City, San Mateo, California[6]; married Martha Sorg; born 18 Jan 1877 in Minnesota[7]; died 15 Jan 1971 in Costa Mesa, Orange County, California[8].

Notes for **James E. Knapp**:

His obituary in the Redwood City, California newspaper lists his full name as James Richard Knapp, address 739 Chestnut Street. This eldest son of James K. Knapp may have lived in Seattle, Washington and worked as a carpenter in the early 1890's. Later on, he was by family accounts a chimney sweep whose business during Prohibition disguised a bootlegging operation. This report comes chiefly from my father who recounted seeing him around Madison Lake, driving an old flatbed truck from which hung an array of sooty chains and brushes and which had beneath its swing out truck bed a secret compartment containing large jugs of pure grain alcohol. He appeared this way once visiting his sister Estella, my father's mother, brought out one or more of these jugs and proceeded to get roaring drunk—to the consternation of his sister who became angry enough to kick him off the place.

He had a reputation for heavy drinking. His wife Martha Sorg abandoned him and their four small children at some point, and they in turn may have become one of several family broods raised by the redoubtable "Grandma Knapp." (Margaret Murphy). His obituary describes him as a widower living alone in a cabin. Margaret Casper has told me that his estranged wife actually showed up at his funeral where she was shunned by the rest of the family. I don't have a reason to question this tale, and it suggests to me that at least some of the children had re-established contact with her and notified her of his death.

For a few years at the turn of the century he owned a farm in central Minnesota in the Crosby/Deerwood area. It was there that three of his four children were born (according to the Knapp family bible). A Federal Land Office record lists a homestead title to what appears to be 160 acres in Crow Wing County granted to James E. Knapp on 23 October 1901. The farm may have been located on the Cayuna iron range, for the story is still in the family that after they sold out ore deposits were discovered.

James Knapp died as the result of a severe beating at his home by one William Harragan who was subsequently charged with his murder. Robbery may have been a motive. He is buried in the Menlo Park, California cemetery. The California Death Index gives his name as James Richard Knapp. I can find no other record with Richard as his middle name, and cannot account for this discrepancy.

According to the 1910 Federal Census, he and his family were living in Madison Lake with his parents James K. and Margaret Knapp. That together with the report that his youngest son was born in North Dakota, the further report of his work in Washington State, and then finally his residences in Deerwood, Minnesota and in California give us a picture of one who moved around a lot, especially in his early adult years.

Since his estranged wife appears to have died in California, we can conjecture that she left him after the family had moved there. Some of his children at that point may have re-located in Madison Lake and were possibly raised by their grandmother. Laura was married there, and family lore says that Frank accompanied his grandmother Margaret on the train to California for the funeral of George Washington Knapp. his uncle and her son.

ii.     George Washington Knapp, born 07 Mar 1878 in Rochester, Minnesota; died 01 Oct 1930 in California; married (1) Mary A. Olmstead 04 Jul 1897 in Minnesota; born Jul 1876 in Wisconsin[9]; married (2) Luella L. Stimson aka Luella Koetke 10 Apr 1910; born Abt. 1892 in Wisconsin or Washington[10]; died 17 Oct 1934 in San Mateo, California[11].

## Notes for **George Washington Knapp**:

Listed in the 1900 Federal Census as living in Washington State (Fairhaven, Whatcom County) with his wife Mary and son Earl. Since Earl's place of birth is given as Minnesota in 1899, it appears George and his family moved from Minnesota to Washington around the turn of the century.

Here and in subsequent censuses his occupation is given as a carpenter. Later on he settled in southern California where he built houses in the Redwood City area. He was killed in an automobile accident, colliding with a truck. His wife was seriously injured and died about a year later.

More About **George Knapp** and **Mary Olmstead**:
Divorce: Abt. 1906
Marriage: 04 Jul 1897, Minnesota

iii.    Genevieve Margaret Knapp, born 06 Aug 1882 in Rochester, Minnesota; died 25 Jun 1912 in Madison Lake, Minnesota; married Henry Andrew Muellerleile 10 Oct 1905 in Madison Lake, Minnesota; born 30 May 1881 in Minnesota[12]; died 29 May 1964 in Louisville, Kentucky.

More About Henry Muellerleile and Genevieve Knapp:
Marriage: 10 Oct 1905, Madison Lake, Minnesota

iv.   (3) Estella Mary Knapp, born 20 Nov 1884 in Rochester, Minnesota; died 23 Jul 1945 in Madison Lake, Minnesota; married Elmer Francis Casper* 15 Nov 1904 in Madison Lake, Minnesota.


*Generation No. 4*


**8. Johann Kasper,** born 01 Apr 1804 in Grafenhausen, Baden, Germany; died 25 May 1861 in Grafenhausen, Baden, Germany. He was the son of **16. Joseph Anton Kasper** and **17. Katharina Hoegi**. He married **9. Katharina Jaeger** 23 Aug 1831 in Grafenhausen, Baden, Germany.

**9. Katharina Jaeger**[13], born 27 Apr 1808; died 22 Apr 1870 in Kappel, Baden, Germany. She was the daughter of **18. Franz Jaeger** and **19. Maria Anna Wendle**.


Notes for **Johann Kasper**:

Johann seems to have been a farmer. Beyond this we know little about him.

Family fortunes by his day appear to have leveled off or perhaps declined, possibly in response to macro events such as the Napoleonic wars and tensions between northern and southern German states, with southern ones sometimes feeling more aligned with French interests than with Prussian countrymen far to the north. To this day in Lahr, a neighboring village, a gasthaus where Napoleon stopped for a meal advertises the event.

The best argument for a decline in family fortunes is the emigration of two of Johann's three children as both Magdalena and Wendelin settled in America. Meantime Johann's widow twice remarried, and the remaining son Johann inherited what remained of family property and enterprise. Nothing indicates Wendelin and Magdalena received significant financial support in America. The former struggled financially throughout his life.

Today, inscribed above a doorway on the main street of Grafenhausen, can still be seen the initials JK & KJ, representing the names of Johann and his wife Katherina. This is their house from former days, much remodeled and probably changed beyond recognition. To its rear may be remnants of earlier Kasper farm buildings. Pictures will be found elsewhere here.

Notes for **Katharina Jaeger**:

As far as I can determine, the three children of Katherina Jaeger by her previous marriage to Xaver Kern produced no offspring. Her sons did not live to adulthood, and her daughter Maria Eva appears to have had no children. This would leave our family without descendants on this branch.

More About **Johann Kasper** and **Katharina Jaeger**:
Marriage: 23 Aug 1831, Grafenhausen, Baden, Germany

Children of Johann Kasper and Katharina Jaeger are:

      i.      Magdalena Kasper[13], born 16 Apr 1833 in Grafenhausen, Baden, Germany; died Abt. 24 Oct 1906 in Mankato, Blue Earth County, Minnesota[14]; married Kasimir Schaub 20 Aug 1857 in Grafenhausen, Baden, Germany; born 21 Jul 1827 in Grafenhausen, Baden, Germany.

Notes for **Magdalena Kasper**:

Magdalena Kasper and Kasimir Schaub came to America with their children in 1868, probably stayed for a while in Indiana, and then along with Wendelin Kasper and a number of other former residents of Grafenhausen, Baden, settled in LeRay and Jamestown Townships, near Madison Lake, Blue Earth County, Minnesota.

The homesteads of Magdalena Kasper Schaub and her brother Wendelin Kasper were less than a mile apart in LeRay Township. Hers in later times became the Clare Frederick farm where I sometimes hunted pheasants with my dog Nellie in my high school years and where once I played basketball in the barn's hayloft with Clare, Jr. and Joseph Hoehn.

Late in the year 1873 Magdalena was the baptismal sponsor for the christening of Clara Casper at a Lutheran church in Mankato. Nevertheless, she appears to have been Roman Catholic as was her brother, and in later years his wife Wilhelmene Cords.

The genealogical records of Shirley Schaub (*Descendants of Johannes Schaub*) seem to indicate that the marriage of Magdalena and Kasimir Schaub failed sometime in the 1880's, but I am skeptical of this, and think it possible that she has mistaken the marriage of their son Casimir to August Reeske as a subsequent marriage of Kasimir Schaub, Sr. I am researching this further. Neither the Mormon Church Schaub family records nor the Schaub immigration record in Germans to America indicate that Kasimir Schaub had both a son named Kasimir and another named Charles, so a case builds that Karl Kasimir and Charles Schaub are one and the same person.

Various dates provided by the Shirley Schaub record (Magdalena's birth and the births of their children) do not reconcile with dates given in the immigration record Germans to America. The latter strike me as more reliable inasmuch as they have the children all being born subsequent to their marriage. Overall, it seems that both the Shirley Schaub genealogy and the Mormon Church records contain errors with respect to this particular Schaub family. It is also possible that the *Ortsippenbuch Grafenhausen* itself is the source of some of these discrepancies, but I haven't yet had a chance to check that.

*Germans to America*, itself far from error free, lists what we know to be two Schaub families arriving at New York on October 12, 1868:

*...the family of Kasimir Schaub and Magdalena Kasper and the family of Kasimir's brother Xavier and his wife Helena. Kasimir and Magdalena are accompanied by five children: Karoline (spelled Caroline in this record) 9, Katherina (spelled Catherine) 8, Lina 6, Frantz (known as Frank elsewhere) 4, and Kasimir (spelled Casimir) 1. Xavier and Helena Schaub are accompanied by their three children: Lambert 22, Helena 17 (subsequently the marriage witness for Wendelin Kasper and Minnie Cords and the wife of Frederick Heinze of Mankato) and Xavier 13.*

More About **Kasimir Schaub** and **Magdalena Kasper**:
Marriage: 20 Aug 1857, Grafenhausen, Baden, Germany

      ii.      Johann Kasper, born 17 Jul 1835 in Grafenhausen, Baden, Germany; died 24 Nov 1912 in Grafenhausen, Baden, Germany; married Theresia Kurz 18 Jun 1860 in Grafenhausen, Baden, Germany; born 24 Feb 1840 in Grafenhausen, Baden, Germany; died 25 Feb 1899 in Grafenhausen, Baden, Germany.

Notes for **Johann Kasper**:

Johann Kasper II lived his entire life in Grafenhausen and produced many children, most of whom did not survive to adulthood. His descendants are the remaining Kaspers in Grafenhausen and indeed in all of Germany, at least from a direct line of descent.

More About **Johann Kasper** and **Theresia Kurz**:
Marriage: 18 Jun 1860, Grafenhausen, Baden, Germany

   iii.  (4) Wendelin Kasper, born 05 Jul 1845 in Grafenhausen-Kappel, Baden, Germany; died 26 Dec 1922 in Madison Lake, Minnesota; married Wilhelmine Sophia Friedericke Caroline Cords 15 Oct 1872 in Mankato, Minnesota.

  **10. Johann Joachim Carl Friedrich Cords,** born 11 Dec 1811 in Ruest, Mecklenburg, Germany. He was the son of **20. Johann Friedrich Cords** and **21. Catherina Margaretha Sophia Hahn(en)**. He married **11. Hannah Catharina Dorothea Sternberg** 03 Aug 1838 in Mestlin, Mecklenburg, Germany.

  **11. Hannah Catharina Dorothea Sternberg,** born 04 Jul 1820 in Ruest, Mecklenburg, Germany. She was the daughter of **22. Johann Sternberg** and **23. Sophia Eikelberg**.

More About **Johann Cords** and **Hannah Sternberg**:
Marriage: 03 Aug 1838, Mestlin, Mecklenburg, Germany

Children of Johann Cords and Hannah Sternberg are:
  i.  Johann Friedrich Carl Cords, born 11 Oct 1838.
  ii.  Sophia Carolina Dorothea Johanna Cords, born 01 Nov 1840.
  iii.  Maria Frederica Johanna Christine Cords, born 22 Jun 1842.
  iv.  Carl Johann Friedrich Theodor "Charles"[15], born 07 Dec 1844 in Mecklenburg, Germany; died 28 Feb 1911 in Hector Township, Renville County, Minnesota; married Fredericka Koppen 18 Feb 1876 in McPherson Township, Blue Earth County, Minnesota[15]; born 01 Dec 1856 in Germany; died Oct 1936 in Bemidji, Minnesota[15].

More about **Carl "Charles" Cords** and **Fredericka Koppen**:
Marriage: 18 Feb 1876, McPherson Township, Blue Earth County, Minnesota[15]

| v. | Friedrich Carl Heinrich Cords, born 05 Jan 1847. |
| vi. | (5) Wilhelmine Sophia Fredericka Caroline Cords, born 08 Aug 1850 in Ruest, Mecklenburg, Germany; died 18 Feb 1940 in Madison Lake, Minnesota; met (1) Carl Moller in Ruest/Mestlin, Mecklenburg, Germany; married (2) Wendelin Kasper 15 Oct 1872 in Mankato, Minnesota. |
| vii. | Wilhelmine Maria Dorothea Cords, born 24 Dec 1852. |

**12. Ambrose Knapp,** born 03 May 1813 in Connecticut[16]; died 23 Jan 1894 in Madison Lake, Minnesota. He was the son of **24. Ebenezer Knapp** and **25. Eunice Campbell**. He married **13. Jane Ann Moxley** 20 Jul 1841 in Litchfield, Connecticut.

**13. Jane Ann Moxley,** born 26 Dec 1814 in near Rosscarbery, County Cork, Ireland; died 21 Jul 1883 in Mankato, Minnesota. She was the daughter of **26. Richard Moxley** and **27. Unknown**.

Notes for **Ambrose Knapp**:

Ambrose Knapp was born in northwestern Connecticut. Baptismal records from the Quaker Community at nearby Nine Partners, New York give his birth date as 03 May 1813 and list his father as Ebenezer and his mother as Eunice (Campbell) Knapp. This date is at variance with that provided by other sources, but seems the most credible. Again, while his mother—in some Knapp genealogies—is given as Maturah Campbell, Eunice's sister, the Quaker record states otherwise, and that is what I have gone with here.

*The author standing in front of the Quaker meeting house at Nine Partners, Duchess County, New York where Ambrose Knapp was christened.*

Ebenezer Knapp was in fact married to both women, and children resulted from each marriage, so the record is confusing to say the least. As for the Quaker background in all this, I suspect we should look to the Campbell side, for there isn't much in Knapp ancestry to support this religious connection.

Though he was baptized in a Quaker community, nothing suggests Ambrose practiced the Quaker religion during his adult life.

Like many men of his generation, Ambrose moved west in search of work, first to New York, then to Wisconsin, and then finally settling in southern Minnesota. He seems to have begun as a ship's carpenter, working in the ship-building yards of southeastern Connecticut. It is possibly there that he met his future wife Jane Ann Moxley whose uncle Robert Noles may have been similarly employed. We will never know for sure, but as nearby timber resources became depleted, this industry declined and forced men like Ambrose to seek work elsewhere.

In the course of all this he and Jane were married at Litchfield, Connecticut not far from Ambrose's birthplace. The record suggests that Jane was a resident of Litchfield at the time of their marriage. How long she had lived there previously and how she came to be there remain a mystery. We next find the couple in New York State where their first children are born, among them James K. Knapp.

Not long after the latter's birth, Ambrose surfaces in Wisconsin where family lore says he built the first hotel in Milwaukee. I have discovered nothing to substantiate this, but I suppose for a man trained in ship construction, a hotel—especially a small wooden one—wouldn't have been difficult.

The 1850 Federal Census locates the family—Ambrose, Jane, and three children, in Eden, Fond Du Lac Wisconsin where Ambrose's identifies himself as a farmer. Ten years later (the 1860 Federal Census) Ambrose, Jane, and four Knapp children are in Buena Vista, Portage, Wisconsin where Ambrose's occupation is given as a carpenter. From there, as the Civil War loomed, they appear to have migrated to southern Minnesota, living on a farm in the Madelia area before a Sioux Indian uprising forced them to flee to Mankato for safety. There also exists a Minnesota land record showing Ambrose's purchase of 160 acres near St. Peter, Minnesota. Wisconsin land records show that he previously owned land there as well.

The Minnesota Territorial Census of 1865 lists Ambrose, Jane, and their five children in McPherson Township of Blue Earth County, Minnesota. Among the children are Mary Jane, the oldest, and Louisa, the youngest. Neither of these daughters survived their mother at the time of her death in 1883. However, the 1870 Federal Census does list Louisa and Alexander as living with their parents, ages 14 and 19 respectively. At this point an older son, James K. had married and may have been living in Rochester, Minnesota, while Theodore, also married, appears to have returned to the Knapp family roots in Connecticut where he spent the rest of his life.

Family History Diary Entry for 1993:

Somewhere I learned—and I haven't yet retraced my steps to the source of this information--that Ambrose Knapp and his wife Jane Moxley were buried in the Glenwood Avenue cemetery in Mankato, Minnesota. One weekend in September 1993, my sons David, Stephen, Cass, and I made a trip there, as part of what I billed as a family history trip, and looked for a grave site.

We found, in fact, a site with a stone bearing the name of Alexander Knapp, one of Ambrose's sons, his wife, and two unmarked sites in the plot, either empty or perhaps the unmarked grave sites of Ambrose and Jane—we just don't know yet.

I have subsequently consulted records of the Glenwood Avenue Cemetery and have learned that Ambrose Knapp and his wife Jane are indeed buried there alongside their son Alexander.

Another recollection about Ambrose . . . when as a boy, I would occasionally get on the topic of family history with my aunt Ivalue, who seemed to love this stuff, the name of Hannah Rappleye would now and then surface. This appears to have been Ambrose's second wife, a marriage late in life of the May/December sort, and one that I recall Aunt Ivalue indicating had met with considerable disapproval in the family, something borne out by what follows here. . .

Also in my possession, a typed transcript from what appears to be Ambrose Knapp's obituary, or at least a local newspaper account of his death:

January 23, 1894:

*Mr. Ambrose Knapp, an old and respected citizen of this county, died at his home at Madison Lake this morning. He was in his usual health and had gone to bed last night apparently well, intending to come to Mankato today. When the team was sent to his house this morning, his body was found lying in bed, his feet were warm, but there was no pulsation of the heart, and he had evidently just passed away, peacefully, and without any evidence of struggle. Mr. Knapp was living at his home alone, which is situated on the easterly bank of the North bay of Madison Lake and where he has made his home for a number of years. His wife and step-daughter left him last summer and are now living somewhere in the west.*

*Mr. Knapp was born in Connecticut, May 15, 1812 where he resided many years, removing to Minnesota in the summer of 1861 settling at or near Madelia. When the Indian massacre occurred in 1862, he moved with his family to Mankato making this city his home for many years. For eight or ten years, he has resided at Madison Lake where he devoted his time to cultivating vegetables and small fruits which he supplied to cottagers and others at the Point [Point Pleasant]. He was of a happy, social disposition, made many friends at the lake and his daily visits were enjoyed by his patrons and friends. Mr. Knapp was a conscientious man, a hard worker, and until a recent sufferer from the grip was vigorous and hardy. Mr. Knapp was twice married, and he leaves three or four children by his first wife who died 12 or 15 years ago and is buried in Mankato cemetery.*

*The funeral will take place at the lake on Thursday, at 10:00 o'clock and the remains brought to this city for burial.*

I also have some further information about Ambrose Knapp, found in the *Blue Earth County Historical Society* written on his family page, complied by whom I don't know:

*Ambrose Knapp moved from Connecticut to New York in 1843, then went to Milwaukee, Wisconsin in 1844. A year later he was in Fond du Lac, then to Osceola in 1852 and Eureka in 1855, then to Buena Vista, Portage County, Wisconsin in 1858, all before arriving in Madelia, Minnesota in 1861.*

In this record his occupation is given as a ship carpenter. His Blue Earth County death record lists it as a hunter. Mankato, Minnesota newspapers of the period occasionally display advertisements indicating that he sold and traded horses and practiced as a veterinarian, which in those days just about anybody could do, hence the epithet "*horse doctor.*"

Various items from an early Mankato, Minnesota newspaper, *The Review*, pertaining to Ambrose Knapp:

**08 June 1880** Dr. *Ambrose Knapp, veterinary, offers his professional services to the public in a card elsewhere, endorsed by some pretty good names.*

Advertisement: *Drs. A. Knapp & Son, Veterinary Surgeons*

**25 July 1882** *Ambrose Knapp offers 8 or 10 horses for sale, very cheap.*

Putting all this together, we have a man who begins adult life as a ship's carpenter on the East Coast and ends it in the Midwest growing fruit and vegetables which he sells to weekend tourists and others at the Point Pleasant Resort, Madison Lake, Minnesota. In between he had been a land speculator, a farmer, a veterinarian of sorts, and a horse trader. Three sons survived him, and from these three extend the surviving branches of our Knapp family as we know it today.

Notes for **Jane Ann Moxley:**

I am certain that Jane's family name was ***Moxley***, rather than *Maxley*, as it appears to be written in the family pages of the Knapp family bible and shows up elsewhere in various genealogies. This is an unfortunate example of an error being endlessly repeated over the internet. Elsewhere her name is clearly given as Moxley, the signature on the letter from her father (transcribed elsewhere here) strongly favors Moxley as the spelling, and Moxley is in fact that English/Irish name that one encounters to this day in County Cork.

She was born in Ireland, County Cork, near the village of Rosscarbery, a rather small town on the south-east coast. Northwest of there but a few miles is the countryside known as Ballyroe, meaning the "red lands," and this is where the Moxley family of Jane's time lived. Even in the present day Moxleys live in the vicinity.

An Ambrose Knapp family page located in the Blue Earth County Historical Society says that she immigrated to Montreal, Canada in 1824, and that she also lived at Prescott, western Canada. Prescott is a village in southeastern Ontario which in those days would have been referred to as western Canada, even though it is far east in Canada as we know it today.

Her obituary mentions that she lived in Ontario in the care of an uncle. I presume this to be accurate, and if so, perhaps Canadian information records should be searched for her. From Montreal somehow, she would have made her way to Connecticut where the Knapp family bible lists her marriage in Litchfield to Ambrose Knapp in 1840.

For several reasons, including details provided in her father's letter of 1838, transcribed elsewhere here, I surmise that Jane may have been the youngest in her family, that her mother died when she was quite young, and an aunt—perhaps her mother's sister or sister-in-law—assumed responsibility for her care, bringing her to America when she and her husband—Robert Noles— subsequently emigrated. If this is correct, then one possibility is that Jane's mother was a Noles or Knowles by birth. The fact that both her obituary and Richard Moxley's letter to his daughter refer to her uncle rather than to her aunt gives this some support, suggesting that the uncle was in fact her blood relative.

Jane's obituary in Mankato, Minnesota newspapers provide the following account:

*"Died in West Mankato Sunday morning the 22nd of July 1883 Mrs. Jane Ann Knapp, consort of Ambrose Knapp, aged 69 years.*

*Got breakfast and partook as usual. Complained of pain in heart —prayed—sang hymns—took farewell of all of family and died.*

*Born near Ross Canberry [sic] Co. Cork, Ireland in 1814.*

*Landed at Montreal, Canada when only ten years old --in care of an uncle.*

*Married Ambrose Knapp, July 20, 1840 at Litchfield, Conn.*

> *moved to Madelia, 1860,*
> *fled to Mankato for safety in 1862,*
> *remained here ever since,*
> *had 9 children, 7 boys, 2 girls.*

> *3 boys survive:*
> > *James K.*
> > *Theodore A.*
> > *Alexander N.*

*Joined the Episcopal Church when 15 years old.*

*Kind to the poor,*
*Conspicuous on her attendance at church,*
*Cheerfully contributing of her limited means to its support."*


Note: It's interesting that she is said to have joined the Episcopal Church when she was 15 years old. This argues that the Moxleys and/or the Noles were Church of Ireland (Anglican) members, and perhaps this accounts for the family's migration to Canada rather than the United States where so many Catholic Irish went. The name Moxley is in fact British Irish, nor is the name Noles, and so it is most likely that early generations of Moxleys in Ireland were Church of Ireland Anglicans. Later generations included Roman Catholics as well. Jane herself appears to have been a Methodist in her Minnesota years.

More About Ambrose Knapp and Jane Moxley:
Marriage: 20 Jul 1841, Litchfield, Connecticut

Children of Ambrose Knapp and Jane Moxley are:
    i.        Wolcott Knapp[17], born 1842.

Notes for **Wolcott Knapp**:
No further information available.

    ii.       Mary Jane Knapp, born 29 Jun 1843 in New York[18]

Notes for **Mary Jane Knapp**:
Not a trace of her in later records.

    iii.      (6) James K. Knapp, born 18 Feb 1845 in Madison County, New York; died 11 Mar 1927 in Madison Lake, Minnesota; married Margaret J. Murphy 03 Jul 1868 in Cedarburg, Ozaukee County, Wisconsin.
    iv.      Theodore A. Knapp, born 19 Oct 1848 in Wisconsin[19]; died 23 Jul 1907 in Waterbury, Connecticut; married Anne Jones 10 Oct 1868; born May 1848 in Ireland[20]; died Aug 1908.

Notes for **Theodore A. Knapp**:
Reported to have been killed in an accident at a Waterbury Brass works.

More About Theodore Knapp and Anne Jones:
Marriage: 10 Oct 1868

    v.       Alexander N. Knapp, born 10 Nov 1851 in Wisconsin[21]; died 1898 in Mankato, Blue Earth County, Minnesota; married Mary Ellen Taylor 28 Oct 1882; born 08 Feb 1863 in Mankato, Blue Earth County, Minnesota; died 1936 in Mankato, Blue Earth County, Minnesota.

Notes for **Alexander N. Knapp**:
Resident of Blue Earth County since 1859. Prominent member of Hook and Ladder Company #2. Lived in West Mankato. Carpenter. . . Died of Typhoid fever at age 47, and is buried with his wife in Glenwood Cemetery, Mankato—in the same plot as his parents.

The 1870 Mankato census lists Alexander as still living at home, age 19, occupation as a teamster.

More About Alexander Knapp and Mary Taylor:
Marriage: 28 Oct 1882

    vi.       Louisa Knapp[22], born Abt. 1856; died Aft. 1870.

Notes for **Louisa Knapp**:

The 1870 census of Mankato lists Louisa Knapp, daughter of Ambrose and Jane, age 14, born in Wisconsin. This is the first mention of her that I have found among Knapp family records. She is not mentioned in the Knapp family bible, nor in any other records, and she must have been dead by the time of her mother's death in 1883. At any rate she is not mentioned as a surviving child in her mother's obituary where reference is made to nine children, only three of whom survive. And it is strange that she is overlooked by Knapp family records which otherwise seem so complete.

        **14. John Henry Murphy,** born 1819 in Ireland (possibly County Cork)[23]; died 16 Apr 1859 in Cedarburg, Wisconsin[24]. He was the son of **28. Unknown Murphy** and **29. Katherine**. He married **15. Catherine O'Connell** 06 Jun 1842 in Probably Wisconsin[25].
        **15. Catherine O'Connell,** born 1823 in County Cork, Ireland[26]; died 13 Apr 1877 in St. Clair, Blue Earth County, Minnesota[27]. She was the daughter of **30. Jeremiah (Geoffry) O'Connell** and **31. Catherine Burke or Booke ? (a widow)**.

Notes for **John Henry Murphy**:

Jayne Joyce Staley in her extensive research on the Murphy/O'Connell branch suspects that John Henry Murphy hailed from the Castletownbere area of the Beara Peninsula, West Cork just as our O'Connell ancestors appear to have. She bases this hunch on the fact of his settling in a Wisconsin region where many recent Castletownbere immigrants settled. This has some inductive value, but as she recognizes is far from conclusive. I myself have problems placing our O'Connell kin out on the Beara Peninsula since the genealogy of Beara has been pretty extensively researched without producing a sign of them. West Cork in the vicinity of the Beara Peninsula seems to me a safer bet.

A hunch of my own, based on Irish naming patterns, is that Daniel's father was named Stephen, hence probably the middle name of his firstborn son Daniel S. Murphy. John J. Murphy, the second son may have had the middle name of Catherine's father Jeremiah/Geoffry O'Connell. We may get closer to the truth eventually where this is concerned. Jayne Staley's research gives Stephen's middle initial as C rather than S. Unfortunately, I have not sourced my record of this.

One could hardly find names more challenging to research than John Murphy and Catherine O'Connell (See my note for Catherine). Many Irish men and women in the same era had these names. Even many John Henry Murphys are to be found among Irish immigrants. The result is an almost hopeless tangle of possibly mistaken identities.

What those of us who have researched the matter suspect is that our Murphy branch at first settled in Massachusetts at about 1840. Though conditions they left behind in Ireland were already bad, fortunately for them the Potato Famine was not yet underway. They thus avoided an ordeal that has been compared to the Holocaust. Some of our Murphys probably settled more or less permanently in Massachusetts. Their descendants might well be there in the present day. Many others in this large family of what seems to have been several brothers, their spouses, and children migrated west to Wisconsin, settling on farms near Milwaukee.

John Henry Murphy and Catherine O'Connell, already married, may have been among them. No record of their marriage has been located in either state, but we do know all of their children were born in Wisconsin.

John Henry died, possibly of tuberculosis, at a very young age, leaving his widow and six surviving children, three sons and three daughters. Within a few years his family moved to a farm in Minnesota near St. Clair. Like a great many other immigrant families first settled in Wisconsin, they were attracted to farmland available in Minnesota after the Civil War and the Sioux Indian uprising had been quelled.

## Notes for **Catherine O'Connell**:

The O'Connell genealogy from Catherine's father back should not be taken as established fact. It is based upon an earlier O'Connell family history compiled by O'Connell family members Curran J. DeBruler and June Joyce Larson, who in turn based their work on Irish genealogical sources of questionable reliability, most notably O'Hart's Irish Peerages. That the Library of

Congress holds a copy of both books should not be taken as acknowledging their historical accuracy.

O'Hart's work has often been characterized as inaccurate and unreliable. It is also clear from a letter in my possession written by Rose Murphy DeBruler to her aunt Maggie (Margaret J. Murphy) that this history was aimed at constructing an O'Connell family story celebrating its heroic Catholicism and its close ties to Daniel O'Connell, known as the Liberator. Such genealogies are often afflicted with assumptions and hasty conclusions supporting the desired result.

Moreover, Irish genealogy in general is chronically afflicted with obstacles and challenges, including fragmentary, lost, and destroyed records and problems identifying specific individuals when names, both surname and given, are shared by multiple individuals within a specific region and era. Ireland and even County Cork was home to many Catherine O'Connells at the time our Catherine was born there, dwelled there, and finally left for America. One ship after another during the peak years of Irish migration carried a Catherine O'Connell to America. Sometimes there were two or more on the same ship. The same holds true for O'Connells with other common given names, Daniel, Stephen, Richard, Mary, and Ellen for example. The same holds true for droves of Murphys.

It's easy to give in to frustration where all this is concerned and take a "shot in the dark" as its often called: here's a ship arriving in an American port with a Catherine O'Connell registered as a passenger. Given other information at hand, the date seems right where others at hand don't quite fit as puzzle pieces. So, the conclusion forms that surely this must be the Catherine O'Connell we seek and others of that name on the same ship must surely have been family members. It's not an established fact, not even close. It could be another Catherine and only the most distantly related O'Connell clan, but the frustrated family historian, eager to fill a blank or two, writes it all down as established fact, and leaves it as such without even a note of caution for other family historians to pick up and repeat. I don't want to make that mistake. Family historians should be in the business of correcting, not compounding errors.

DeBruler and Larson may have compounded errors when approaching O'Hart's work, accepting without question the O'Connell relationship leaps leading to Daniel, the Liberator and beyond, all the way back actually to the King of Munster. It has been sometimes said derisively that every Irishman is related to a king. It can also be said that almost every O'Connell claims direct kinship with the great Daniel. Wishful thinking can be an obstacle to sound scholarship. If from a selection of Richards and Maurices, only one of each leads in the desired direction, tie those two together as son and father, though they might have been nephew and uncle or even distant cousins.

I am not accusing DeBruler and Larson of proceeding this way, or even saying that O'Hart did. The point is we just don't know and probably never will, and the potential for confusion and inaccuracy is high, sufficiently high to leave much in doubt once we go beyond Catherine's father Jeremiah in the O'Connell line.

So where does this leave us with respect to Catherine and the O'Connell genealogy? The Rose Murphy DeBruler letter proves that at least some of the O'Connell family history research was undertaken while children of John Henry Murphy and Catherine O'Connell were still living and might have been in a position to corroborate certain details. Enclosed with the letter was a family tree apparently culled from O'Hart. This family tree was passed on to Margaret Murphy Knapp's granddaughter Ivalue Casper and from there it came to me.

Since it seems likely that the children of John Murphy and Catherine O'Connell would have heard their grandparents' names mentioned in family conversations, and would have immediately identified a mistake, we might assume that the given name of Catherine O'Connell's father is correct along with possibly certain background details. The problem is we are given two names, and the names Jeremiah and Geoffry are not versions of the same name. Did DeBruler and Larson seem to think otherwise, and perhaps attach information about the one to the other and from that point on locate our O'Connell family on the wrong branch of the extended family tree? Did they attribute details drawn from the life of one to the life of the other? Did these details instead apply to an O'Connell of an earlier generation?

Still, some details about Jeremiah/Geoffry O'Connell are sufficiently extraordinary—military surgeon stationed in India, formerly married to a Dutch woman, etc. —to make a narrative the Murphy children might have heard firsthand from their O'Connell mother. As family lore alone, as a story passed from mother to children detailing the life of their grandfather, it would almost certainly be true, at least in its broad outlines. But we don't know when Jeremiah/Geoffry died. Presumably his second marriage (to a widow Catherine Burke) came later in life, and he might have died before his daughter Catherine was even old enough to remember him.

The story might have been passed to her secondhand from her mother who herself might have confused details. Sometimes such stories are misinterpreted by those who hear them. References to father and grandfather, mother and grandmother can be ambiguous, and are sometimes applied by the listener to one generation and one side of the family, when in fact they are about an earlier generation on the other side of the family. A surgeon stationed in India might in fact have been in the East or West Indies. The Dutch wife might have been a grandfather's, not a father's. These kinds of confusions abound in family lore and can take on a life of their own, especially if they involve something sufficiently interesting or notable to be worth repeating.

Most recently an online publication under the general title of NOT ONE IN TEN THOUSAND KNOW YOUR NAME has posted a brief biography of one Richard O'Connell, surgeon in various Regiments of Foot, including the Irish 43rd. A number of important details from Richard's military career replicate those mentioned by DeBruler and Larson in their account of Jeremiah. Jeremiah was said to have been a surgeon in the 43rd. and stationed in India. Richard, a surgeon, was in the 43rd as well as other regiments of foot at various times. Records of the 43rd tell us that the regiment was never in India in this era, but it was in the West Indies for a time in the mid 1790's. Toward the apparent end of his military career, Richard was stationed in the Netherlands. All this invites speculation that family anecdotes confuse Jeremiah with his father Richard. We can't of course prove this, nor can we prove that this Richard is one and the same as the one mentioned in the DeBruler-Larson history. Still it does make pretty good sense to think so.

Genealogist Basil O'Connell has left three tracts delineating various lines of the O'Connell family. So far as I can tell, none of these deals directly with our supposed line, a work he mentions but never got around to. Reading through these tracts, one gets a sense of the numerous O'Connells of the same name—John, Richard, Daniel, Maurice, Catherine, etc—that makeup this easily tangled history. One even finds—in apparently another line—reference to a renowned O'Connell soldier/surgeon stationed in the West Indies. Who knows but this may be our man, only distantly related? I doubt that even Catherine O'Connell herself, were she alive today, could say for sure.

The best we can say here is that her father was probably named either Jeremiah or Geoffrey. I favor the former and suspect the matter might be close to established if we knew he middle name of her son John J. Murphy. Jeremiah/Geoffry or his father or grandfather or perhaps all three may have been military physicians, and one or more of them was probably stationed in the East or West Indies. I favor either over India, especially the East, given the report of Jeremiah/Geoffry's Dutch wife. Still we can't completely reject the idea that it might have been India and the story is simply wrong when it comes to the 43rd Regiment of Foot. See my notes for Richard and Jeremiah O'Connell.

Jeremiah/Geoffry's military background may be somewhat corroborated by the report of his being stationed on the Beara Peninsula after his years in India or the Indies. Elsewhere I have read that Beara and adjacent Bear Island were frequented by pirates, and military were stationed there to intercept them.

Family lore insists that Catherine was born in County Cork. I see no reason to question this, but it is an interesting instance of the confusion I have described above that both my father and my aunt Ivalue were certain that her daughter Margaret Murphy Knapp, their grandmother, had also been born in County Cork. We know for certain that she was born in Wisconsin. No doubt they had been told, "Grandma was born in County Cork," and applied this to their grandmother rather than their grandmother's mother. I doubt very much that their Grandmother Knapp intended to deceive them. It's just a good example of what happens when family lore is passed along.

The dates 1823 and 1826 are both given for Catherine O'Connell's birth. I favor the former as provided in the 1850 Federal Census. In subsequent censuses she appears to have taken the opportunity to subtract a few years, something a County Cork genealogist suggested women of that era almost always did when given the opportunity. Only her late husband would have been the wiser. On the other hand, she might have mislead her husband concerning her age, not wishing at the time of her marriage to declare herself as young as she was. If born in 1826, she would have married at about age 16. Again, we will probably never know.

## A family sketch of Catherine O'Connell

I have the original scrap of paper on which she wrote out the names and dates of her husband and children. Here we have a firm record at least.

Catherine O'Connell is buried in the Catholic cemetery at St. Clair, Minnesota. She appears to have moved to Minnesota from the Milwaukee, Wisconsin area about 1867, having been widowed by the death of her husband eight years before. The 1850 Federal Census record indicate she continued to run the family Wisconsin farm after her husband's death, employing live-in hired hands for assistance as needed. Later, as her sons grew up, they most likely carried on their father's work.

Along with a great many other rural families, she and her children moved from Wisconsin to southern Minnesota, in a covered wagon after the Sioux uprising resulted in the Indians native to the area being forcibly relocated in South Dakota. She is said to have purchased a farm near St. Clair, and there she lived with one or other of her children until her death in 1877.

The obituary of her daughter Catherine Murphy says that her mother purchased a farm near St. Clair in 1868 and moved there with her daughters and a son.

We will probably never know much more than this.

Catherine's middle name may have been Marie, Maria, or Mary.

Marriage Notes for **John Murphy** and **Catherine O'Connell**:

Many years ago, when I was not quite started in this family history project, my aunt Ivalue Casper Hilgers showed me an old wedding invitation announcing the marriage of John Henry Murphy and Catherine O'Connell. I distinctly recall seeing the O'Connell name and perhaps the date 1842. This invitation unfortunately appears to have been lost in the turmoil of her possessions after her untimely death, leaving whatever other facts it might have contained a matter of conjecture.

More About John Murphy and Catherine O'Connell:
Marriage: 06 Jun 1842, Probably Wisconsin[28]

Children of John Murphy and Catherine O'Connell are:
    i.       Mary A. Murphy, born 03 Jan 1844 in Cedarburg, Ozaukee County, Wisconsin[29]; died 19 Jun 1904 in St Clair, Minnesota; married Michael Neary Abt. 03 Sep 1865; born 20 Feb 1833 in Ireland; died 29 Apr 1930 in Mankato, Minnesota.

More About Michael Neary and Mary Murphy:
Marriage: Abt. 03 Sep 1865

ii.   Daniel S. Murphy, born 27 Jan 1846 in Milwaukee, Wisconsin[29]; died 08 Aug 1913 in Madison Lake, Minnesota[30]; married Sarah Ann Couillard aka. Sarah Kohler Jul 1871 in Wisconsin; born 18 May 1854 in Oconto County, Wisconsin; died 07 Sep 1899 in Blue Earth County, Minnesota[31].

More About Daniel Murphy and Sarah Kohler:
Marriage: Jul 1871, Wisconsin

iii.   John J. Murphy, born 06 Oct 1847 in Milwaukee, Wisconsin[32]; died 08 Aug 1918 in Mankato, Blue Earth County, Minnesota; married Mary A. Donahue; born 19 Jun 1852 in Woodstock, Illinois; died Oct 1934 in Spokane, Washington.

Notes for **John J. Murphy**:
Owned a hardware and general merchandise store in Mankato, Minnesota.

iv.   (7) Margaret J. Murphy, born 15 Oct 1849 in Milwaukee, Wisconsin; died 05 Oct 1931 in LeRay Township, Blue Earth County; married James K. Knapp 03 Jul 1868 in Cedarburg, Ozaukee County, Wisconsin.
v.   Catherine Murphy, born 06 Oct 1852 in Cedarburg, Wisconsin[33]; died 09 Apr 1929 in Mankato, Blue Earth County, Minnesota.

Notes for **Catherine Murphy**:
Some early Mankato newspaper notices:

14 September 1880 --*Miss Kate Murphy --vocal & instrumental music instruction*

27 September 1881 -- *Musical entertainment given at opera house.*

Owned a millinery and dress shop on Front Street in Madison Lake, Minnesota before 1920.

vi.   Ellen Murphy, born 08 Apr 1853 in Cedarburg, Ozaukee County, Wisconsin[34]; died Bef. 1857 in Cedarburg, Ozaukee County, Wisconsin.
vii.   Stephen A. Murphy[35], born 26 Dec 1854 in Wisconsin[36]; died 21 Jan 1895 in Minnesota[37]; married Margaret Jane O'Connor 25 Feb 1884 in Minnesota; born 22 Jun 1860 in Fond du Lac County, Wisconsin; died 27 Mar 1936 in Minnesota.

More About **Stephen Murphy** and **Margaret O'Connor**:
Marriage: 25 Feb 1884, Minnesota

viii.     Ellen "Nellie" Murphy, born 03 Mar 1857 in Cedarburg, Ozaukee County, Wisconsin[38]; died 15 Jan 1936 in possibly Palo Alto, California; married Patrick Murphy, Jr. 1888 in Minnesota; born Abt. Jan 1868 in Minnesota.

More About **Patrick Murphy** and **Ellen Murphy**:
Marriage: 1888, Minnesota

*Generation No. 5*

**16. Joseph Anton Kasper**[39], born 13 Apr 1777 in Grafenhausen, Baden, Germany; died 18 Feb 1850 in Grafenhausen, Baden, Germany. He was the son of **32. Johannes Kasper** and **33. Anna Maria Ursula Ehinger**. He married **17. Katharina Hoegi** 11 Oct 1802.
        **17. Katharina Hoegi,** born 28 Apr 1778; died 08 May 1810.

Notes for **Joseph Anton Kasper**:

*Ortsippenbuch Grafenhausen* describes Joseph Anton as a "burgermeister" (mayor) in 1836. Here, about a century after the first of our family arrived in Grafenhausen, we see what appears to be a significant rise in prosperity and stature.

Part of this might be explained by the preponderance of female offspring in earlier generations. Joseph's father and grandfather between them produced seven daughters and only three sons. Daughters married into other village families, and sometimes these "matches" brought additional stature. With fewer sons to inherit, wealth accumulated in one generation could be concentrated in the next. Added to this advantage, we may assume that these earliest generations of Grafenhausen family were ambitious and productive to a remarkable degree.

Joseph Anton appears to have been notably successful, so here is another candidate for the family lore about the wealthy mayor or judge who had "wheelbarrows full of money." At the same time, all this should be seen against the background of a nineteen century German village where to have a little money might be seen as having a lot, compared to most people.

We should also note that two of Joseph Anton's sons, Gabriel and Raphael, finding local prospects sufficiently bleak, became early emigrants to America. In the subsequent lives of both there is little indication of significant financial support from their father easing their way.

For further information and discussion, see THREE HUNDRED YEARS IN THE LIFE OF A FAMILY.

More About Joseph Kasper and Katharina Hoegi:
Marriage: 11 Oct 1802

Children of Joseph Kasper and Katharina Hoegi are:
  i.    (8) Johann Kasper, born 01 Apr 1804 in Grafenhausen, Baden, Germany; died 25 May 1861 in Grafenhausen, Baden, Germany; married Katharina Jaeger 23 Aug 1831 in Grafenhausen, Baden, Germany.
  ii.   Matthias Kasper, born 14 Feb 1806 in Grafenhausen.
  iii.  Gabriel Kasper (Casper), born 26 Mar 1808 in Grafenhausen; died in Probably in New Jersey; married Rosena; born Abt. 1806 in Baden, Germany.

Notes for **Gabriel Kasper (Casper)**:
Koebele indicates that Gabriel Kasper emigrated to America. He and his brother Raphael, uncles of Wendelin Kasper, were probably the first of our Grafenhausen Kasper family to emigrate to America.

The 1850 Federal Census for New Jersey lists Gabriel Casper's occupation as a tailor. In the 1870 Federal Census, he is still residing in New Jersey (Hackensack, Bergen County) and is occupation is given as a grocer.

  iv.   Raphael Kasper, born 08 May 1810 in Grafenhausen; died Aft. 1870 in Probably Mascoutah, St. Clair County, Illinois; married Marie; born Abt. 1811 in Hanover, Germany.

Notes for **Raphael Kasper**:

Koebele indicates that Raphael Kasper emigrated to America along with his brother Gabriel, both uncles of Wendelin Kasper and among the very first German immigrants from Grafenhausen. He shows up as Raph Kasper in 1870 Federal Census for Mascoutah, St. Clair County, Indiana. His occupation is a "turner."

Raphael's location in southern Illinois may be the source of the family report that Wendelin stopped off in "Indiana" on his way to Minnesota about 1869-70.

A search of Federal census records from 1860 forward to 1920 suggests that the sons of Raphael Kasper listed here remained single throughout their lives and died without children, the last of them Fritz in an "old soldiers'" home in Leavenworth, Kansas.

Raphael was probably buried in a pioneer cemetery on the outskirts of Mascoutah where most memorials have been lost, though the cemetery itself is identified by a roadside plaque.

**18. Franz Jaeger,** born in Ichenheim, Baden, Germany. He married **19. Maria Anna Wendle**.

**19. Maria Anna Wendle**

Children of Franz Jaeger and Maria Wendle are:
- i. (9) Katharina Jaeger, born 27 Apr 1808; died 22 Apr 1870 in Kappel, Baden, Germany; married (1) Xaver Kern 02 May 1825; married (2) Johann Kasper 23 Aug 1831 in Grafenhausen, Baden, Germany; married (3) Jakob Sutter 11 Aug 1862.
- ii. Karolina Jaeger, born 1797 in Ickenheim; died 1830 in Grafenhausen; married Jacob Koebele.
- iii. Maria Juditha Jaeger, born 1806 in Ickenheim; died 1852 in Grafenhausen; married Georg Anton Rees.

**20. Johann Friedrich Cords,** born 18 Jun 1780 in Ruest/Mestlin, Mecklenburg, Germany. He was the son of **40. Johann Joachim Diederich Cords** and **41. Anna Maria Ilsabe Dieckmann**. He married **21. Catherina Margaretha Sophia Hahn(en)** 20 Nov 1807 in Ruest/Mestlin, Mecklenburg, Germany.

**21. Catherina Margaretha Sophia Hahn(en),** born 11 Apr 1785 in Ruest/Mestlin, Mecklenburg, Germany. She was the daughter of **42. Johann Friedrich Christoph Herman Hahn** and **43. Anna Dorothea Ilsabe Cords**.

More About Johann Cords and Catherina Hahn(en):
Marriage: 20 Nov 1807, Ruest/Mestlin, Mecklenburg, Germany

Children of Johann Cords and Catherina Hahn(en) are:
- i. Maria Margaretha Dorothea Cords, born 03 Oct 1808.
- ii. Sophia Maria Dorothea Cords, born 25 Sep 1810.

iii.     (10) Johann Joachim Carl Friedrich Cords, born 11 Dec 1811 in Ruest, Mecklenburg, Germany; married Hannah Catharina Dorothea Sternberg 03 Aug 1838 in Mestlin, Mecklenburg, Germany.

iv.     Johann Carl Friedrich Cords, born 21 Aug 1818.

v.     Sophia Dorothea Maria Cords, born 07 Mar 1821.

vi.     Sophia Caroline Dorothia Cords, born 23 Dec 1822.

vii.     Johann Joachim Friedrich Cords, born 25 Sep 1828 in Ruest/Mestlin, Mecklenburg, Germany; died 06 Nov 1883 in St. Clair, Blue Earth County, Minnesota; married Sophia Ehlers; born Abt. 1838 in Mecklenburg, Germany; died in probably St. Clair, Minnesota.

**22. Johann Sternberg,** born in Ruest, Mecklenburg, Germany. He married **23. Sophia Eikelberg**.

    **23. Sophia Eikelberg**

Child of Johann Sternberg and Sophia Eikelberg is:

i.     (11) Hannah Catharina Dorothea Sternberg, born 04 Jul 1820 in Ruest, Mecklenburg, Germany; married Johann Joachim Carl Friedrich Cords 03 Aug 1838 in Mestlin, Mecklenburg, Germany.

    **24. Ebenezer Knapp[40],** born 24 Oct 1771 in Norfolk, Connecticut[41]; died 05 Nov 1833 in North Canaan, Connecticut. He was the son of **48. Samuel Knapp III** and **49. Mercy Bouton**. He married **25. Eunice Campbell**.

    **25. Eunice Campbell[42],** born Abt. 1776; died 18 Oct 1824. She was the daughter of **50. John Campbell** and **51. Mary**.

Notes for **Ebenezer Knapp**:

I am fairly certain of its accuracy from the generation of Ebenezer Knapp and Maturah Campbell forward. First, because it became the basis for a nearest next-of-kin estate settlement whose research was carried out by a competent court-appointed genealogist. Second, because of an important piece of anecdotal evidence gleaned from an interview with my cousin Sam Casper whose father was James K. Knapp's grandson and who had apparently heard him say that somehow, we Casper/Knapps had some Scottish blood in us. Well, as far as I can tell, that must have been a reference to James K. Knapp's grandmother Eunice Campbell, for searching all over in his vicinity I can't find another Scot among his immediate ancestors. This would seem to tie us to Ebenezer Knapp through James K. and his father Ambrose. Beyond that, when one gets to the string of Samuel Knapps between Ebenezer and Caleb, son of Nicholas, the possibility of error increases greatly in my view. There seem to have been many Samuel Knapps in various Knapp branches during this period of a hundred years or so.

My information on the wives and children of Ebenezer Knapp was provided by professional genealogist Francis M. Fransson of West Hartford, Connecticut and was part of her work as court-appointed genealogist determining next-of-kin in the Katherine Knapp Milburn estate matter previously mentioned.

In documents provided to the Court, Ms. Fransson does not provide specific birth dates for the Ebenezer Knapp children, but following genealogy convention, I assume, does list them in birth order from left to right across the page. I have kept this order here. Elsewhere I am less than sure that Ms. Fransson's order of listing indicates anything since the main interest of her research is in determining when Knapp family members died.

--------------------------------------------------------------------------------

Child: Benjamin Knapp Reference ID: 2
Gender: male
Birth Date: 15 Aug 1810
Parents: Ebenezer Knapp; Eunice Knapp
Comment: born in Norfolk, Conn.
Source: Quaker Births, Nine Partners Monthly Meeting, Dutchess County
Nine Partners Quaker Meeting: 1758-1876
Location: Town of Washington, Dutchess County --- Denomination: Quaker

--------------------------------------------------------------------------------

Child: Ambrose Knapp Reference ID: 17
Gender: male
Birth Date: 3 May 1813
Parents: Ebenezer Knapp; Eunice Knapp

Comment: born in Norfolk, Conn.
Source: Quaker Births, Nine Partners Monthly Meeting, Dutchess County
Nine Partners Quaker Meeting: 1758-1876
Location: Town of Washington, Dutchess County --- Denomination: Quaker

---------------------------------------------------------------------------------

Child: Jane Knapp Reference ID: 108
Gender: female
Birth Date: 7 Dec 1826
Parents: Ebenezer Knapp; Dafiny Knapp
Source: Quaker Births, Nine Partners Monthly Meeting, Dutchess County
Nine Partners Quaker Meeting: 1758-1876
Location: Town of Washington, Dutchess County --- Denomination: Quaker

Notes for Eunice Campbell:
Name: Ebenezer Knapp
Spouse's Name: Eunice
Child Name: John; Benjamin; Ambrose
Child's Birth Date: -; 15 Aug 1810; 03 May 1813
Child's Death Date: -; 01 Dec 1810; -
Family's Comments: Cert fr Galway 11-20-1805, rem to Norfolk, Conn

Children of Ebenezer Knapp and Eunice Campbell are:
    i.      John Knapp, born Bef. 1810.
    ii.     Benjamin Knapp, born 15 Aug 1810[43]; died 01 Dec 1810.
    iii.    Paulina Knapp, born Aft. 1812; married Jesse Knapp.
    iv.    **(12)** Ambrose Knapp, born 03 May 1813 in Connecticut; died 23 Jan 1894 in Madison Lake, Minnesota; married (1) Jane Ann Moxley 20 Jul 1841 in Litchfield, Connecticut; married (2) Hannah Rappleye 05 Mar 1886 in Rochester (?) Minnesota.
    v.     Nicholas Knapp, born Aft. 1814.
    vi.    Eunice Knapp, born Aft. 1817.

**26. Richard Moxley,** born in England; died Aft. 1838 in Ballyroe (near Rosscarbery), Ireland. He married **27. Unknown.**

    **27. Unknown,** born in England.

Notes for **Richard Moxley**:

We would not know Richard Moxley's name but for his letter to his daughter Jane, long preserved in family records, most recently by Ivalue Casper Hilgers. His letter is a reply to one she had written, and it contains both news of marriages, children, etc. since her departure, and a plea for money. Her County Cork family appears to be desperately poor, without even money to pay a dowry enabling one of Jane's sisters to live with her husband.

Richard himself seems to be in poor health, and we can safely assume this is the last his daughter heard from him. Perhaps for this reason, the letter was kept and handed down in the Knapp family where it has become the lone detailed record of our Moxley family in County Cork at the time of Jane's emigration to America. The names and dates included here are all based upon this letter.

The 1880 Federal Census reports that Jane Moxley Knapp's parents were both born in England and were, in fact, English rather than Irish. To this day, the Moxley name can be found in England, especially in the Southwest and in London. Perhaps church birth records for both Richard and Jane's mother could be found, but without more to go on, anything definitive seems unlikely.

There is nothing unusual about an English family emigrating to Ireland in search of work at a time when much of Ireland was controlled by British landlords, one of whom must have been Mr. Abraham Morris whose recent death is reported in Richard's letter. In fact, English families would sometimes move back and forth, between the two countries from one generation to the next, depending on where work was to be found.

It is possible that some of Jane's siblings eventually emigrated to America. Others may have died in the famine a decade later. The Moxley names Stephen and Richard can be found in various records from southeastern Ontario and the northeastern United States. In both areas the Moxley name still occurs. This is also true of the County Cork area where Jane was born. Some of these Moxleys, including those yet living in Cork, are probably distant cousins.

One of these is Clair Wills whose mother grew up in County Cork. Clair is writer and teacher at Queen Mary - London University.

What follows is a transcription of Richard Moxley's letter, parts of which are illegible:

*Ballyroe, Febry. 12th 1838*

*My Dear Daughter*

*I have your letter and was happy to hear of your safe arrival in America. and to know that you were doing well. As you were so good as to make inquiry about your youngest sister Ellen, I have to inform you that she married Michael Connor, son to _____ Connor the _________; and your brothers Stephen and Richard and I promised ________________________________ not able to give them anything afterwards, and as a consequence of which he would not live with her, therefore she was under the necessity of going in service, and as you well know it is not easy to get service here. She is often out of place and then she lives with me. If you could possibly send her some money her husband and she might do well as he is a good tradesman and would gladly live with her if we could give her anything. Your brothers and I return many thanks for you for your kind offer, and if they had the means, there is nothing would give them more pleasure than to go to you as any change would better than as they are. Stephen is married to Ellen _______ and has two children, daughters. I am sorry to inform you that mr. Abraham Morris of Ballyroe died on the 1st of Oct. 183_ and Mr. _________ Morris is residing where he lived since March 1833. I have a house from him and as I am now nearly beyond my labour I shall leave the wants of an aged parent rest with yourself to consider of. I am happy to tell you that your sisters Mary and Elizabeth are well and each of them living where they were when you left home. Let me know in your next letter how your Uncle Robert Noles acted toward you and how his family are getting on. I remain as always your affect. Father*

*Richard Moxley*

Aspects of this letter suggest it was *dictated* and is not in Richard's own hand, for instance the peculiarity of Richard using Jane's uncle's full name and his own full name at the end. For this we can be grateful, because otherwise we would know neither.

The letters reference to Jane's safe arrival in America suggests that she had only recently left Ireland. However, this doesn't seem to be the case, as the letter itself makes clear from the news it brings after what must have been a lapse of years. A possibility is that Jane's letter brought news of her moving from southeastern Ontario where she seems to have lived at first to Connecticut where she subsequently married Ambrose Knapp in the village of Litchfield.

Richard Moxley and Jane's mother are likely buried in a rural Ballyroe cemetery near her place of birth, a picture of which is included in this record.

*Ballyroe, County Cork graveyard where Richard Moxley and his wife are probably buried.*

Children of Richard Moxley and Unknown are:
    i.       Stephen Moxley, born Abt. 1812.
    ii.     Richard Moxley[44], born Abt. 1813.

## Notes for **Richard Moxley**:

I have in my Moxley file an internet report of a Richard Moxley posted by Allen Craig. This Richard was born in Ireland about 1815, married an Elizabeth Templeton in 1835, emigrated to

Gloucester Township, near Ottawa, Ontario, and had a son named Richard born in 1847. There is an outside chance this could be our Richard, son of Richard. I base this on two circumstances: his year of birth in Ireland and his emigration to a part of Canada where Jane Moxley is reported to have first settled.

Another possible Richard is listed in the Irish Records Extraction data base as having married Honora Forrest in County Cork 1939.

County Cork church records should be researched.

iii.      Elizabeth Moxley, born Bef. 1814.
iv.      Mary Moxley, born Bef. 1814.
v.      **(13)** Jane Ann Moxley, born 26 Dec 1814 in near Rosscarbery, County Cork, Ireland; died 21 Jul 1883 in Mankato, Minnesota; married Ambrose Knapp 20 Jul 1841 in Litchfield, Connecticut.
vi.      Ellen Moxley, born Abt. 1820.

       **28. Unknown Murphy**[45], born in Ireland. He married **29. Katherine** Abt. 1812 in Ireland.
       **29. Katherine**[45], born in Ireland.

Notes for **Unknown Murphy**:
Note on sources:

With the exception of John Henry's Murphy's descendants through Margaret Murphy Knapp, which I have been able to research on my own using family records, Murphy information from this point on is mainly the research work of Kathleen M. Curry (descendant from Daniel Murphy and Joanna Crowley) and Jayne Joyce Staley (descendant of John Henry Murphy and Catherine O'Connell through their son Stephen A, Murphy). I acknowledge with thanks their willingness to share the result of their extensive work.

The evidence pointing to this as the family of our John H. Murphy may be largely circumstantial via Kathleen Curry, based upon immigration records, proximity of farms in Wisconsin, I gather, family anecdote, and perhaps other things I am unaware of. I myself know of no official document definitely acknowledging these relationships. In the absence of such documentation, this list of John H. Murphy's siblings must be regarded as tentative, albeit probably correct.

At the same time, Kathleen Curry has compiled a careful and impressive record of painstaking research, and on that account alone much that follows here should be regarded as highly credible.

More About Unknown Murphy and Katherine:
Marriage: Abt. 1812, Ireland

Children of Unknown Murphy and Katherine are:
 i.  Dennis Murphy?[46], born Bet. 1810 - 1815 in Ireland; married Unknown Nancy Abt. 1838; born Abt. 1812 in Ireland.

Notes for Dennis Murphy?:
Kathleen Curry, the Murphy family historian, regards it as highly probable that this Dennis Murphy was an older brother of our John Henry Murphy, but at this point the question mark must remain.

More About Dennis Murphy? and Unknown Nancy:
Marriage: Abt. 1838

 ii.  Mary Murphy, born Abt. 1815 in Ireland; died Bef. Jun 1901; married Patrick O'Neal 28 Sep 1837 in Charlestown, Suffolk County, Massachusetts; born Abt. 1810 in Ireland; died Abt. 1857 in Wisconsin?.

More About Patrick O'Neal and Mary Murphy:
Marriage: 28 Sep 1837, Charlestown, Suffolk County, Massachusetts

 iii.  (14) John Henry Murphy, born 1819 in Ireland (possibly County Cork); died 16 Apr 1859 in Cedarburg, Wisconsin; married Catherine O'Connell 06 Jun 1842 in Probably Wisconsin.
 iv.  Daniel Murphy, born 06 Apr 1823 in Ireland[47]; died 20 Feb 1900 in Twin Deer Creek, Outagamie, Wisconsin[47]; married Johanna Crowley Abt. 1856 in St. Malachy, Beaver Dam, Dodge County, Wisconsin[47]; born Abt. 1836 in Ireland[47]; died 01 Nov 1877 in Bear Creek, Outagamie, Wisconsin[47].

More About **Daniel Murphy** and **Johanna Crowley**:
Marriage: Abt. 1856, St. Malachy, Beaver Dam, Dodge County, Wisconsin[47]

|      |                                              |
|------|----------------------------------------------|
| v.   | Patrick Murphy, born Aft. 1828 in Ireland.   |
| vi.  | Julia Murphy, born 25 Mar 1832 in Ireland.   |

**30. Jeremiah (Geoffry) O'Connell,** born Abt. 1780; died Bef. 1840 in Ireland. He was the son of **60. Richard O'Connell**. He married **31. Catherine Burke or Booke ? (a widow)**.

**31. Catherine Burke or Booke ? (a widow),** born in Ireland.

Notes for **Jeremiah (Geoffry) O'Connell ***:

Sometimes known as Geoffry or Geoffrey though these names are not interchangeable with Jeremiah, possibly accounting for confusion in what follows:

According to the O'Connell Family History (Curran J. DeBruler & June Joyce Larson), he was a surgeon attached to the 43 Foot Regiment spending 21 years in India. While on duty there he appears to have been married to a woman from Holland of Dutch background who apparently died in India. (My speculation) If they had children, it is possible that they either returned to Ireland with their father, or that they went to Holland where presumably their mother's family lived, or they may have remained in India where to this day O'Connells can be found. Thus, there may be O'Connell cousins in the Netherlands today who are thoroughly Dutch, or there may be O'Connell cousins in Ireland who have some Dutch ancestry, or there may be O'Connell cousins in India. In any event, much of the above may be traceable through British military records or records of the East India Trading Company, which should be available in London. Another possibility is that Jeremiah was never married to a Dutch woman. See my notes for Richard O'Connell.

Jeremiah married an Irish woman, a widow named Catherine, whose surname was probably Burke sometime after his return to Ireland. From that marriage a daughter Catherine (our Catherine) and possibly a son Jeremiah were born. Or it is possible that Catherine had a Dutch half-brother named Jeremiah. The two of them may have come to America together via Liverpool about 1840. That would have been when Catherine was only 14, so I speculate that by that time one or both of her parents may have died.

21 November 1998

Further research calls into question much of the above. It is possible that family lore sometimes confuses Jeremiah with his father Richard, and that military service in India in fact took place in the West Indies. I have found no firm record of Catherine having a brother Jeremiah, and if we can trust the ship's immigration lists located by Kathleen Curry in the course of her research, no one of the O'Connell name accompanied Catherine on the voyage to Halifax, Nova Scotia in 1840.

A much more extensive review of all this can be found in my notes for Richard and Catherine O'Connell.

03 March 2009

Notes for Catherine Burke or Booke ? (a widow):
If Burke, raises the possibility of kinship with descendants of the Irish philosopher Edmund Burke. The Burke and O'Connell names frequently cross paths in County Cork.

Child of Jeremiah O'Connell and Catherine widow) is:
1.   (15) Catherine O'Connell, born 1823 in County Cork, Ireland; died 13 Apr 1877 in St. Clair, Blue Earth County, Minnesota; married John Henry Murphy 06 Jun 1842 in Probably Wisconsin.

Child of Jeremiah O'Connell and Unknown woman is:

*Generation No. 6*

**32. Johannes Kasper**[48], born 11 Dec 1725 in Grafenhausen, Baden, Germany; died 30 Apr 1786 in Grafenhausen, Baden, Germany. He was the son of **64. Michael Kasper** and **65. Anna Maria Nopper**. He married **33. Anna Maria Ursula Ehinger** 14 Nov 1768 in 14 November 1768.

**33. Anna Maria Ursula Ehinger,** born 30 Jan 1743/44 in Grafenhausen, Baden, Germany; died 18 Mar 1814 in Grafenhausen, Baden, Germany.

Notes for **Johannes Kasper**:
ORTSIPPENBUCH GRAFENHAUSEN also describes him as a shoemaker/cobbler, no doubt having learned the trade from his father and inheriting his business.

More About **Johannes Kasper** and **Anna Ehinger**:
Marriage: 14 Nov 1768, 14 November 1768

Children of Johannes Kasper and Anna Ehinger are:
 i.  Katharina Kasper, born 1770 in Grafenhausen; died 1818 in Grafenhausen.
 ii.  Lorenz Michael Kasper, born 1773 in Grafenhausen, Baden, Germany; died 1852 in Grafenhausen, Baden, Germany.

Notes for Lorenz Michael Kasper:
This Kasper line needs to be seriously researched for descendants.

 iii.  (16) Joseph Anton Kasper, born 13 Apr 1777 in Grafenhausen, Baden, Germany; died 18 Feb 1850 in Grafenhausen, Baden, Germany; married (1) Katharina Daibach; married (2) Katharina Hoegi 11 Oct 1802; married (3) Appollonia Koebele 21 Oct 1811.
 iv.  Maria Anna Kasper, born 04 Sep 1780 in Grafenhausen; died 1780 in Grafenhausen.


**40. Johann Joachim Diederich Cords** He married **41. Anna Maria Ilsabe Dieckmann** 26 Nov 1773 in Mestlin, Mecklenburg, Germany.

 **41. Anna Maria Ilsabe Dieckmann** She was the daughter of **82. Hans Dieckmann**.

More About **Johann Cords** and **Anna Dieckmann**:
Marriage: 26 Nov 1773, Mestlin, Mecklenburg, Germany

Child of Johann Cords and Anna Dieckmann is:
 i.  (20) Johann Friedrich Cords, born 18 Jun 1780 in Ruest/Mestlin, Mecklenburg, Germany; married Catherina Margaretha Sophia Hahn(en) 20 Nov 1807 in Ruest/Mestlin, Mecklenburg, Germany.


 **42. Johann Friedrich Christoph Herman Hahn,** born 01 Jan 1760 in Klein Updahl/Lohmen, Mecklenburg, Germany. He was the son of **84. Heinrich Daniel Hahn** and

**85. Ilse Passow**. He married **43. Anna Dorothea Ilsabe Cords** 13 Nov 1783 in Mestlin, Mecklenburg, Germany.

> **43. Anna Dorothea Ilsabe Cords**

More About **Johann Hahn** and **Anna Cords**:
Marriage: 13 Nov 1783, Mestlin, Mecklenburg, Germany

Child of Johann Hahn and Anna Cords is:

    i.      (21) Catherina Margaretha Sophia Hahn(en), born 11 Apr 1785 in Ruest/Mestlin, Mecklenburg, Germany; married Johann Friedrich Cords 20 Nov 1807 in Ruest/Mestlin, Mecklenburg, Germany.

**48. Samuel Knapp III,** born 1726 in Danbury, Connecticut; died 12 Mar 1816 in Norfolk, Connecticut[49]. He was the son of **96. Samuel Knapp II** and **97. Sarah Hoyt**. He married **49. Mercy Bouton** Abt. 15 Mar 1747/48 in Stamford, Connecticut.

**49. Mercy Bouton,** born Abt. 1730 in Danbury, Connecticut; died Abt. 1828 in Stamford, Connecticut. She was the daughter of **98. Samuel Bouton** and **99. Abigail (unknown last name) Bouton**.

Notes for Samuel Knapp III:
Another source lists Samuel's death date as 16 November 1816.

More About **Samuel Knapp** and **Mercy Bouton**:
Marriage: Abt. 15 Mar 1747/48, Stamford, Connecticut

Children of Samuel Knapp and Mercy Bouton are:

    i.      Samuel Knapp IV, born Abt. 1768 in Norfolk, Litchfield County, Connecticut; died 1841 in Litchfield County, Connecticut[50]; married Lois Lake 20 Feb 1799 in Washington, Litchfield County, Connecticut[51]; born 01 Jul 1770 in Washington, Litchfield County, Connecticut.

More About Samuel Knapp and Lois Lake:
Marriage: 20 Feb 1799, Washington, Litchfield County, Connecticut[51]

    ii.     (24) Ebenezer Knapp, born 24 Oct 1771 in Norfolk, Connecticut; died 05 Nov 1833 in North Canaan, Connecticut; married (1) Maturah Campbell; married (2) Eunice

Campbell; married (3) Daphne Stevens 23 Nov 1825 in Canaan, Litchfield County, Connecticut.


**50. John Campbell** He was the son of **100. Charles Campbell** and **101. Mary Stuart**. He married **51. Mary**.

    **51. Mary**

Children of John Campbell and Mary are:

    i.      Maturah Campbell[52], born 1774 in New Marlborough, Massachusetts[5354]; married Ebenezer Knapp; born 24 Oct 1771 in Norfolk, Connecticut[55]; died 05 Nov 1833 in North Canaan, Connecticut.


Notes for **Maturah and Eunice Campbell**:

Family History Diary Entry 28 November 1997

Today I visited with my cousin Sam Casper. In the course of exchanging family history stories, he mentioned that his father (Dayton Casper) once told him that J. K. Knapp said his family had Scottish origins. This, I think, is interesting corroboration of Maturah and Eunice Campbell as being wives of Ebenezer, Eunice being the mother of Ambrose. I know of no other possible Scottish connection in this family.

As for Maturah Campbell and her sister Eunice, Ebenezer's first wife, so far, I have been unable to locate them in any census or Campbell family tree. Mrs. Frannson, the genealogist cited elsewhere here, also appears to have come up empty-handed where they are concerned. One possibility I have not pursued is that they came from Canada and somehow account for how Ebenzer's son Ambrose and Jane Moxley met.

Further notes for **Ebenezer Knapp**:

The Nicholas Knapp Genealogy is an excellent example of what can go most wrong in genealogical research, especially in the present era when information can be electronically published without proper source citation and editorial critique, and then is picked up and used by others who regard it as true, so that questionable research findings and errors are multiplied many times over and further disseminated until the whole topic becomes a tangle of facts, assumptions, errors, and rumors repeated like gossip and regarded as true. Genealogists are especially vulnerable to all this because most of them are untrained in proper research technique, and their eagerness to succeed in their endeavors to uncover information from ever more remote times and ever more distant family branches leads them to embrace enthusiastically many things that they ought to regard with caution, if not outright suspicion.

In the case of Nicholas Knapp, both his ancestors and his descendants, one would need to be especially vigilant because the Knapp family is an enormous one here in the United States, and many uncritical hands have delved into its history, while many other hands have received the results as if they came from a family bible, and even family bibles contain errors. It strikes me as especially messy with respect to his English ancestors and his descendants from the second or third generation forward when the family has become so prolific and certain naming so common that within the same generation, often in the same general geographical area, we will find several Knapps with the same given first name. And so entire family branches can be mistakenly attached to others of the same name.

I cannot positively say that such errors exist in what I have recorded here, but there is some probability that they do. Therefore, anyone reviewing the Knapp branch of our family tree needs to do so with a questioning attitude, and perhaps even undertake to do the necessary research to either support what is here or correct its errors as they are discovered. Not an easy thing to do, or I would have already done it!

I am fairly certain of its accuracy from the generation of Ebenezer Knapp forward. First, because it became the basis for a nearest next-of-kin estate settlement whose research was carried out by a competent court-appointed genealogist. Second, because of an important piece of anecdotal evidence gleaned from an interview with my cousin Sam Casper whose father was James K. Knapp's grandson and who had apparently heard him say that somehow, we Casper/Knapps had some Scottish blood in us. Well, as far as I can tell, that must have been a reference to James K. Knapp's grandmother Eunice Campbell, for searching all over in his vicinity I can't find another Scot among his immediate ancestors. This would seem to tie us to Ebenezer Knapp through James K. and his father Ambrose. Beyond that, when one gets to the string of Samuel Knapps between Ebenezer and Caleb, son of Nicholas, the possibility of error increases greatly in my view. There seem to have been many Samuel Knapps in various Knapp branches during this period of a hundred years or so.

My information on the wives and children of Ebenezer Knapp was provided by professional genealogist Francis M. Fransson of West Hartford, Connecticut and was part of her work as court-appointed genealogist determining next-of-kin in the Katherine Knapp Milburn estate matter previously mentioned.

In documents provided to the Court, Ms. Fransson does not provide specific birth dates for the Ebenezer Knapp children, but following genealogy convention, I assume, does list them in birth order from left to right across the page. I have kept this order here. Elsewhere I am less than sure that Ms. Fransson's order of listing indicates anything since the main interest of her research is in determining when Knapp family members died.

Child: Benjamin Knapp Reference ID: 2
Gender: male
Birth Date: 15 Aug 1810
Parents: Ebenezer Knapp; Eunice Knapp
Comment: born in Norfolk, Conn.
Source: Quaker Births, Nine Partners Monthly Meeting, Dutchess County
Nine Partners Quaker Meeting: 1758-1876
Location: Town of Washington, Dutchess County --- Denomination: Quaker

Child: Ambros Knapp* Reference ID: 17
Gender: male
Birth Date: 3 May 1813
Parents: Ebenezer Knapp; Eunice Knapp
Comment: born in Norfolk, Conn.
Source: Quaker Births, Nine Partners Monthly Meeting, Dutchess County
Nine Partners Quaker Meeting: 1758-1876
Location: Town of Washington, Dutchess County --- Denomination: Quaker

*Our Ambrose Knapp, father of James K. Knapp

Child: Jane Knapp Reference ID: 108
Gender: female
Birth Date: 7 Dec 1826
Parents: Ebenezer Knapp; Dafiny Knapp
Source: Quaker Births, Nine Partners Monthly Meeting, Dutchess County
Nine Partners Quaker Meeting: 1758-1876
Location: Town of Washington, Dutchess County --- Denomination: Quaker

ii.        (25) Eunice Campbell, born Abt. 1776; died 18 Oct 1824; married Ebenezer Knapp.


**Richard O'Connell** He was the son of **120. Maurice O'Connell** *

Notes for **Richard O'Connell**:

A Richard O'Connell is identified as the father of Jeremiah in the DeBruler-Larson family history. Since it is likely Catherine O'Connell would have known the name of her grandfather, and she in turn might have passed his name on to her children who were living at the time of this history's publication, I think there is every reason to trust its accuracy. Our next problem is to pinpoint a Richard O'Connell among possible candidates.

The DeBruler-Larson family history identifies Richard O'Connell who was "Captain of the Maillebois Legion in the service of Holland" and a cousin twice removed from a Daniel O'Connell who was the cousin of Daniel O'Connell, the Liberator. This particular Richard hardly seems possible since according to Burke's HISTORY OF THE COMMONERS OF GREAT BRITAIN AND IRELAND (p. 567) he was the grandson of one Maurice O'Connell who died in 1715. We don't know Maurice's age at death, but grandparents are usually at least forty, and this would mean he was born no later than 1675. Since grandchildren are usually 40 to 70 years younger than their grandparents, this Richard at the youngest would have been born in 1745 at the very latest, making him almost 80 when Catherine O'Connell, his granddaughter was born. Possible, but a stretch, I think.

One attraction of this Richard is that he does allow our O'Connell family to trace its relationship to Daniel, the Liberator, and this relationship at least in general terms is also something Catherine O'Connell probably asserted among her children. The minute we look closely at all this, however, we see problems with dates and possible name confusion, there being among the O'Connells a plethora of men of the same given name. Daniel O'Connell, the Liberator, was so popular among Catholic Irish of this period that virtually anyone of that surname would have wanted to claim a relationship with him.

Another Richard O'Connell has recently come to light in an internet biography of Napoleon era soldiers. His brief biography included under the general title NOT ONE IN TEN THOUSAND KNOW YOUR NAME offers several details that parallel the life of Jeremiah O'Connell in the account from DeBruler and Larson. He was for a time in the 43rd. Regiment of Foot and a military surgeon throughout a career of perhaps the approximate number of years attributed to Jeremiah. Though he was never stationed in India, as DeBruler and Larson would have it, he was probably with the 43rd. in the West Indies in 1794-95 when many of that regiment were lost to Yellow Fever. It appears that the Regiments of Foot to which Jeremiah was said to belong, the 41st and 43rd, were never stationed in India during this era, inviting the conclusion that the Indies became confused with India as the story was handed down.

Putting all this together, a fairly good case can be made for this Richard O'Connell as our direct ancestor. If so, the stories of Richard and Jeremiah got confused and garbled as they were handed down over family generations. This often happens in family lore owing to ambiguities in the picture when people speak of father and grandfather without clearly stating what generation they have in mind. For a fuller account of this and related matters, see my notes for Catherine O'Connell.

For want of a better candidate and in view of a number of parallels between the life of this Richard O'Connell and Jeremiah of the DeBruler-Larson account, I am tentatively identifying him as the father of Jeremiah, and explaining the discrepancy as father-son, father-grandfather confusion.

Richard's internet biographical sketch identifies his wife as Elizabeth Brice, daughter of Edward Brice using Burke's A GENEALOGICAL AND HERALDIC HISTORY OF LANDED GENTRY (p. 152) as its source. This also opens up some fascinating possibilities. The Brice family, formerly Bruce, seems to have been quite prominent in County Antrim, Northern Ireland and would have been almost certainly Protestant Presbyterian inasmuch as the name is Scottish. Northern Ireland Protestants to this day identify themselves as "Orange" because of a connection with the reign of William, the Duke of Orange, a Protestant British monarch who defended their interests against English/Irish Catholics. William was from the Netherlands, hence Dutch. Thus we are provided another possible explanation for the DeBruler-Larson report that Richard/Jeremiah married a "Dutch" woman, which in this case could have meant a Northern Ireland Protestant. At the same time, it's certainly possible that he or his son Jeremiah really did marry a woman from the Netherlands We're unlikely ever to know for certain. This, along with a great many other things in the O'Connell family story.

It also happens, again according to Burke (p. 152) that Elizabeth Brice had a Brice uncle who "died shortly after his return from the West Indies." This uncle, possibly an officer, may have been in one of the Regiments of Foot withdrawn from the West Indies in 1795-96. We can then speculate, without stretching the matter beyond belief, that Richard O'Connell may have met him there in his surgeon's role. (His biographical sketch as noted above only summarizes his career from 1803 onwards, but this doesn't preclude its beginning earlier since the narrative only concerns itself with his service in the Napoleonic period.) If these two men were stationed in the West Indies at the same time, perhaps they met in the course of Richard providing treatment for whatever wound or disease ultimately killed Elizabeth's uncle. Upon returning to Ireland, Richard visited the latter in County Antrim, and so he and his future wife met. Further research might be possible where all this is concerned.

One source of O'Connell Family genealogical information are the O'Connell tracts of one Basil O'Connell. I have perused various of these which were published by Browne & Nolan, presently at Botanic Road #9 in Dublin: tracts 2 & 3 may be found in the National Library of Ireland, while another tract is the Library of the London Society of Genealogists. None of these shed light on the family lore of a connection between our O'Connells and Daniel, the Liberator, and the whole O'Connell clan of County Kerry. We certainly are not direct descendants of Daniel, but we may well be connected via a cousin in the O'Connell branch. The immediate O'Connell ancestry of our family appears to originate in West County Cork and then perhaps earlier in Kerry. Irish genealogical research is difficult at best because of the loss of so many records, then more difficult with common surnames like O'Connell and Murphy having a plethora of Catherines, Kates, Maurices, Daniels, Richards, Johns, and even Jeremiahs, and then finally most of Basil O'Connell's records—30 years' worth—appear to have been lost in Singapore in 1948 where he was stationed in the military when Chinese Communists overran the place.

It must be said that family historians are always over eager to embrace connections with famous people whose surnames they share, and as mentioned above you will hardly find an O'Connell who doesn't think he is somehow Daniel, the Liberator's direct descendant. My aunt Ivalue thought we were related both to him and to the actress and singer Helen O'Connell, something I have never come close to establishing, and of course elsewhere in these pages you can find out about our family's alleged connection with the famous Revolutionary War hero Ethan Allen. There's hardly an Allen who isn't so connected! Nevertheless, sometimes all our vanity concerning such things to the contrary notwithstanding—as in the case of actor Robert Taylor— these family folk lore tales turn out to be true.

Still the details that have come down to us concerning Captain Jeremiah O'Connell (son of the above Richard), for example his service on the Beara Peninsula and his second marriage, etc. are so precise that one would have to regard them as having an historical basis. We just don't know whether these things apply to Richard or to Jeremiah. If to Jeremiah, then it's possible that Elizabeth Brice was his mother. Otherwise, Elizabeth may have been the first wife who died, and no relationship to our O'Connell branch whatsoever.

**The DeBruler-Larson family history from the point of Richard's father, grandfather, etc. is so problematic I have chosen to include it here only for whatever value it may have as a starting point for further research.** Richard's father was identified as a Maurice O'Connell. This may have been the case, but the wrong Maurice, since dates and relationships don't work out to form a plausible genealogy. Maurice was said to have had a brother John, both brothers the sons of a Daniel O'Connell, a cousin of Daniel, the Liberator's grandfather. Nothing I have discovered in my research creates a convincing pathway from all this to Jeremiah and his daughter Catherine O'Connell, our direct ancestors in this family branch. This isn't to say that a connection of some sort doesn't exist. So far though it has eluded all but those researchers most interested in making it happen by stretching the account to a point of breaking.

Child of Richard O'Connell is:

    i.      **(30)** Jeremiah (Geoffry) O'Connell, born Abt. 1780; died Bef. 1840 in Ireland; married (1) Catherine Burke or Booke ? (a widow); married (2) Unknown Dutch woman.

*Generation No. 7*

**64. Michael Kasper**[56], born in Prechtal, Baden-Wurtemburg, Germany; died 04 Nov 1761 in Grafenhausen, Baden, Germany. He married **65. Anna Maria Nopper** 27 Sep 1723.
    **65. Anna Maria Nopper,** died 28 Sep 1767 in Grafenhausen, Baden, Germany.

Notes for **Michael Kasper**:

Ortsippenbuch Grafenhausen describes him as a "Schuster, aus Prechtal" (a shoemaker from Prechtal). A shoemaker or cobbler would have also made and repaired belts, harnesses, and other necessary leather products. We can assume that he settled there in response to an opportunity created when another shoemaker died or moved away. German villages of this period were remarkably self-sufficient with produce from adjacent farms providing raw materials for resident craftsmen whose goods and services met the everyday needs of villagers. In this environment, losing a baker, a blacksmith, a tailor, or a cobbler, etc. could be a crisis, requiring strenuous efforts to find a replacement.

Here begins almost three centuries of Kasper presence in Grafenhausen, a fuller account of which can be found in my family history monograph *Three Hundred Years in the Life of a Family*

More About Michael Kasper and Anna Nopper:
Marriage: 27 Sep 1723

Children of Michael Kasper and Anna Nopper are:
    i.      (**32**) Johannes Kasper, born 11 Dec 1725 in Grafenhausen, Baden, Germany; died 30 Apr 1786 in Grafenhausen, Baden, Germany; married Anna Maria Ursula Ehinger 14 Nov 1768 in 14 November 1768.
    ii.     Anna Maria Kasper, born 15 Aug 1727 in Grafenhausen.
    iii.    Maria Barbara Kasper, born 1729 in Grafenhausen; died 1780 in Grafenhausen.
    iv.    Maria Anna Kasper, born 27 Jun 1734 in Grafenhausen.
    v.     Maria Eva Kasper, born 1735 in Grafenhausen; died 1765 in Grafenhausen.
    vi.    Justina Kasper, born 1739 in Grafenhausen, Baden, Germany.

**82. Hans Dieckmann,** died 1773.

Child of Hans Dieckmann is:
    i.      (**41**) Anna Maria Ilsabe Dieckmann, married Johann Joachim Diederich Cords 26 Nov 1773 in Mestlin, Mecklenburg, Germany.

**84. Heinrich Daniel Hahn,** born Abt. 1725. He married **85. Ilse Passow** 06 Jan 1753 in Lohmen, Mecklenburg.
    **85. Ilse Passow,** born Abt. 1730. She was the daughter of **170. Michael Passow**.

More About Heinrich Hahn and Ilse Passow:
Marriage: 06 Jan 1753, Lohmen, Mecklenburg

Child of Heinrich Hahn and Ilse Passow is:

    i.       (42) Johann Friedrich Christoph Herman Hahn, born 01 Jan 1760 in Klein Up-dahl/Lohmen, Mecklenburg, Germany; married Anna Dorothea Ilsabe Cords 13 Nov 1783 in Mestlin, Mecklenburg, Germany.

**96. Samuel Knapp II,** born Abt. 1698 in Danbury, Connecticut[57]; died Abt. 1740 in Danbury, Connecticut. He was the son of **192. Samuel Knapp** and **193. Hannah Bushnell.** He married **97. Sarah Hoyt.**

    **97. Sarah Hoyt**[57]. She was the daughter of **194. John Hoyt.**

Child of Samuel Knapp and Sarah Hoyt is:

    i.       (48) Samuel Knapp III, born 1726 in Danbury, Connecticut; died 12 Mar 1816 in Norfolk, Connecticut; married (1) Phoebe Lockwood Bef. 1747; married (2) Mercy Bouton Abt. 15 Mar 1747/48 in Stamford, Connecticut.

**98. Samuel Bouton** He married **99. Abigail (unknown last name) Bouton.**

    **99. Abigail (unknown last name) Bouton**

Child of Samuel Bouton and Abigail Bouton is:

    i.       (49) Mercy Bouton, born Abt. 1730 in Danbury, Connecticut; died Abt. 1828 in Stamford, Connecticut; married Samuel Knapp III Abt. 15 Mar 1747/48 in Stamford, Connecticut.

**100. Charles Campbell**[58], born Abt. 1696 in County Tyrone, Ulster, Ireland[58]; died May 1770. He was the son of **200. Robert Campbell** and **201. Janet Stuart.** He married **101. Mary Stuart.**

    **101. Mary Stuart**

Child of Charles Campbell and Mary Stuart is:

    i.       (50) John Campbell, married Mary.

**120. Maurice O'Connell,** died 1715. He was the son of **240. Daniel O'Connell** and **241. Alice Seagrave.**

Notes for **Maurice O'Connell**:
Brother of John O'Connell.

According to some handwritten notes—possibly taken from a genealogical work identified *as O'Hart's Irish Peerages*—passed down through the family, and a photocopy of which is in my possession—Maurice O'Connell was the first in the family to undergo persecution by the English for his religious views. He sent his son Richard to Europe to be educated there, and he secured for him a Captain's commission in the Mallebois Legion in Holland.

This same Maurice O'Connell, younger brother of John, would have been the uncle of Daniel, the Irish Liberator. O'Connell papers taken off internet and, in my file, speak of a much-celebrated Maurice O'Connell (1727-1825) known as "Hunting Cap" who was the "uncle" of Daniel O'Connell. This Maurice seems almost too old to be Daniel's uncle, so perhaps he was a grand-uncle and hence a brother of our Maurice's father Daniel. All most confusing—we shall have to see—but at this point we must regard all this is highly doubtful.

Child of Maurice O'Connell is:
    i.        **(60)** Richard O'Connell.


*Generation No. 8*


**170. Michael Passow,** died 1753.

Child of Michael Passow is:
    i.        **(85)** Ilse Passow, born Abt. 1730; married Heinrich Daniel Hahn 06 Jan 1753 in Lohmen, Mecklenburg.


      **192. Samuel Knapp**[59], born Abt. 1668 in Stamford, Connecticut; died 1739 in Danbury, Connecticut. He was the son of **384. Caleb Knapp** and **385. Hannah Smith**. He married **193. Hannah Bushnell** Abt. 1696.
      **193. Hannah Bushnell**[59], born 22 Aug 1676 in Norwalk, Connecticut; died Abt. 1722. She was the daughter of **386. Francis Bushnell** and **387. Hannah Seymour**.

More About **Samuel Knapp** and **Hannah Bushnell**:
Marriage: Abt. 1696

Child of Samuel Knapp and Hannah Bushnell is:

i.      (96) Samuel Knapp II, born Abt. 1698 in Danbury, Connecticut; died Abt. 1740 in Danbury, Connecticut; married Sarah Hoyt.


## 194. John Hoyt

Child of John Hoyt is:

i.      (97) Sarah Hoyt, married Samuel Knapp II.


**200. Robert Campbell**[60], born 1673 in Campbelltown, Argyshire, Scotland. He married **201. Janet Stuart**.

**201. Janet Stuart,** died 1729.

Child of Robert Campbell and Janet Stuart is:

i.      (100) Charles Campbell, born Abt. 1696 in County Tyrone, Ulster, Ireland; died May 1770; married Mary Stuart.


**240. Daniel O'Connell** He married **241. Alice Seagrave**.

**241. Alice Seagrave** She was the daughter of **482. Christopher Seagrave**.

Notes for Daniel O'Connell:
This Daniel is known as *Daniel of Aghagabar*.

This Daniel O'Connell is *alleged* to be the family's common ancestor with Daniel O'Connell, known as the Irish "Liberator." The latter is descendant from an oldest son John, while the O'Connells in our family descend from Maurice, a younger son. Thus Daniel O'Connell, the Irish Liberator, would have been the first cousin of Maurice O'Connell.

This family connection was of great interest to Ivalue Knapp (Hilgers), my aunt, who would spare no occasion to talk about it whenever an opportunity arose. And it was from her that I learned of another O'Connell connection, the actress *Helen O'Connell*, but whether this is true or simply speculation of a common sort in families I don't know at this point.

Children of Daniel O'Connell and Alice Seagrave are:
    i.       John O'Connell

Notes for John O'Connell:
Great-grandfather of Daniel O'Connell, the Liberator.

    ii.      **(120)** Maurice O'Connell, died 1825.


*Generation No. 9*


**384. Caleb Knapp,** born Abt. 20 Jan 1636/37 in Watertown, Massachusetts; died Abt. 1675. He was the son of **768. Nicholas Knapp** and **769. Eleanor (aka Elinor) (Disbrow) Lockwood**. He married **385. Hannah Smith** Abt. 1660 in Stamford, Connecticut.
    **385. Hannah Smith** She was the daughter of **770. Henry Smith**.

More About Caleb Knapp and Hannah Smith:
Marriage: Abt. 1660, Stamford, Connecticut

Child of Caleb Knapp and Hannah Smith is:
    i.      **(192)** Samuel Knapp, born Abt. 1668 in Stamford, Connecticut; died 1739 in Danbury, Connecticut; married Hannah Bushnell Abt. 1696.


**386. Francis Bushnell,** born 06 Jan 1647/48 in Guilford or Saybrook, Connecticut; died 1697 in Danbury, Connecticut. He was the son of **772. William Bushnell** and **773. Rebecca Chapman**. He married **387. Hannah Seymour** 12 Oct 1675 in Norwalk, Connecticut.
    **387. Hannah Seymour,** born 12 Dec 1654 in Norwalk, Connecticut. She was the daughter of **774. Thomas Seymour** and **775. Hannah Marvin**.

More About **Francis Bushnell** and **Hannah Seymour**:
Marriage: 12 Oct 1675, Norwalk, Connecticut

Child of Francis Bushnell and Hannah Seymour is:
    i.      **(193)** Hannah Bushnell, born 22 Aug 1676 in Norwalk, Connecticut; died Abt. 1722; married Samuel Knapp Abt. 1696.

### 482. Christopher Seagrave

Child of Christopher Seagrave is:

    i.        (241) Alice Seagrave, married Daniel O'Connell.


*Generation No. 10*


**768. Nicholas Knapp,** born Abt. 16 May 1592 in Suffolk, England; died 16 Apr 1670 in Stamford, Fairfield, Connecticut. He was the son of John Knapp and Margaret Blois. He married **769. Eleanor (aka Elinor) (Disbrow) Lockwood.**

*Scenes from Suffolk village where Nicholas Knapp may have lived prior to his emigration to the American colonies in about 1629.*


**769. Eleanor (aka Elinor) (Disbrow) Lockwood,** born Abt. 1609; died 16 Aug 1658 in Stamford, Fairfield, Connecticut.


**Notes for Nicholas Knapp:**

In the privately printed *DAWES-GATES ANCESTRAL LINES (1943)*, Volume 1, page 369 there is to be found the following reference to a Knapp, possibly Nicholas:

*"The next year [1658] he [Robert Jennison] and his son-in-law Richard Bloise contracted to pay 5 pounds per year for the use of the meadow and corn land belonging to 'Ould Knop' (Knap), an aged man who was being cared for by the town."*

Other records indicate that Nicholas whose first wife had died re-married in 1658 and possibly fathered a couple more children! Yet it's interesting to question, given the few Knapps in the county at this time who might have been old enough to be so described, if this reference isn't to Nicholas or his brother William, who is it then?

The above reference to Richard Bloise is especially interesting since at least one set of genealogical records in *Family Tree Maker Archives* identifies a Margaret Blois as the mother of Nicholas Knapp. Is it possible that the Jennison/Bloise land rental came about because of some connection between Richard Bloise and the Nicholas and William Knapp families on their mother's side? Margaret Blois's father was also named Richard, which lends a bit more support to the theory.

Children of Nicholas Knapp and Eleanor Lockwood are:
  i.      Jonathan Knapp, born Nov 1631.
  ii.     Timothy Knapp, born 14 Dec 1632.
  iii.    Joshua Knapp, born 05 Jan 1634/35.
  iv.     (384) Caleb Knapp, born Abt. 20 Jan 1636/37 in Watertown, Massachusetts; died Abt. 1675; married Hannah Smith Abt. 1660 in Stamford, Connecticut.
  v.      Sarah Knapp, born 05 Jan 1638/39.
  vi.     Ruth Knapp, born 06 Jan 1640/41.
  vii.    Hannah Knapp, born 06 Mar 1643/44.
  viii.   Moses Knapp, born 1645.
  ix.     Lydia Knapp, born 1647.

**770. Henry Smith,** born in London, England; died in Stamford, Connecticut(?). He was the son of Thomas Smith.

Child of Henry Smith is:
  i.      (385) Hannah Smith, married Caleb Knapp Abt. 1660 in Stamford, Connecticut.

**772. William Bushnell,** born in England; died 12 Nov 1683 in Saybrook, Connecticut. He married **773. Rebecca Chapman** Abt. 1643.
     **773. Rebecca Chapman**

More About William Bushnell and Rebecca Chapman:

Marriage: Abt. 1643

Child of William Bushnell and Rebecca Chapman is:
  i.     **(386)** Francis Bushnell, born 06 Jan 1647/48 in Guilford or Saybrook, Connecticut; died 1697 in Danbury, Connecticut; married Hannah Seymour 12 Oct 1675 in Norwalk, Connecticut.


**774. Thomas Seymour,** born 15 Jul 1632 in *Sawbridgeworth**, Hertfordshire, England; died 22 Sep 1712 in Norwalk, Connecticut. He was the son of Richard Seymour and Marcy or Mercy Ruscoe. He married **775. Hannah Marvin** 05 Jan 1653/54 in Norwalk, Connecticut.
   **775. Hannah Marvin,** born Abt. Oct 1634 in Essex, England; died Aft. 1680. She was the daughter of Matthew Marvin and Elizabeth (last name unknown) Marvin.

*

Sawbridgeworth churchyard in a village from which our Knapp family
may have originated.


More About Thomas Seymour and Hannah Marvin:
Marriage: 05 Jan 1653/54, Norwalk, Connecticut

Child of Thomas Seymour and Hannah Marvin is:

i. (387) Hannah Seymour, born 12 Dec 1654 in Norwalk, Connecticut; married Francis Bushnell 12 Oct 1675 in Norwalk, Connecticut.

*Endnotes*

1. 1870 Minnesota census.
2. Research of Betty Lou Cords.
3. Blue Earth County Courthouse records.
4. Knapp family bible.
5. A handwritten account probably by Catherine O'Connell, copy of which is in my possession.
6. California Death Index.
7. 1910 Federal Census, Jamestown, Blue Earth County, Minnesota.
8. Social Security Death Index.
9. 1900 Federal Census, Fairhaven, Whatcom County, Washington.
10. 1930 Federal Census, San Mateo, California.
11. California Death Index.
12. 1900 Federal Census for Madison Lake, Minnesota.
13. Albert Koebele, *Ortssippenbuch Grafenhausen*, (1971).
14. Shirley Schaub, *"Descendants of Johannes Schaub"*, (Privately published), "Electronic."
15. Cords Family History by Betty Lou Cords.
16. Baptismal Record recorded in New York State, Town of Dutchess, Washington County Quaker Births Nine Partners Monthly Meeting.
17. Sharon McClintock mentions him in a letter dated 03 October 2003.
18. James K. Knapp family Bible.
19. 1900 Federal Census for.
20. 1900 Federal Census, Waterbury, New Haven, Connecticut.
21. Knapp family bible.
22. 1870 Minnesota census.
23. 1850 United States Federal Census for Wisconsin.
24. Handwritten family record probably by Catherine O'Connell, copy of which is in my possession.
25. No record has been found.
26. 1850 United States Federal Census for Wisconsin.
27. Cemetery grave marker at St. Clair, Minnesota
28. No record has been found.
29. account probably written by Catherine O'Connell, copy of which is in my possession.
30. Minnesota Death Index.

31. from grave marker in cemetery at St. Clair, Minnesota

32. by Catherine O'Connell, copy of which is in my possession.

33. by Catherine O'Connell, copy of which is in my possession, and also obituary.

34. by Catherine O'Connell, copy of which is in my possession.

35. Murphy genealogy of Jayne Joyce Staley.

36. by Catherine O'Connell, copy of which is in my possession.

37. Murphy genealogy of Jayne Joyce Staley.

38. by Catherine O'Connell, copy of which is in my possession, and published here in the latter's scrapbook.

39. Albert Koebele, *Ortssippenbuch Grafenhausen*, (1971).

40. As cited by Mrs. Frances M. Fransson in 01 August 1976 letter to James T. Casper, *Nicholas Knapp Genealogy*.

41. Linda Guilmart, 18 April 2000 posting, Knapp Family Genealogy Forum. Nicholas Knapp Genealogy (p. 181) puts date for Ebenezer's birth 1761/64.

42. As cited by Mrs. Frances M. Fransson in 01 August 1976 letter to James T. Casper, *Nicholas Knapp Genealogy*.

43. Nine Partners New York State Quaker Records.

44. Richard Moxley letter to his daughter Jane Ann, Ballyroe, Ireland 12 February 1938, now in my possession.

45. Genealogical research of Kathleen M. Curry.

46. Kathleen Curry's Murphy Genealogy.

47. Murphy Genealogy of Kathleen M. Curry.

48. Albert Koebele, *Ortssippenbuch Grafenhausen*, (1971).

49. Nicholas Knapp Genealogy as cited by genealogist Mrs. Frances M. Fransson in letter to James T. Casper dated 01 August 1976

50. Linda Guilmart, *Knapp Family Genealogy Forum*, (Posted on web site 18 April 2000), "Electronic," 18 April 2000 posting.

51. Linda Guilmart, *Knapp Family Genealogy Forum*, (Posted on web site 18 April 2000), "Electronic."

52. As cited by Mrs. Frances M. Fransson in 01 August 1976 letter to James T. Casper, *Nicholas Knapp Genealogy*.

53. Linda Guilmart, *Knapp Family Genealogy Forum*, (Posted on web site 18 April 2000), "Electronic."

54. As cited by Mrs. Frances M. Fransson in 01 August 1976 letter to James T. Casper, *Nicholas Knapp Genealogy*.

55. Linda Guilmart, 18 April 2000 posting, Knapp Family Genealogy Forum. Nicholas Knapp Genealogy (p. 181) puts date for Ebenezer's birth 1761/64.

56. Albert Koebele, *Ortssippenbuch Grafenhausen*, (1971).

57. As cited by Mrs. Frances M. Fransson in 01 August 1976 letter to James T. Casper, *Nicholas Knapp Genealogy*, page 36.

58. *Lindy Guilmart Knapp Genealogy @ Ancestry.com.*

59. As cited by Mrs. Frances M. Fransson in 01 August 1976 letter to James T. Casper, *Nicholas Knapp Genealogy*, page 15.

60. *Lindy Guilmart Knapp Genealogy @ Ancestry.com.*

# 9 Note on the Kasper/Casper Name

As has been previously seen, our branch of this enormous family originally spelled its name *Kasper*, a name of most ancient origin, probably originating in the Persian region with a meaning that suggests a person having something to do with gold or treasure. It seems to have originated as a given name, over time evolving into a surname, and is most notable as the name of one of the legendary three magi who visited the infant Jesus as Bethlehem. These reasons—its associations with gold and ancient legend and its widespread use as a given name—probably account for its occurrence in so many forms and so many parts of the European and Eurasian world. One finds the name in the ancient *Cas bah* of Algiers and other Arab cities, in the Caspersens of Denmark, southern European Casperellas, central European Caspari, and even Kasparov, most recently the name of a famous Russian chess player. Indeed, most middle eastern and western European nations have one or more variations of the name within their populations.

The German branch of this family is indeed a large one, and today in virtually every region of that country one finds both *Kaspers* and *Caspers*. As far as I can tell, in the late 17th and early 18th centuries, Kaspers were especially present in southern Germany, within 50 or so miles in all directions from Stuttgart, with other branches of the family in the adjacent German state of Wurttemberg, in Bavaria, and also in Switzerland. One also finds numerous Caspers across the Rhine in Alsatian France, Kaspers east of the Danube in Czechoslovakia, and others spelling the name either way in northern German states.

In our particular Kasper family, there appears to have been a gradual evolution in the direction of the *Casper* spelling. Early LeRay Township census and land records spell the name either way, apparently the whim of whomever recorded it. The earliest family gravesite, in the Eagle Lake, Minnesota cemetery, contains memorials bearing the name as *Kasper*, leaving no doubt about how the family wished to be remembered at the end of the nineteenth century. Later family graves in the Madison Lake, Minnesota cemetery are uniformly *Casper*. Wendelin Kasper, the pioneer founder of our American family, seems to retain the original spelling in official records bearing his signature. An umlaut over the *a* is evident in one or other of these, and one explanation I have for this was that it was his attempt to indicate an accent most consistent with his particular southern Baden dialect.

With World War I, generating a wave of anti-German feeling in the United States, many German people felt the need to obscure their ethnic origins, or at least to publicly demonstrate that they were first and foremost Americans. One device was to give children Anglo-Saxon sounding first names, and with similar intent to alter the spelling of surnames. So names like Karl, Fritz, and Otto were replaced by Charles, Francis, and Louis, and surnames beginning with the letter *K* were changed to letter *C,* which was much less commonly used in Germany. Thus, from the 1920's forward, our Kasper family became Casper for all time.

Wendelin never seems to have formerly changed his name to Casper. Various census and land records spell it that way, but this is simply at the whim of record keepers who went by sound alone. It is also a fact that even in Germany many people with this name spell it as *Casper,* and that way of spelling it is far and away the most common in the many nations where this name and its variants are to be found. The earliest family grave marker in this country is that of young Louis (Lewis) Kasper, Wendelin's son buried in the Eagle Lake cemetery in 1894. This leaves no doubt about how the family wished to be remembered as the last century drew to a close.

An interesting family anecdote concerning all this (from Margaret Casper) relates how sometime during the 1930's Wendelin Kasper's oldest son John suggested to his mother that he might adopt the original spelling.[87] Her advice to him was to leave it as it was, advice he apparently followed, for there is no evidence anywhere of any of our family after World War I and Wendelin's time spelling the name in its original form. Even Wendelin's obituary in the *Madison Lake Times* and even his own memorial spell it as Casper.

As a final note, the Casper name had gone through an evolution typical of many significant ancient names once associated with the ruling class. Names like Oscar, Percival, Henry, and Alphonse come to mind—all once the names of princes and kings, while today any child unfortunate enough to have been so burdened by his parents would be the laughing stock of his classmates in school. The name Casper has a particularly unlucky history including its identification with a likable cartoon character known as the *Friendly Ghost.* Earlier it became attached to a simpering coward named *Caspar Milquetoast,* a comic strip character creation of the American cartoonist H. T. Webster. In Germany, a *Kasper* is a puppet clown featured in a

---

87 Interview with Margaret Casper.

*Punch and Judy* show, equally unflattering. There is also the children's moral tale of the boy *Suppen-Kasper* who steadfastly refused to eat his soup and subsequently starved to death.

*Illustration of a Kasper puppet theater at a German village festival.*

And, finally, there was the sensational Kaspar Hauser, the "wild boy" discovered in a marketplace in Nuremberg in 1828 whose mind was said to have been a complete blank, and who—it was claimed—had been kept in a hole his entire life by a man who prevented him from knowing anything till the day he surfaced. Philosophers of innate ideas and later psychologists took an active interest in this young man who died under strange circumstances in 1833, and left behind himself a wealth of rumor, suspicion, and speculation. Nowadays, *Casper* has emerged as a popular name for a pet. Any search of the internet will locate dozens of pictures of cats, dogs, and birds by that name.

*Cartoon illustration of Suppen Kasper, the boy who refused to eat his soup and grew thinner and thinner until he simply vanished. . .*

So with all these allusions and uses still readily at hand, some days it isn't easy being a Casper, and I myself have sometimes felt a cringe or a pang of embarrassment out on a playground or in a classroom, even over the telephone, when somebody made the connection to one or other of these most famous *Caspers*. When I was still a young man, I learned to anticipate *Casper, the Friendly Ghost* by bringing up the connection myself before anyone else had the chance, and then adding wryly that he was the most famous and successful member of our family. This worked and got me ahead of the game where some fool would call me *the friendly ghost* or just plain *ghost* or joke about how haunting I was, as if he were the first person who ever thought of it. Nowadays I will even instruct somebody in the correct spelling of my name by simply suggesting, "It's the same as the Friendly Ghost." It's always better to have a joke upon yourself rather than letting someone else have the joke on you.

I conclude by urging any Casper who may read this to view lightheartedly its modern-day transformation, even while keeping in mind that is was the name of a legendary king who followed the star of Bethlehem and brought a gift of gold to the infant Jesus. It is a name with great prominence in geography, history, and mythology, found alike in the Caspian Sea and in the name of the mythic prophet Cassandra whose fate it was to prophecy doom and never be believed. I have always thought it a foolish vanity for people to take excessive pride in their names, but neither should any Casper feel chagrin at the latter-day ridicule associated with this fascinating and significant name, for it is a badge that can be worn proudly.

# 10 Family Genealogical Charts and Records

## *Descendants of Michael Kasper*

**Michael Kasper**
*b: in Prechtal, Baden-Wurtemburg, Germany*

*d: 04 Nov 1761 in Grafenhausen, Baden, Germany*

**Anna Maria Nopper**

*m: 27 Sep 1723*

*d: 28 Sep 1767 in Grafenhausen, Baden, Germany*

Children

**Johannes Kasper**
*b: 11 Dec 1725 in Grafenhausen, Baden, Germany*

*d: 30 Apr 1786 in Grafenhausen, Baden, Germany*

**Anna Maria Ursula Ehing**
*b: 30 Jan 1743/44 in Grafenhausen, Baden, Germany*
*m: 14 Nov 1768 in 14 November 1768*
*d: 18 Mar 1814 in Grafenhausen, Baden, Germany*

**Anna Maria Kasper**
*b: 15 Aug 1727 in Grafenhausen*

**Maria Barbara Kasper**
*b: 1729 in Grafenhausen*

*d: 1780 in Grafenhausen*

**Maria Anna Kasper**
*b: 27 Jun 1734 in Grafenhausen*

**Maria Eva Kasper**
*b: 1735 in Grafenhausen*

*d: 1765 in Grafenhausen*

**Justina Kasper**
*b: 1739 in Grafenhausen, Baden, Germany*

## *Descendants of Johannes Kasper*

**Johannes Kasper**
b: 11 Dec 1725 in Grafenhausen, Baden, Germany

d: 30 Apr 1786 in Grafenhausen, Baden, Germany

**Anna Maria Ursula Ehing**
b: 30 Jan 1743/44 in Grafenhausen, Baden, Germany
m: 14 Nov 1768 in 14 November 1768
d: 18 Mar 1814 in Grafenhausen, Baden, Germany

Children

**Katharina Kasper**
b: 1770 in Grafenhausen

d: 1818 in Grafenhausen

**Lorenz Michael Kasper**
b: 1773 in Grafenhausen

d: 1852 in Grafenhausen

**Katharina Daibach**

**Joseph Anton Kasper**
b: 13 Apr 1777 in Grafenhausen, Baden, Germany

d: 18 Feb 1850 in Grafenhausen, Baden, Germany

**Katharina Hoegi**
b: 28 Apr 1778

m: 11 Oct 1802

d: 08 May 1810

**Appollonia Koebele**
b: 27 Jan 1790 in Grafenhausen, Baden, Germany
m: 21 Oct 1811

d: 26 May 1835 in Grafenhausen, Baden, Germany

**Maria Anna Kasper**
b: 04 Sep 1780 in Grafenhausen

d: 1780 in Grafenhausen

## *Descendants of Joseph Anton Kasper*

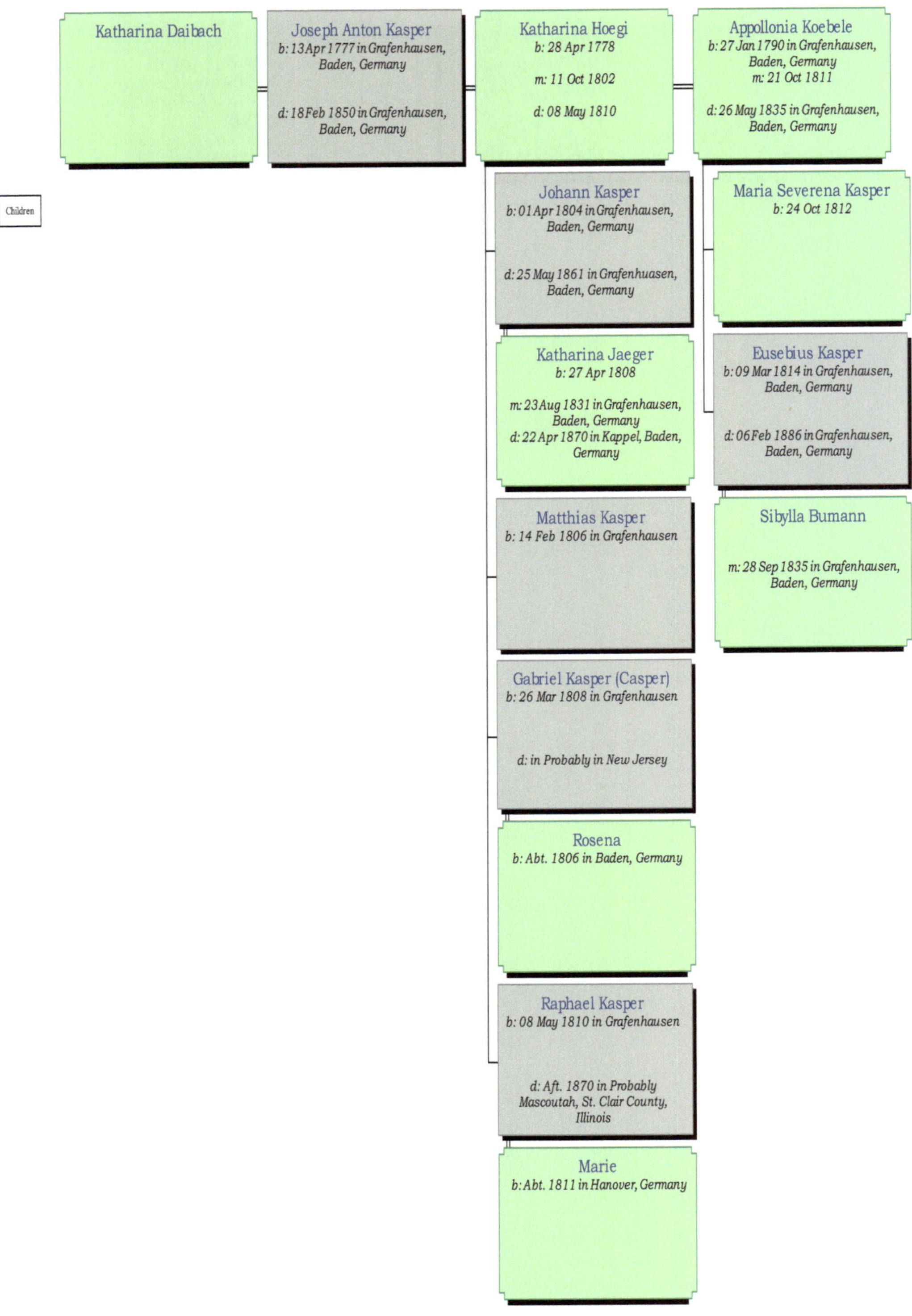

**Johann Kasper**
b: 01 Apr 1804 in Grafenhausen, Baden, Germany

d: 25 May 1861 in Grafenhuasen, Baden, Germany

**Katharina Jaeger**
b: 27 Apr 1808

m: 23 Aug 1831 in Grafenhausen, Baden, Germany
d: 22 Apr 1870 in Kappel, Baden, Germany

Children

**Magdalena Kasper**
b: 16 Apr 1833 in Grafenhausen, Baden, Germany

d: Abt. 24 Oct 1906 in Mankato, Blue Earth County, Minnesota

**Kasimir Schaub**
b: 21 Jul 1827 in Grafenhausen, Baden, Germany
m: 20 Aug 1857 in Grafenhausen, Baden, Germany

**Johann Kasper**
b: 17 Jul 1835 in Grafenhausen, Baden, Germany

d: 24 Nov 1912 in Grafenhausen, Baden, Germany

**Theresia Kurz**
b: 24 Feb 1840 in Grafenhausen, Baden, Germany
m: 18 Jun 1860 in Grafenhausen, Baden, Germany
d: 25 Feb 1899 in Grafenhausen, Baden, Germany

**Wendelin Kasper**
b: 05 Jul 1845 in Grafenhausen-Kappel, Baden, Germany

d: 26 Dec 1922 in Madison Lake, Minnesota

**Wilhelmine Sophia Friede**
b: 08 Aug 1850 in Ruest, Mecklenburg, Germany
m: 15 Oct 1872 in Mankato, Minnesota
d: 18 Feb 1940 in Madison Lake, Minnesota

## *Descendants of Wendelin Kasper*

**Wendelin Kasper**
b: 05 Jul 1845 in Grafenhausen-Kappel, Baden, Germany

d: 26 Dec 1922 in Madison Lake, Minnesota

**Wilhelmine Sophia Friede**
b: 08 Aug 1850 in Ruest, Mecklenburg, Germany

m: 15 Oct 1872 in Mankato, Minnesota
d: 18 Feb 1940 in Madison Lake, Minnesota

Children

**John Charles Casper**
b: 26 Aug 1872 in LeRay Township, Madison Lake, Minnesota

d: 22 Jun 1940 in Janesville Township, Waseca County, Minnesota

**Rozetta Florence Compton**
b: 1878

m: 10 Jan 1897

d: 08 Nov 1970 in Minneapolis, Hennepin County, Minnesota

**Clara Leona Casper**
b: 26 Sep 1873 in LeRay Township, Blue Earth County, Minnesota

d: 02 Dec 1963 in St. Clair, Blue Earth County, Minnesota

**Johann Heinrich Carl "Jo**
b: 1868

m: 15 Mar 1894

d: 1939 in St. Clair, Blue Earth County, Minnesota

**Minnie Kasper**
b: 10 Jan 1877 in LeRay Township, Madison Lake, Minnesota

d: 21 Jan 1887 in LeRay Township, Madison Lake, Minnesota

**Lewis "Louis" Kasper**
*b: 1879 in LeRay Township, Madison Lake, Minnesota*

*d: 12 Jun 1894 in LeRay Township, Madison Lake, Minnesota*

**Elmer Francis Casper***
*b: 27 Dec 1883 in LeRay Township, Blue Earth County, Minnesota*

*d: 14 May 1953 in Madison Lake, Minnesota*

**Estella Mary Knapp**
*b: 20 Nov 1884 in Rochester, Minnesota*

*m: 15 Nov 1904 in Madison Lake, Minnesota*
*d: 23 Jul 1945 in Madison Lake, Minnesota*

**Albert Casper**

*d: Abt. 1884*

**Albert A. "Bert" Casper**
*b: 04 Jul 1885 in LeRay Township, Madison Lake, Minnesota*

*d: 04 Oct 1963 in New Ulm, Minnesota*

**Laura J. Knapp**
*b: 22 Feb 1899 in Deerwood, Minnesota*

*d: Mar 1924 in Madison Lake, Minnesota*

# 11 Acknowledgements

Few family historians work alone, and most willingly share information they have gathered with others who share their interest in the family.

Among the several who have been most helpful, I must first mention my aunt, **Ivalue Casper**; my cousin **Robert James Knapp**, and **Betty Lou Cords**, conscientious historian of the Cords family, for providing information about the extended family of Wendelin Kasper's wife Minnie Cords. Her chance discovery of Wendelin's sister Magdalena Kasper created my path to locating our Kasper family origins in Grafenhausen, Baden. Equally significant was her discovery of the tiny Mecklenburg village of Ruest as the origin of our Cords family, mentioned in the obituary of Minnie's brother Charles Cords. Without her cheerful help, much of great interest would be absent from this account.

**Jayne Joyce Stayley** has been especially generous in sharing her Murphy-O'Connell family research. I would also like to thank **Sharon Schaub** for sharing details about the descendants of Magdalena Kasper and Kasimir Schaub. My old friend **Joe Hoehn** recently forwarded valuable information about his own family's roots in Grafenhausen. **Judy Bushlack** provided further valuable assistance with facts about the Casper family descendants of Wendelin's son John. **Sam Casper** and **Faye Casper Michaletz** have been most helpful, as was my cousin the late **Margaret Casper Schroepfer**.

A special thank you to my wife Kate whose wonderful bell-like laughter keeps me going and has warmed our recently discovered German Kasper cousins sufficiently to overcome what might have been a language barrier. She has done so much to make this all possible, traveling with me to far-off lands, visiting so many distant family, driving the car, taking pictures, hearing the story over and over again, and catching dozens of errors in a final proofreading of the manuscript. I couldn't have gotten so far with all this without her patience, encouragement, assistance, and willingness to share my enthusiasm for family history.

# About the Author

**James Casper** was born and grew up in southern Minnesota. Apart from living in various Minnesota locales, he has resided in Boston, St. Louis, eastern Tennessee, and London, England. He and his wife of twenty-eight years have traveled extensively. Rome is one of their favorite places. He is happiest walking from lock to lock along the Thames.

Website: FarhavenPress.com

# More by James Casper

***Everywhere in Chains: Secrets of the North Shore*** is a moving story about a young girl whose real father's whereabouts is kept a secret to "protect her" from the truth. Ultimately, she is reunited with him, along the way proving that the path to healing takes a lot of courage and strength. The story provides a way forward for families who are victims of priest sexual abuse and for those who have a loved-one in prison.

### An Accidental Pope
The Catholic Church faces one of the greatest scandals in its history. Only the reader will know the whole story of how the Vatican came to have its secret pope.

### The Far End of the Park
Explore a year of turmoil, revelation, and change in the life of Jude Henley. Here is a story that will make you laugh, cry, and remember what it felt like to be growing up.

And finally, if you have enjoyed reading this compilation of family history, please leave a short review online at Amazon or elsewhere. We realize, these will probably only come from family members in the case of *Three Hundred Years in the Life of a Family,* and those would add to the ongoing story of the Casper family.

# Room for Notes
# Pictures
# Your Family Tree